The Gold-Seekers
A Tale Of California

By

Gustave Aimard

Double9
BOOKS

The Gold-Seekers
A Tale Of California
by Gustave Aimard

Copyright © 2024

All Rights reserved.

ISBN: 978-93-61421-04-4

Published by

DOUBLE 9 BOOKS
2/13-B, Ansari Road
Daryaganj, New Delhi – 110002
info@double9books.com
www.double9books.com
Tel. 011-40042856

This book is under public domain

ABOUT THE AUTHOR

Gustave Aimard wrote multiple volumes about Latin America and the American frontier. Oliver Aimard was born in Paris. As he previously stated, he was the offspring of two married individuals, "but not to each other". His father, François Sébastiani de la Porta (1775-1851), was a commander in Napoleon's army and a representative of the Louis Philippe government. Sebastiani was married to the Duchess of Coigny. In 1806, the couple had a daughter, Alatrice-Rosalba Fanny. The mother died shortly after she was born. Fanny was reared by her grandmother, Duchess of Coigny. Aimard was placed as a baby with a family that were paid to raise him. By the age of nine or twelve, he was sent off on a herring boat. Later, about 1838, he served briefly with the French Navy. After one more trip to America (when he claims he was adopted into a Comanche tribe), Aimard returned to Paris in 1847, the same year his half-sister, Duchess de Choiseul-Pralin, was cruelly killed by her noble husband. Reconciliation or acknowledgement by his biological family did not occur. After serving briefly in the Garde Mobil, Aimard returned to the Americas.

CONTENTS

PREFACE

The "Gold-Seekers" must be regarded as forming the connecting link between the "Tiger-Slayer" and the "Indian Chief," the concluding volume of this series. It must not be forgotten that the author is dealing with real characters, and that the hero lived and died in the way hereafter to be described; and the three volumes may be considered a life-history of a very remarkable man. Although they may be perused separately with equal interest, I feel confident that those readers who have gone so far with me will desire to know the conclusion of this strange eventful history.

LASCELLES WRAXALL.

PROLOGUE

I
THE MEETING

On the 5th of July, 184-, at about six in the evening, a party of well-mounted horsemen started at a gallop from Guadalajara, the capital of the state of Jalisco, and proceeded along the road that traverses the village of Zapopan, celebrated for its miraculous virgin. After crossing the escarped summits of the Cordilleras, this road reaches the charming little town of Tepic, the usual refuge of those Europeans and rich Mexicans whom business carries to San Blas, but to whom the insalubrity of the air breathed in that port, the maritime arsenal of the Mexican union, would be mortal.

We have said that six o'clock was striking as the cavalcade passed the gateway. The officer of the watch, after bowing respectfully to the travellers, watched them for a long time, then re-entered the guardroom, shaking his head, and muttering to himself,—

"Heaven save me! What can Colonel Guerrero be thinking of, to set out on a Friday, and at such an hour as this? Does he fancy that the *salteadores* will allow him to pass? Hum! He will see what they are about at the *barranca del mal paso* (the gorge of the evil step)."

The travellers, however, probably unaffected by the superstitious fears that ruled the worthy officer, rapidly sped on the long poplar alley that extends from the town to Zapopan, caring neither for the advanced hour nor the ill-omened day of the week.

They were six in number—Colonel Sebastian Guerrero, his daughter, and four peons, or Indian criados. The colonel was a tall man, with harsh, marked features, and a bronzed complexion. The few silvery threads mingled with his black hair showed that he had passed middle life, although his robust limbs, upright stature, and the brilliancy of his glance denoted that years had not yet gained the mastery over this vigorous organisation. He wore the uniform of a Mexican field officer with the ease and nonchalance peculiar to old soldiers; but, in addition to the sabre hanging by his side, his holsters held pistols; and a rifle laid across the saddle-bow proved that, in case of need, he would offer a vigorous resistance to any robbers who ventured to attack him.

His daughter, Doña Angela, rode on his right hand. In Europe, where the growth of girls is not nearly so precocious as in America, she would only have been a child; for she counted scarce thirteen summers. As far as could be judged, she was slight, but graceful, and perfectly proportioned; her features were delicate and noble; her mouth laughing; her eyes black, quick, and flashing with wit; while her brown hair fell in two enormous tresses down upon her horse. She was wrapped up coquettishly in her *rebozo*, and laughed madly at every bound of her steed, which she maliciously tormented, in spite of her father's reiterated remonstrances.

The servants were powerfully-built Indians, armed to the teeth, and appeared capable of defending their master in case of need. They rode some ten paces behind the colonel, and led two mules loaded with provisions and baggage—an indispensable precaution in Mexico, if travellers do not wish to die of hunger by the way.

Mexico combines all the climates of the globe. From the icy peaks of the Cordilleras, down to the burning coasts of the ocean, the traveller in that country undergoes every temperature. Hence this vast territory has been divided into three distinct zones: *las tierras calientes*, or hot lands, composed of the plains on the seashore, and which produce sugar, indigo, and cotton in truly tropical abundance; *las tierras templadas*, or temperate lands, regions formed by the Cordilleras, and which enjoy an eternal spring, great heat and extreme cold being equally unknown there; and lastly, *las tierras frias*, or cold lands, which include the central plateaux, and where the temperature is relatively much lower than in the other zones.

Still we should remark that in Mexico the expressions "heat," and "cold," have not an absolute value as in Europe, and that the lofty plateaux, known as the *tierras frias*, enjoy a temperature like that of Lombardy, which would seem to any European a very pleasant climate. Owing to its position, Guadalajara shares in two of the three zones that divide Mexico. Situated on the limit of the *tierra caliente* and the *tierra templada*, the tepid breezes and pure sky reveal the warm regions of the seaboard, which extend thus far. The arid sands are succeeded by fertile and well-cultivated plains, fields of sugar-cane, Indian corn, bananas, goyaviers, and other productions of the tropical flora. By degrees the gloomy black oaks and pines, which only grow on the mountains, become rarer, and eventually disappear entirely, to make room for poplars, fan-palms, calabash trees, sumachs, Peru trees, and thousands of others, which proudly wave their superb crowns over the spontaneous vegetation that surrounds them.

In *las tierras calientes*, where the heat of the day is stifling, persons generally only travel from five to eleven A.M., and from three in the afternoon till ten at night, so as to enjoy the morning and evening freshness. Colonel Guerrero had, therefore, only conformed to the general custom by commencing his journey in the evening; but, as so often occurs, he had started later than he wished, owing to those numberless obstacles which ever supervene at the moment of departure, and cause a lengthened delay for no visible reason. But the colonel cared little about the advanced hour: a night march possessed no terrors for him, as he had been accustomed for years to modify his humour by circumstances, and yield to the exigencies of the situation in which he found himself.

The sun set behind the Peak of Teguilla, and the Cerro del Col disappeared in the centre of the chain of tall, abrupt hills which borders the Rio Tololotlan: gradually the scene was veiled in darkness. The travellers progressed gaily conversing together, while following the winding and accidented course of the Rio Grande del Norte, along whose banks their road ran. The latter was wide, well made, and easy to follow. Hence the colonel, after taking a careful glance around to assure himself there was nothing suspicious in the neighbourhood, trusted entirely to the vigilance of the criados, and resumed the conversation with his daughter, which he had for a moment broken off.

"Angela, my child," he said to her, "you are wrong to tease your horse so. Rebecca is a good beast, very gentle, and very sure-footed; and you should be more merciful to her than you are."

"I assure you, papa," the pretty girl answered with a laugh, "I am not in the least teasing Rebecca; on the contrary, I am only tickling her to render her lively."

"Yes, and to make her dance too, as I can plainly see, little madcap. That would be all very well if we were only taking a ride for a few hours, instead of a journey which will last a month. Remember, niña, that a rider must also treat his horse carefully if he wish to reach his destination safe, and sound. You would not like, I fancy, to be left on the road by your horse."

"Heaven forbid, father! If it be so, I will obey you. Rebecca may be at ease in future; I will not tease her."

And, while speaking thus, she bent over her horse's neck and gently patted it.

"There!" the colonel continued, "now that peace, as I suppose, is made between you, what do you think of our way of travelling? Does it please you?"

"I think it charming, father; the night is magnificent, the moon lights us as if it were day; the breeze is fresh, and yet not cold. I never was so happy."

"All the better, my child. I am the more pleased to hear you speak thus, because I so feared the effects of such a journey for you, that I was on the point of leaving you at the convent."

"Thank you, father, for having changed your mind, and bringing me with you. I was so wearied with that wretched convent; and then it is so long since I have seen my dear mother, whom I long to embrace."

"This time, child, you will have ample leisure to do so for I propose leaving you with your mother."

"Then I shall not return to Guadalajara with you?"

"No, child; you will live at my large *hacienda*, Aguas Frescas, with your mother and my most faithful servants, during the period of my absence; for so soon as I have ended the urgent business that demands my presence at San Blas, I shall go to Mexico and join General Santa Anna. His Excellency has done me the honour to send for me."

"Oh!" she said, clasping her hands in entreaty, "you ought to take me with you to the *ciudad*."

"Little madcap, you know perfectly well that is impossible; but on my return I will bring you and your mother the finest things from the Portales des Mercaderes and the Parian, in order that you may eclipse the most coquettish señoras of Tepic, when it may please you to walk on the Alameda of the Pueblo."

"Oh! That is not the same thing," she said with a charming pout; "and yet," she added, suddenly regaining her good humour, "I thank you, father; for you are kind—you love me; and when you do not satisfy my whims, it is because you find it impossible."

"I am glad that you recognise that fact, and at length do me justice, little rattle-brain; for you spend your life in teasing me."

The girl began laughing, and by a sudden impulse letting her reins fall, she threw her arms round her father's neck and kissed him several times.

"Take care what you are about," the colonel said, at once happy and alarmed. "If Rebecca were to bolt you would be killed. Take up your reins at once, I say!"

"Nonsense!" she said, laughing, and shaking her brown tresses carelessly; "Rebecca is too well trained to behave in such a way."

Still she caught up her reins and settled herself in her saddle.

"Angelita mia," the father continued, perhaps more seriously than the circumstances demanded, "you are no longer a child. You ought to begin to grow more reasonable, and moderate the vivacity of your character."

"Do you scold me for loving you, my father?"

"Heaven forbid, my child! I only make a remark which I consider just; for, if you yield in this way to your first impressions, you will prepare great grief for yourself at a future day."

"Do not think that, my kind father. I am quick, careless, impressionable, that is true; but, by the side of those defects, I have the family pride I derive from you, and which will defend me from many faults."

"I hope so, my daughter."

"Do not assume that stern air for a harmless act of folly, father, or I shall fancy that you are angry with me." Then she added, with a laugh, "I remember that our family descends in a straight line from the Mexican king, Chimalpopocatzin, who, as his name indicates, had for his emblem a buckler from which smoke is issuing. You see, father, our character has not degenerated since that valorous king, and we have ever remained as firm as he was himself."

"Come, come," the colonel said good-humouredly, "I shall give up scolding you in future, for I see that it is labour wasted."

The girl smiled maliciously, and was about to reply, when a flash of light was seen in front of the party.

"What is that?" the colonel asked, raising his voice. "Is there anyone on the road?"

"I think so, colonel," one of the domestics answered at once, "for that flash seems to me produced by the flint of a *mechero.*

"That is my opinion too," the colonel said. "Let us hasten on, in order to see this delayed smoker."

The little band, which had hitherto proceeded at a slow pace, broke into an amble. At the expiration of an hour, at the same time as the sound of a horse's hoofs reached the travellers, they also heard the shrill and discordant sounds of a *jarana* (guitar), and the refrain of the following song, so familiar in Mexico, was borne on the breeze:—

"Sin pena vivamos
En calma feliz:
Gozar es mi estrella,
Cantar y reir." [1]

"Bravo!" the colonel shouted, who reached the singer at this moment. "Bravely and joyously said, comrade!"

The latter, with a husk cigarette in his mouth, bowed his head in affirmation, and defiantly twanged an air on his jarana; then, throwing it across his shoulder, where it was held by a species of brace, he turned to his addresser, and ceremoniously doffed his vicuna-skin hat.

"May God protect you, caballero!" he said politely. "It seems that the music pleases you."

"Greatly," the colonel answered, scarce able to retain his laughter at the sight of the singular person before him.

He was a tall fellow of eight-and-twenty at the most, marvellously thin, dressed in a ragged jacket, and haughtily folded in a cloak, whose primitive colour it was impossible to recognise, and which was as full of holes as a sieve. Still, in spite of this apparent wretchedness and starving face, the man had a joyous and decided expression about him, which it was a pleasure to look upon. His little black eyes, which looked as if pierced by an auger, sparkled with humour, and his manner had something *distingué* about it. He was mounted on a horse as thin and lanky as himself, against whose hollow flanks beat the straight sword called a *machete*, which the Mexicans continually wear at their side, passed through an iron ring instead of a sheath.

"You are very late on the road, compañero," the colonel continued, whose escort had by this time caught him up. "Is it prudent for you to travel alone at this hour?"

"What have I to fear?" the stranger replied. "What salteador would be such a fool as to stop me?"

"Who knows?" the colonel remarked with a smile. "Appearances are often deceitful, and it is not a bad plan to pretend poverty, in order to travel in safety along the high roads of our beloved country."

Though uttered purposelessly, these words visibly troubled the stranger; still he at once recovered, and continued in a hearty voice,—

"Unfortunately for me, any feint is useless. I am really as poor as I seem at this moment, although I have seen happier days, and my cloak was not always so ragged as you now see it."

The colonel, perceiving that the subject of conversation was disagreeable to his new acquaintance, said, —

"As you did not stop either at San Pedro or at Zapopan, for I presume that, like myself, you came from Guadalajara — —"

"It is true," the stranger interrupted him; "I quitted the city about three in the afternoon."

"I suppose," the colonel continued, "that you intend to halt at the mesón of San Juan; so, if you have no objection, we will proceed thither together, for I intend to halt for the night there."

"The mesón of San Juan is a good hostelry," the other said, respectfully lifting his hand to his hat; "but what shall I do there? I have not an *ochavo* to expénd uselessly, and have far to go. I will bivouac on the road; and while my horse, poor brute, is sucking its bit, I will smoke cigarettes, and sing that romance of King Rodrigo, which, as you are aware, commences thus."

And quickly bringing his guitar to the front, he began singing in a loud voice, —

> "Cuando las pintadas aves
> Mudas están, y la tierra
> Atenta escucha los rio
> Que al mar su tributo llevan:
> Al escaso resplandor—" [2]

"Eh!" the colonel exclaimed, brusquely interrupting, "what musical rage possesses you? It is frenzy."

"No," the singer replied in melancholy mood; "it is philosophy."

The colonel examined the poor fellow for a moment; then drawing nearer to him, —

"I am Colonel Don Sebastian Guerrero de Chimalpos. I am travelling with my daughter and a few servants. Grant me the honour of your company for this night: tomorrow we will separate, and go our several ways."

The stranger hesitated for a moment, and frowned. This shade of dissatisfaction, however, soon disappeared.

"I am a proud fool," he replied with affecting frankness; "misery renders me so susceptible that I fancy people are ever trying to humiliate me. I accept your gracious invitation as frankly as it is offered. Perhaps I may be able to prove my gratitude to you ere long."

The colonel paid no great attention to these words, because, just at the moment, the party arrived at the mesón of San Juan, whose lighted windows had revealed its proximity to the travellers for some time past.

[1] Let us live without annoyance in a happy calm: playing is my star, singing and laughing.

[2] When the spangled birds are dumb, and the attentive earth listens to the rivers that bear their tribute to the sea by the weak light—.

II
EL MESÓN DE SAN JUAN

A great deal has been written about the cool and inhospitable way in which Spanish and Sicilian landlords receive the travellers whom Providence sends them; but it is evident to us that those who write in such wise are not acquainted, even by hearsay, with the *mesoneros* or Mexican hosts. Were it so, they would doubtlessly, at their own risk and peril, have rehabilitated those worthy fellows, to discharge the whole weight of their indignation on the *huéspedes* of New Spain.

It is a justice to render to the Spanish and Sicilian landlords, that if they are utterly unable to satisfy in any way the exigencies of travellers, by giving the latter the provisions they demand, still they greet them with so affable a countenance, and veil their refusal under such an exquisite politeness, that in nine cases out of ten the traveller is compelled to allow that he was himself to blame for not laying in the necessary provisions, and therefore sups on apologies.

In Mexico things are very different. On the few high roads formerly constructed by the Spaniards, and which the neglect of the different governments that succeeded them has left in such a state that they will soon disappear completely, there stand, at long distances from each other, vast buildings which resemble fortresses, for they are nearly all surrounded by embattled and loopholed walls. These buildings are the *mesones*, or inns.

The interior is composed, first, of an enormous court, with a *noria*, or well, intended to water the horses. Corrals for the beasts of burden occupy the four corners of this yard. In a separate building are the travellers' *cuartos*; that is to say, miserable dens furnished only with a frame of oak, covered with a cowhide, which serves as a bed. These cuartos are numbered, and all open on long corridors. Each traveller is obliged to bring with him the indispensable bedding, for the host only supplies the alfalfa for the horses' provender, and water from the noria.

It was about ten at night when Colonel Guerrero arrived at the door of the mesón of San Juan, which was hermetically closed. Upon the repeated blows dealt by one of the servants, a wicket pierced in the wall, about two paces from the gate, at length opened; an ill-tempered face was visible, and a rough voice shouted,—

"Who dares to make such a disturbance at the gate of so honest and respectable a mesón as this?"

"Travellers have arrived, Don Cristoval Saccaplata," the colonel answered. "Come, open quickly, for we have made a long journey, and are tired."

"Hum! They all say the same thing," the host growled. "What do I care for that? I shall not open, it is too late; so go your way, and Heaven protect you!"

And he prepared to close the wicket.

"One moment. Confound you!" the colonel shouted, "you will not let us bivouac in front of your door? That would not be at all honourable for you."

"Bah! A night is soon passed," the host replied with a grin; "besides, you can go on to the mesón del Salto: they will open to you there."

"Don't you know that is eight miles off?"

"Of course I do."

"Come, open, Señor Saccaplata: you would not have the barbarity to leave us out here?"

"Why not?"

"Because, if you do open, you will be rewarded in a way which you will not repent of."

"Yes, yes, all travellers are the same; they make plenty of promises so long as they are outside; but once in, they are not in a hurry to untie their purse-strings."

"That will not be the case with us."

"How do I know?" the *huésped* said, shrugging his shoulders. "My house is full; I have no room left."

"We will find some, dear Saccaplata."

"Halloh! Who are you, pray, who know me so well? Maybe you are one of those *caballeros de la noche* who have been ransacking the country for some time past."

"You are mistaken grossly, and I will prove it to you," the colonel answered, anxious to cut short this open-air conversation. "Take that first," he said, throwing two ounces through the wicket; "and now, to prevent any misunderstanding, know that I am Don Sebastian Guerrero."

The worthy landlord was only sensible to one argument—that which the colonel had so judiciously employed to overcome his resistance. He stooped, picked up the two ounces, which disappeared in a second, and again addressing the travellers, but this time with a tone which he strove to render more amiable,—

"Come," he said, "I must e'en do what you wish, I am too good-hearted. You have provisions, I hope?"

"We have everything we require."

"All the better, for I could not have supplied you. Do not be impatient; I am coming down."

He disappeared from the wicket, and within five minutes could be heard unbarring the door, growling fearfully the while. The travellers then entered the yard of the mesón. The huésped had lied like the true landlord he was; he only had in the house two or three muleteers with their animals, and three travellers, who, by their dress, seemed to be hacenderos from the vicinity.

"Halloh!" Don Sebastian shouted, "someone to take my horse."

"If you begin in that way we shall not be friends long," the huésped said in the sharp tone he had previously employed. "Here, everyone, big or little, waits on himself, and attends to his own horse."

The colonel was far from being of a patient temper. If he had previously endured the host's insolence, it was solely because it was impossible to chastise him; but that reason no longer existed. Sharply dismounting, he drew his pistols from his holsters, thrust them in his belt, and walking boldly toward Señor Saccaplata, seized him by the collar and shook him roughly.

"Listen, master rogue!" he said to him. "A truce to your insolence, and wait on me, unless you would repent it."

The host was so amazed at this brusque way of replying to him, and this assault on his inviolability, that for a moment he remained dumb through confusion and wrath. His face became crimson, his eyes rolled, and he at length shouted in a strangled voice,—

"Help! Help me! Such an insult! By the body of Christ, I will not overlook it! Leave my house at once!"

"I shall not go," the colonel answered peaceably, but firmly; "and you will attend to me immediately."

"Oh! We shall see that. Here, help, Pedro, Juan, Jacinto! Come, all of you, and on to these rascals!"

Seven or eight servants rushed from the corrals at the sound of their master's voice, and ranged themselves behind him.

"Very good," the colonel said, raising his pistols. "I'll blow out the brains of the first scamp who moves a step toward me with bad intention."

We need not say that the peons remained motionless, as if they had suddenly been changed into blocks of granite. One of the colonel's servants had assisted Doña Angela from her horse, and accompanied her to a cuarto, in which he installed her; then he returned in all haste to his master's side, foreseeing that his co-operation would be speedily needed.

The courtyard of the mesón offered a most singular aspect at this moment by the light of the torches of ocote wood, passed through iron rings along the walls. On one side stood the host and his servants; on the other, Don Sebastian's four footmen, with their hands on their weapons, and the guitar player, with his jarana on his back, and his hands folded on his chest; a little on one side, the travellers and arrieros previously arrived; and in the centre, alone, with his pistols in his hand, the colonel, with frowning brow and flashing eyes.

"Enough of this, scoundrel!" he shouted. "For a long time you have been plundering and insulting the travellers whom Providence sends to you. By heavens! If you do not on the instant demand my pardon for your insolence, and if you do not serve me with all that politeness I have a right to demand from you, I will inflict on you, upon the spot, a correction which you will remember your life long."

"Take care what you are about, my master," the huésped answered ironically. "You see that I have men to help me. If you do not decamp at once, all the worse for you. I have witnesses, and the *juez de letras* shall decide."

"Good heavens!" the colonel shouted, "that is too much, and removes all my scruples. The scoundrel threatens me with the law. Level your pieces, men, and fire on the first who stirs!"

The domestics obeyed. Don Sebastian then seized the host, despite his cries and desperate resistance, and in a second had him down on the ground.

"I believe I shall do a service to all the travellers whom their evil star may in future bring to this den," he continued, "by punishing this scamp as he deserves."

The witnesses of this scene—peons, arrieros, or travellers—had not made a move to help the host. It was evident that all, for certain reasons, were in their hearts pleased with what was happening to him. Not one of them would have dared to take on himself the responsibility of such an act; but as there was someone ready to do so, they were careful not to offer the slightest obstacle to him. By the peremptory order of the colonel, the poor landlord was fastened by two of his own servants to the long pole of the noria, and debarred from making the slightest movement.

"Now," the colonel continued, "each of you take a *reata*, and thrash him till he confesses himself conquered, and consents to do what I ask of him."

Despite their feigned repugnance, the host's two peons were compelled to obey the colonel; for his orders were supported by four rifles and two pistols, whose gaping muzzles were directed point blank at them. To honour the truth, we must confess that, either through terror or for some other cause, the two peons conscientiously performed their duty.

The host howled like a bull. He was mad with rage, and writhed like a viper in the bonds which he tried in vain to break. The colonel stood stoically by his side, only asking him from time to time, ironically, how he liked his arguments, and if he would soon make up his mind to yield. Human strength has limits which it cannot pass. In spite of all his fury and obstinacy, the host was forced to confess to himself, aside, that he had to do with a man more obstinate than he was, and that, if he did not wish to die under the lash, he must resolve to endure the humiliation imposed on him.

"I surrender," he said, in a voice broken as much by anger as by pain.

"Already!" the colonel remarked coldly. "Pooh! I fancied you braver. Why, you have hardly received thirty lashes. Stop, you fellows, and unfasten your master!"

The peons eagerly obeyed. When free, the host tried to rise, but his strength failed him, and he fell back on the ground, where he lay for several moments powerless to move. At length he made a desperate effort, and picked himself up. His face was pale; his features were contracted; an abundant perspiration stood on his temples, which throbbed as if ready to burst; he had a buzzing in his ears; and tears of shame poured from his eyes. He took a few tottering steps toward the colonel.

"I am at your orders, caballero," he said, bowing his head humbly. "Speak: what must I do?"

"Good!" the latter remarked. "Now you are reasonable; you are much better so. Give some provender to my horses, and assist my servants to wait on me."

"Pardon, caballero!" the huésped said. "Will you allow me to say two words to you?"

The colonel smiled contemptuously.

"To what end? I know them, and I will repeat them myself. You wish to warn me that, obliged to yield to superior force, you have done so, but you will avenge yourself on the first opportunity. Is not that it?"

"Yes," he muttered in a hollow voice.

"Very well; you are quite at liberty to do so, master host; but take your precautions, for I warn you that, if you miss me, I shall not miss you. So now wait on me, and make haste."

And, shrugging his shoulders, the colonel turned his back on him with a smile of disdain.

The host watched him depart with a hateful expression, which imparted something hideous to his face; and when he saw that the colonel was out of the yard, he shook his head twice or thrice, muttering to himself,—

"Yes, I will avenge myself, demon, and sooner than you imagine."

After this aside, he composed his face and attended to his household duties with an activity and apparent indifference that caused his servants to be thoughtful, for they knew his rancorous character. Still he did not complain; he made no allusion to the cruel punishment he had undergone, but, on the contrary, waited on the travellers with an attention and politeness they had not been accustomed to prior to this unlucky day; and they took advantage of the change, while keeping on their guard.

Still nothing apparently happened to justify their suspicions—all went on calmly: the travellers retired to bed one after the other; then the host made his round to assure himself that all was in order, and retired to the room reserved for his private use.

The colonel had already been asleep some hours, and was in a deep sleep, from which he was suddenly aroused by a noise he heard at his door.

"Who's there?" he asked.

"Silence!" someone answered outside. "Open; it is a friend."

"Friend or foe, tell me who you are, that I may know with whom I have to deal."

"I am," the voice made answer, "the man you met on the road."

"Hem! What do you want with me? Why are you not asleep at this hour, instead of coming to rouse me?"

"Open, in Heaven's name! I have important news to tell you."

The colonel hesitated for a moment, but soon reflecting that this man, to whom he had done no harm, could have no motive, for being his enemy, he decided on getting up. Still, through prudence, he cocked one of his pistols, which he had placed by his side on retiring to bed, and went to open the door. The stranger walked in quickly, and closed it after him.

"Speak low," he said hurriedly. "Listen to me: the host is forming some scheme against you."

"I suspect it," the colonel said, who, while speaking, had lit a candle; "but whatever he may do, I am out of his reach, and the scoundrel will be crushed if he attack me."

"Who knows?" the stranger said.

"Come, you know something positive. Have I any plot to fear inside the house?"

"I do not think so."

"Tell me what you have discovered, then."

"I will do so; but in the first place, as I am a total stranger to you, allow me to tell you my name."

"For what good?"

"No one knows what may happen in this world: it is useful to be able to distinguish one's friends from one's enemies."

"Speak; I am listening."

"You nearly guessed the truth. Under my starving appearance I conceal a certain monetary value. My name is Don Cornelio Mendoza. I am a student. I had at Guadalajara an aunt, who, on dying, appointed me her heir. I am carrying with me in my belt one hundred and fifty gold ounces, and in my portfolios bills for an equal amount payable at San Blas. You see that I am not so poor as I appear to be. But the road between the two cities is long and dangerous, and I assumed this disguise to escape the robbers, if that be possible."

"Very good, Don Cornelio: you can now, if you please, change your attire, for I hope that we shall pursue our journey together."

"With all my heart; but if it make no difference, I will retain my lepero dress provisionally."

"As you please; but now to the fact. What have you to tell me?"

"Not much, but yet enough to put us on our guard. Our landlord, after making his round and assuring himself that everyone had retired, woke up one of his servants, the very one who thrashed him with such good will."

"Yes, I remember that rogue's face."

"Very good. After calling him into his room, he remained shut up with him for ten minutes; then he opened a window, the peon leaped out on the highway, and ran off at full speed."

"Oh, oh!" the colonel said.

"The landlord looked after him till he disappeared, then muttered several words I could not understand, excepting one name, which, thanks to Heaven, reached my ear."

"What was it?"

"El Buitre (the Vulture)."

"Hum! Is that all?"

"Yes."

"It does not teach me much; but how did you learn all this? The landlord did not make you his confidant, I suppose?"

"No, not a bit in the world. I became his confidant in spite of himself, and in the most natural way. My cuarto is just over his room. I heard him open a window, and I listened."

"Yes, but unfortunately you heard nothing."

"Yes, a name."

"But a name which has no meaning for us."

"On the contrary, it is of enormous significance."

"How so?"

"The famous leader of the salteadores, whose band has been desolating the province for a year, is called El Buitre. Do you now understand?"

"Body o' me!" the colonel shouted, as he jumped up hurriedly, "I rather think I do understand."

III
THE GENTLEMEN OF THE ROAD

We will for the moment quit the mesón of San Juan, and proceed about two leagues further on, where certain persons, with whom the reader must form an acquaintance, are assembled.

Hardly one hundred and fifty yards beyond the mesón the road begins to grow narrower; the mountains approach, as if wishful to shake hands, and that so abruptly and unexpectedly, that they form all at once a narrow and long gorge, which is known throughout the country as the *barranca del mal paso*.

After passing through this gorge, the scenery leaves its abrupt and savage aspect to resume a smiling character; the road widens again; a charming valley, intersected by a stream, presents itself to sight; and on all sides the eye surveys a deliciously accidented horizon.

On either side of the barranca begin impenetrable forests, through which a road can only be cut axe in hand, unless the traveller has a deep knowledge of the narrow and almost invisible paths which lead into the interior with innumerable twinings.

We must ask the reader to follow us to one of the most hidden and least known resorts in this forest.

In the centre of a vast clearing, where burned a cedar eighty feet in height, emitting incessant sparks, some twenty men in sordid garments—a horrible medley of luxury and indigence—with faces in which crime was written in capital letters, but all armed to the teeth, were assembled in groups of three or four each, drinking, eating, smoking, and singing.

Not far from them, their horses, saddled and ready to mount at the first signal, were eating their provender of alfalfa and climbing peas; while, on the edge of the covert, four or five men, motionless as bronze statues, were attentively surveying the surrounding country.

A little on one side, two men, seated on low stools, were talking and puffing in each other's faces enormous volleys of smoke. The first and elder of the two appeared about eight-and-twenty years of age; his long, light hair fell in heavy curls on his shoulders; his features were effeminate; but his aquiline nose, his bright blue eyes, and narrow forehead, imparted to his face a character of baseness and cold cruelty. He wore the splendid costume of the Mexican hacenderos, and was carelessly playing with the trigger of a splendid silver-mounted American rifle.

His companion offered a striking contrast to him: while the first was tall, well built, and endowed with pleasing manners, the second was short, stumpy, heavy, and repulsive in face, gestures, and even in language. The richness of his attire only seemed to render more striking the hideousness imprinted as an indelible stigma on this odious person. Everything announced in him the prowling jackal, that possesses all the ferocity of the lion, but none of that animal's nobility or courage.

The clearing we have described was one of the principal haunts of the Vulture, that terrible bandit who, at the time we write of, was ravaging the state of Guadalajara. The men collected in it formed his band, and the two men we have just introduced were, the first, *El Buitre* himself; the second, *El Garrucholo*, his lieutenant and dearest friend.

At the moment we bring them on the stage, these two interesting personages were engaged, as we shall see, in a confidential conversation. We may observe that, strangely enough, this conversation was not held in Spanish, but in English.

"Hem!" El Garrucholo said, as he inhaled a mouthful of smoke, which he immediately sent forth again from his mouth and nostrils. "What do you find so disagreeable in our profession, John? For my part, I consider it delightful. These worthy Mexicans are gentle as lambs; they allow themselves to be plundered with unequalled patience; and you will agree with me, my dear fellow, that we gain more by cutting the buttons from their *calzoneras* than by easing the richest gentleman down there."

"All that is possible, my friend," El Buitre answered, throwing away his cigarette with a gesture of impatience. "I do not assert the contrary. Assuredly the profit is large, and the risk nothing, I grant; but—"

"Well, why do you stop? Go on."

"In a word, I was not born for such a trade."

El Garrucholo gave vent to a hearty laugh.

"That's where the shoe galls you, then?" he said, with a shrug of his shoulders. "You are mad, comrade: every man is born for the trade he carries on, especially when he chose it himself."

"Would you assert by that——?"

"What I say I mean. When I picked you up in Mexico, under the arcades of the Plaza Mayor, with a dagger buried in your breast up to the hilt, and not a real in your pockets, I should have done better, deuce take me, to let you die like a masterless dog, instead of curing you; at least, I should not have heard such nonsense from you."

"Why did you not do so? At any rate I should have died without dishonouring an honourable name."

"Deuce take the honourable name, and the man who bears it! My dear fellow, you annoy me by your ridiculous pretensions; you forget, with your mania for nobility, that you are only a foundling."

El Buitre frowned and seized his lieutenant's arm.

"Enough on that subject, Red Blood; you know that I have already warned you that I would not suffer any jesting on that head."

"Bah! What's the odds about being a foundling? A man ought not to feel annoyed at that; it is one of those accidents for which the most honest fellow cannot be responsible."

"You are my friend, Red Blood; or, at least, seem to be so."

"In your turn, my noble Mr. John Stanley," the bandit sharply interrupted him, "do not express such doubts about me; they grieve and insult me more than I can express. I am attached to you as the blade of my bowie-knife is to the hilt I am yours, body and soul. I have only that one virtue, if it be one; so pray do not strip me of it."

El Buitre remained silent for a moment, and then continued in a conciliating voice, —

"I am wrong. Pardon me, brother; in truth, I have had sufficient proofs of your friendship to have no right to doubt it. Still it seems to me so strange, that I at times ask myself how it comes that you, Red Blood, who hate humanity in a mass—you to whom nothing is respectable or sacred—feel for me a friendship which rises to the most complete abnegation and the most utter weakness. That appears to me so extraordinary, that I would give much to hold the solution of the problem."

"You are an ass, John!" the bandit replied in a mocking tone. "What is the use of telling you why I love you? You would not understand me. Suffice it for you to know that it is so. Do you believe me, then, a perfect ferocious brute, incapable of generous instincts?"

"I do not say that."

"You think it, which comes to the same thing. But it is of no matter to me: I dispense you from gratitude; you may even hate me, and I should not care. I do not love you for yourself, but for myself. But suppose we talk of something else, if you are agreeable?"

"I wish nothing better, for I see that I should lose as much time in trying to draw a good reason from you as in washing a blackamoor white."

"Ta, ta, ta! You are an ass, I repeat. But let me alone; if a certain thing I am now scheming succeed, we shall soon bury El Buitre to bring John Stanley to life again."

The salteador quivered.

"May Heaven hear you!" he exclaimed involuntarily.

"You had better appeal to the other place if you wish to succeed," the bandit said with a grin; "but you trust to me. Soon, I hope, we shall so completely change our skins that fellows will be very clever who recognise us. Look ye, John: in, this world all that is needful is to take the ball on the bound and turn with the wind."

"I confess, my good fellow, that I do not understand a syllable of what you are saying to me."

"Eh! What do you want to understand for? You never were the worse off for leaving me to guide you. Two words are as good as a thousand. Before long we shall turn our coats, and change, not the trade we carry on so agreeably, but the name under which we do it, to assume one better sounding and more lofty. Look there!" he added, pointing sarcastically at his comrades. "What an imposing collection of honest fellows we shall restore to circulation under our auspices! Will it not be magnificent, after having so long plundered individuals, to become suddenly the defenders of a nation to the prejudice of the government?"

"Yes," El Buitre said thoughtfully, "I have always dreamed—"

"Of carrying on our trade on a grand scale, eh? You were right: there is nothing like doing things properly, if you wish to be held in estimation. Well, be at ease; I will procure that pleasure. At any rate, if luck desert you, you will have the advantage of being shot instead of being hanged or garotted, and that is a consolation."

"Yes," El Buitre said quickly; "in that way a man dies like a gentleman."

"And is not dishonoured, I allow. Ah! The filibusters of old were lucky fellows; they conquered empires, and handed down their names to posterity, the exploits of the hero easily causing the crimes of the bandit to be forgotten."

"Will you never be serious?"

"I am only too much so, on the contrary; for, as you see, although you did not confide in me, I am preparing you a place by the side of the Cortez, the Almagros, and Pizarros, whose glory has so long prevented you sleeping."

"You may jest, Red Blood," the salteador said with an accent of profound emotion; "but if, as I suppose, you appreciate my character at its true value, you know that I only seek one thing—to regenerate these unhappy races, whom a brutalising subjection has plunged during so many centuries into a degrading barbarism."

"You only wish for the welfare of humanity of course," the bandit said with an ironical laugh. "We should not be worthy sons of Uncle Sam, that land of liberty and theoretical philanthropy, did we not dream of the amelioration of society. That is the reason why, while biding our time, we have become of our private authority redressers of wrong, and gentlemen of the road—a charming trade, I may remark parenthetically, and which we carry on conscientiously."

"Go to the deuce, you inexplicable scamp!" the young man exclaimed in a passion. "Shall I never know how to speak or how to deal with you?"

"No," he replied seriously, "no, John, so long as you try to play at hide and seek with me, who know every thought of your heart. Cease to display these pretensions to honesty, which deceive nobody, not even yourself, and become frankly a bandit chief till you can be something else. When the moment has arrived it will be time to put on a cloak of hypocrisy, which will deceive the fools, and consolidate the position you have acquired."

At this moment the shriek of the owl was heard in the thickest part of the forest.

"What's that?" El Buitre asked, not sorry to break off a conversation which was taking a personal turn rather disagreeable to him.

"A signal given by a sentry," El Garrucholo answered; "a spy who doubtlessly brings us news. We are awaiting, as you know, the passing of certain travellers."

"I know it; but they are said to be well armed, and under good escort."

"All the better; they will defend themselves, and that will be a change."

"The truth is, that those we have stopped for some time past seemed to have agreed to let themselves be plundered without a murmur."

"If the information I have received be exact, that will not be the case with the present party."

The owl cry was heard a second time, but now much nearer.

"It is time," El Garrucholo observed.

The two chiefs then put on black velvet masks, and almost immediately a man appeared, led by two bandits. On entering the clearing this individual threw around a glance rather of astonishment than terror: nothing in his conduct showed that he had fallen into an ambuscade, for his face was calm, though rather pale, and his step was assured.

The bandits who escorted him led him before the two chiefs, who examined him attentively through the holes in their masks. El Buitre then addressed the bandits in Spanish.

"Where the deuce did you catch that scoundrel?" he said in a rough voice. "He has not an ochavo about him. Hang him, and let us have no more bother."

"Yes," the lieutenant observed, "he is only fit for that, as he was such an ass as to rush into the net prepared for more noble game."

"Permit me, excellency," one of the bandits said, bowing respectfully; "this man was not caught by us."

"How is he here, then?"

"Because, illustrious captain, he earnestly asked to be led into your excellency's presence, as he had matters of the utmost importance to impart to you."

"Ah!" the chief said, but added, "I know the fellow; he is, if I am not mistaken, the huésped of the mesón of San Juan."

The prisoner bowed in affirmation.

It was really the worthy Saccaplata himself. After sending off his criado, and while Don Cornelio was with the colonel, the host thought that nobody could do one's business so well as one's self; and as he was probably anxious that it should succeed, he had started off after the peon, whom he had no difficulty in catching up, for the poor fellow was not at all anxious to execute the commission his master had intrusted to him. Saccaplata sent him back to the mesón; and, while the peon returned in delight, had himself attempted the adventure.

"Indeed!" the lieutenant remarked. "Does Señor Saccaplata wish to enter into business relations with us? That would be an excellent idea."

"I do not say no, honourable caballero," the landlord replied in a honeyed voice. "Business is very bad at this moment, and it is certain that a little extra profit, honestly come by, would be acceptable; but, for the present, I only desire—"

"To the point," El Buitre suddenly interrupted him; "we have no time to lose in silly remarks."

The landlord understood that he must be brief, if he did not wish to bring down certain unpleasantnesses on himself.

"The fact is this," he said: "I have in my house, at the present moment, several rich travellers."

"We know it. What next?"

"Among them is the Señor Colonel—"

"Don Sebastian Guerrero, proceeding to Tepic with his daughter and four servants," the lieutenant interrupted him. "What next?"

"What next?" the landlord said, sadly discountenanced.

"Yes, what next?"

"That is all."

"What, you scoundrel! And you had the effrontery to venture among us, only to tell us a thing we knew as well as yourself?" El Garrucholo exclaimed.

"I thought I was doing you a service."

"You wished to be a spy on us."

"I!"

"Of course. Do you take us for fools like yourself, you wretch? But you shall remember this visit. The *orejada*" he added, turning to the two bandits, who had remained by the landlord's side.

"One moment," the captain said.

Saccaplata, fancying he should escape with the fright, grimaced a smile.

"I will tell you," the captain continued, "why you came to us. You want to revenge yourself on Colonel Guerrero, who a few hours back inflicted on you a well-merited correction."

"But—" the landlord ventured.

"Silence! Do not attempt to deny it. I was there. I saw what occurred. As you are too great a coward to dare to avenge yourself, you thought of us, supposing that we should not refuse to render you that slight service. What do you say—is that the truth?"

"Hum! I would not venture to contradict your excellency," the landlord said, now beginning to regret having entered this wasp's nest.

The bandits, attracted by the colloquy, had gradually drawn nearer, and formed a circle round the speakers, while laughing cunningly to each other. Still, although accustomed to the pleasing eccentricities of their worthy chief, they were far from anticipating the *dénouement* of this scene.

After having proved to Saccaplata as clearly as the day that he knew the motive that led him to offer his good services to the salteadores, the captain continued in these terms, while smiling cunningly:—

"Dear huésped of my heart, we do not refuse to undertake revenging you, the more so as we had already made up our minds to stop the colonel."

"Ah!" the landlord said, beginning to feel easier.

"Yes: still, after reflecting on it thoroughly, we gave up the plan. The colonel is brave—he will defend himself; moreover, he has with him four well-armed and determined men. My faith, it was too great a risk; but if you insist—"

"Immensely!" the other exclaimed, deceived by the bandit's feigned kindliness.

"Very good," the other answered, changing his tone; "then it is a matter of business between us. Now, such things are always paid for, as you know, my scamp."

Saccaplata turned involuntarily toward the other salteadores, who were grinning affably at him.

"Consequently," the captain continued with perfect calmness, "you will pay me twenty ounces for your vengeance, which I take on my own account, and ten for your ransom."

"Heaven save me!" the landlord said, clasping his hands in despair. "I never possessed such a sum, not even in a dream."

"That is a matter of perfect indifference to me. I never recall my decision under any circumstances. Another time you will think twice before venturing so rashly into the claws of El Buitre. The orejada—"

"Oh, my lord!" the luckless Saccaplata exclaimed, as he fell on his knees, "I am a poor devil. Have pity on me, noble captain, I implore you!"

"Come, put an end to this."

In spite of his cries and protestations, the landlord was seized and haled off by his guardians, amid the laughter and sarcasms of the bandits, whom the sight promised by the captain delighted.

"Stop!" the huésped suddenly exclaimed; "I think I have a little money about me."

"No, no!" the salteadores shouted. "Give him the orejada all the same."

El Garrucholo made a sign, and order was restored.

"Let us see," he said.

The wretch gave a sigh, and with extreme difficulty, after ransacking all his pockets with many a protestation that he was utterly ruined, which the bandits listened to with stoical indifference, he at last succeeded in making up a little more than half the sum.

"Hum!" the lieutenant said as he pocketed the money, "that is nothing; but I am a good fellow. You have no more?"

"Oh! I swear it, excellency," he said, turning out all his pockets.

"Well," El Garrucholo continued philosophically, "no man is bound to do impossibilities, and as you have only that—"

"I am sure of it," the other said, fancying himself saved.

"Well, then," the lieutenant continued, "let him be only attached by one ear: we must be honest."

An immense burst of laughter from the whole band greeted this proposition. The landlord was carried off to a tree, and before he understood what they meant to do to him, he uttered a frightful yell of pain. A bandit had fastened him to the tree by the right ear, by simply driving his knife through it.

"There, that's settled," the lieutenant said. "Now, I warn you that, if you continue to howl, I will have you gagged."

"Traitors, dogs, assassins, kill me!"

"No. But listen; that wound is nothing. It is easy for you to deliver yourself by a slight tug. Your ear will be torn, I allow, but you can't have everything. As soon as you are free, return home; one of our friends will accompany you, and you will pay him the rest of the sum."

"Never!" the landlord howled, "Never! I would sooner die!"

"Very good; then you shall die, and after that we will carry off the contents of the hiding place you have so cleverly made in the wall of your cuarto, by placing before it a picture of Nuestra Señora de Guadalupe. Eh! What do you think of that?"

The lieutenant had hardly finished speaking ere the landlord, by a sharp movement, had regained his liberty. Without thinking of his frightfully-mutilated ear, he threw himself at the feet of El Garrucholo.

"I accept, my lord, I accept; but I implore you, do not ruin me."

"I was certain you would understand. Be off, scoundrel; and if it is any consolation, know that you will be avenged on the colonel."

"Yes," the landlord muttered to himself, "but who will avenge me on you? Thanks," he added aloud; "that promise causes me to forget my suffering."

"All the better; but mind you, no treachery, or we shall manage to get hold of you again."

Saccaplata bowed, but made no reply. He understood that it would have been better for him to remain at home, and allow matters to follow their course, without seeking a problematic vengeance which cost him thirty gold ounces and an ear. On reaching the mesón he paid the rest of his ransom, and banging the door in the face of the bandit who accompanied him, and thanked him with an air of mockery, he sank on a bench, and overcome by so many terrible emotions, fainted away.

IV
THE BARRANCA DEL MAL PASO

The rest of the night passed, apparently at any rate, calmly and tranquilly, and nothing occurred to disturb the rest enjoyed by the guests at the mesón of San Juan. About four in the morning the doors of the travellers' cuartos began to open one after the other, and lights flashed in the patios. The shouts of the muleteers, and the bells of their animals, aroused the colonel and his daughter, warning them that it was time to prepare for their departure.

Don Sebastian, after the suspicions Don Cornelio had suggested to him, did not at all wish, as he had a young lady with him, to start before sunrise, especially as he had to traverse the gorge we have already described, and where it would be easy to form an ambuscade.

By the sunlight he had a better chance, for two reasons: in the first place, the servants who accompanied him were old soldiers, accustomed to war, and greatly attached to him; the second was, that the Mexican brigands are usually great cowards, and whenever they meet with any serious resistance from those they attack, they immediately give up the game.

These two reasons, and, before all, the fear of alarming his daughter, and uselessly exposing her to danger during the darkness, obliged the colonel to let all the other travellers at the mesón start before him; and, in fact, they soon quitted the hostelry, and dispersed in various directions.

The Señor Saccaplata, with pallid face, compressed eyebrows, and head bandaged up, was walking up and down the patio, with his arms behind his back, every now and then raising his eyes angrily to the colonel's window, and growling in a low voice,—

"Body and bones! Will not that trumpery colonel make up his mind to start soon, if he is so ready to give the bastinado to poor folk? But let him do what he will, he will not escape the fate that awaits him."

At this moment a young man appeared in the patio, strumming a guitar, and singing in a low voice,—

"No sabo donde mirar,
De todo teme y rezela,

Si al cielo teme su furia,
Porque hizo al cielo ofensa." [3]

These verses, taken from the romance of King Rodrigo, though probably sung without any malignant meaning, still referred so closely to the landlord's present position, that he turned furiously to the unlucky singer, and attacked him in a brutal voice.

"Deuce take your howling! Why do you come buzzing in this way in my ears, when you ought, on the contrary, to be preparing for your departure?"

"Why, it is our worthy huésped," Don Cornelio replied with that joyful accent peculiar to him. "What! You are not fond of music? You are wrong, my worthy friend, for what I am singing to you is really fine."

"That is possible," the other said in a rough voice; "but I should feel obliged by your giving me no more of it."

"Oh, oh! You are not in a good temper this morning. What's the matter with you, that you are so bandaged up? On my soul, you must be ill. Oh! I see what it is; you slept with your window open, and have caught a toothache."

The landlord turned green with impotent fury.

"Caballero," he shouted, "take care."

"Of what?" Don Cornelio said peacefully. "Toothache is not catching, as I am aware. Poor man! Pain causes him to wander. Take care of yourself, my good man; take care of yourself, I advise you."

And without further ceremony he turned his back on him, and began again the song which so annoyed the landlord at the point where he broke it off.

"Hum!" the latter growled, shaking his fist at the singer; "I hope that you will catch something in the row. Ah!" he added, "the sun is rising: perhaps that will induce him to come down."

In fact, the sun appeared at this moment in a bed of vapour, and after a twilight, whose duration was almost nothing, the day succeeded, as it were, immediately to night.

Don Cornelio, aided by the colonel's servants, fed the horses and saddled the mules—preparations which brought a smile to the landlord's lips which would have caused the colonel to feel uncomfortable had he seen it.

Suddenly a sound of horses was heard outside, and two men trotted into the patio, through the gateway left open after the departure of the arrieros and other travellers. At this unexpected arrival the landlord turned as if a viper had stung him.

"Confusion!" he muttered; "day has hardly broken ere these accursed fellows come across my path."

The two arrivals troubled themselves in no way about their host's ill-temper, but dismounted, and taking the bridles off their horses, led them to the noria to let them drink.

The travellers were dressed in the garb of the frontier men, and appeared to be from forty to forty-five years of age. Like all wayfarers in this blessed country, where every man must depend on himself alone, they were armed; but, in lieu of the lance or fusil usual in the interior, they had excellent Mexican rifles—a peculiarity which, in addition to their *zarapés* of Indian manufacture, and their fiery and half-wild mustangs, allowed them to be recognised as Sonorians, or at least men domiciled in that state.

The landlord, seeing that the newcomers did not appear to trouble themselves in the least about him, decided at length on walking toward them and addressing them.

"What do you want?" he said to them.

"Nothing just at present," the elder replied; "but so soon as our horses have finished drinking, you will give each of them a measure of maize and a truss of alfalfa."

"I am the mesonero, and not a peon. It is not my place to wait upon you," he said brutally.

The traveller who had spoken looked askance at the host.

"I don't care whether it is you or your criados who do it," he answered dryly, "provided that the order I have given is executed promptly, for I am in a hurry."

In the face of this rebuff, and especially the glance that accompanied it, the huésped judged it prudent to draw in his horns and assume a more conciliatory tone. For the last few hours poor Saccaplata had not been fortunate with his travellers. All those Heaven sent him had the air of young bulls escaped from the *toril*.

"Your excellencies are doubtless anxious to set out again?" he said in an insinuating voice.

The strangers made no answer.

"Not to be too curious," the landlord continued, not yet discouraged, "may I ask in what direction your honourable seigneuries intend to proceed?"

One of the travellers then raised his head, and, looking the indiscreet mesonero full in the face, said with a mocking air, —

"If you are asked, you will answer that you do not know. Come, my good fellow, have us attended to, and blow your own *puchero*, without troubling yourself about ours: you might find it too hot for you."

The host shrugged his shoulders and slipped away, the more nimbly because he noticed the colonel entering the patio at the moment, and felt no desire to come in contact with him.

The two strangers exchanged a smile, and, without further remark, watched the peon who was giving their horses the provender they had ordered.

Don Sebastian was ready to start: he had come to give a final glance to the horses before leading his daughter downstairs. Don Cornelio walked up to him so soon as he saw him, and after wishing him good day, drew him a little aside and whispered, —

"Look there, colonel," and he pointed to the two strangers; "those are sturdy fellows, if I am not mistaken."

"They are so," Don Sebastian made answer; "I did not notice them before."

"They have only just arrived. They would be famous recruits added to our party, if they would consent to travel with us. What do you think of it?"

"I think you are right; but will they consent?"

"Why not? If they are going the same road as ourselves they will derive the same benefit from our presence as we shall from theirs."

"That is true. Have you spoken to them?"

"No: as I told you, they arrived this moment. You ought to try to persuade them."

"I see no harm in attempting it, at least," the colonel answered.

Hereupon, leaving Don Cornelio, he advanced toward the strangers, and saluting them politely, said, —

"You have magnificent horses, caballeros. I see that they come from the prairies."

"Yes, they are real mustangs," one of the strangers replied, returning the bow.

"You are finishing your journey at a very early hour," the colonel continued. "With horses like yours a deal of ground could be covered."

"What makes you suppose, caballero, that our journey is ended?"

"Why, your arrival at this hostelry at so early an hour."

"Ah! You might be mistaken."

"Pardon my indiscretion, caballeros. Do you come from Guadalajara, or are you going there?"

"Caballero," the stranger replied dryly, who had hitherto spoken, "we the more readily pardon your indiscretion, because it appears that in this hostelry everybody passes his time in asking questions; still, you will permit me not to answer yours. My companion and myself are old travellers, and we know that on the roads of this country men too often repent gossiping about their business, but never of keeping it to themselves."

The colonel drew himself up with an air of pique.

"As you please, caballero," he replied coldly. "I cannot feel annoyed at your prudence; still, I would observe that you have given a wrong meaning to my remarks. I only wished to offer you my escort in crossing an ill-famed gorge, in which the band of the dangerous robber, El Buitre, is at this moment ensconced."

"I know the man by repute," the stranger said in a somewhat more affable tone. "My friend and myself will, I hope, be sufficient to keep him at arm's length; still, though I do not accept your offer, I thank you for the cordiality which urged you to make it."

The conversation broke off here. The two men bowed with all the marks of the most exquisite politeness, and turned their backs on each other. The colonel, annoyed at the way in which his advances had been met, gave the order for departure, and went to fetch his daughter. An instant later he reappeared with her; the band mounted, and, on a signal from Don Sebastian, set out. On passing before the strangers, who watched their departure, the colonel took off his hat, as did Don Cornelio. Doña Angela gave a graceful bow, accompanied by a charming smile. The strangers, in their turn, uncovered and bowed respectfully to the party.

"There, scoundrel," the colonel said as he threw an ounce to the landlord, who watched their departure with a cunning look, "there's a plaster for your wounds."

Saccaplata sharply picked up the ounce, thrust it into his pocket, and crossed himself as he muttered, —

"You will want a good many ounces to cure your wounds, you will. Bah!" he added, with a sinister laugh, "it is now El Buitre's affair; let them settle it together."

When Don Sebastian had left the hostelry he divided his party into three: two of his servants rode in front, gun on thigh; two others behind; while he and Don Cornelio, having Doña Angela between them, rode in the middle. All being thus arranged, and the order given to keep a careful outlook, the cavalcade started at a sharp trot.

In the meanwhile the two strangers, as we have said, remained at the mesón. They watched the little party for a long time, and then, as their horses had finished eating, they put on their bridles and tightened their girths.

"My faith, Don Louis!" the younger of the two at length said, "I can't help it; I must tell you what I have on my mind, or I shall choke."

"Speak, my friend," his comrade said with a sad smile. "I know as well as you do what is troubling your mind."

"Perhaps so; still that would surprise me."

"Listen, then, Belhumeur. You are asking yourself at this moment why I was so rude to that gentleman whom I do not know, and whom I saw for a moment for the first time in my life?"

"By my faith! You have guessed it: that was, in truth, my thought. I seek in vain the reason for such extraordinary conduct on your part, and I confess that I give it up as a bad job."

"Do not trouble yourself any further, my good fellow. I was involuntarily guided by a secret presentiment, by a species of incomprehensible instinct, which forced me to act as I did."

"That is strange."

"Yes, is it not so? You know the feeling of instinctive repulsion one experiences on touching a reptile?"

"Of course."

"Well, when that man advanced toward me, even before I saw him, I felt his presence, if I may say so; my heart beat violently; and when he addressed me I felt a sudden and incomprehensible pain."

Belhumeur regarded him for a moment with fixed attention.

"And you conclude from that?" he said.

"That this man will be my enemy at some appointed moment; that he will stand in my path, gloomy and implacable, and prove fatal to me."

"Come, my friend, that is not possible. You are leaving this country, never to return to it, since, in spite of all your researches, you have been unable to find the man on whose behalf you came. The man you saw this morning is a field officer in the Mexican army, and it is not very likely he will leave his country: everything opposes it. Where can you meet again?"

"I do not know, Belhumeur; I seek neither to guess nor to foresee the future. It is evident that, after leaving you at the Hacienda del Milagro, I shall proceed to Guaymas, where I shall embark, I know not yet for what country; and it is my settled purpose never to set foot in Mexico again. Still I repeat to you, although it may appear absurd, I am convinced that that man will be my enemy some day, and that one of us will kill the other."

"Come, come, I will not discuss that subject with you; it is better for us, I fancy, to start, for we have a long journey before us today."

"That is true, my friend. Let us start, and think no more of my forebodings. They will turn out as Heaven may direct."

"Amen!" Belhumeur said. "That is how I like to see you; thus you resemble my brave Raphael, my dear Loyal Heart, to whom I wish to make you known before leaving you."

"You will afford me the greatest pleasure."

They mounted their horses, paid the landlord, and in their turn quitted the mesón de San Juan, walking their horses in the direction of the barranca del mal paso, where the colonel had preceded them. They proceeded for some time in silence, side by side. At length the Canadian, who could not remain long without speaking, took the word.

"Do you not think, Don Louis, that, supposing the colonel spoke the truth, two men like ourselves would prove very useful to him?"

"What does that concern us?" Don Louis asked sharply.

"Us nothing; and assuredly, if only that soldier, to whom you have such an antipathy, were concerned, I should not trouble myself about him, but leave him to settle with the bandits as best he could."

"Well?"

"Don't you understand me?"

"No, on my honour."

"Did you not notice the charming girl that accompanies him?"

"Of course I did."

"Would it not be frightful—?"

"Good heavens!" the Count de Prébois Crancé, whom the reader has doubtlessly recognised, [4] quickly interrupted him, "that would be fearful. Poor child! Forward, Belhumeur, forward! We must save her."

"Ah!" the Canadian thought to himself, "I was sure I should find the soft place."

The two men bowed over their horses' necks, and started with the velocity of the tempest. They had scarce gone a mile when cries and shots reached their ears.

"Forward—confound it, forward!" the count shouted, urging his horse to increased speed.

"Forward!" Belhumeur repeated.

They rushed into the barranca at headlong speed, and fell like two demons into the midst of the bandits, whom they saluted with two shots; then clubbing their rifles, they employed them like maces, bounding into the medley with indescribable fury.

It was high time for this assistance to reach the colonel. Three of his servants were killed; Don Cornelio was lying wounded on the ground; while Don Sebastian, with his back against a block of granite, was desperately defending himself against five or six bandits who assailed him.

El Buitre had seized Doña Angela, and thrown her across his saddle-bow, in spite of her shrieks and resistance; but suddenly Don Louis dealt the bandit a crushing blow on the head, which hurled him to the ground, and delivered the girl. Belhumeur all this time did not remain inactive; he wounded and trampled under his horse's hoofs all those who dared to oppose his passage.

The salteadores, surprised by this sudden attack, which they were far from anticipating—frightened by the carnage the newcomers caused among their comrades, and not knowing how many foes they might have upon them, were seized with a panic fear, and fled in the utmost disorder, clambering up the rocks. El Garrucholo, at the peril of his life, picked up his captain, whom he would not abandon, and El Buitre once again escaped the garota. The salteadores lost in this skirmish more than two-thirds of their numbers.

When tranquillity was restored, and the bandits had completely disappeared, Don Sebastian warmly thanked the two adventurers for the timely aid they had rendered him. Don Louis received politely, but very coldly, the colonel's advances, confining himself to saying that if he had been so fortunate as to save his life, he found a reward in his own heart, and that was sufficient for him; but, in spite of the colonel's pressing, he refused to tell him who he was, alleging as his sole reason that he was about to leave Mexico for ever, and that he did not wish to lay on him a burden so heavy as gratitude. At this remark Doña Angela drew nearer to Don Louis, and said with a smile of gentle reproach,—

"It is quite natural that you who have saved our lives should forget the fact, or at least attach but slight importance to it; but my father and myself will remember it for ever."

And before Don Louis could prevent it, the lovely girl bounded like a fawn, threw her arms round his neck, and holding up her pure forehead, which was still rather pale,—

"Kiss me, my saviour!" she said, with tears in her eyes.

The count, affected, in spite of himself, by an action full of such simple frankness, respectfully kissed the maiden's brow, then turned away, that she might not read the sweet and yet painful impression so simple an action had produced on him.

Doña Angela, smiling and blushing, sought refuge in her father's arms, leaving in Don Louis' hand a small relic she usually wore round her neck.

"Keep it," she said to him, with that sweet Spanish superstition so full of grace; "it will bring you good fortune."

"Yes, I will keep it, señorita," the count replied, hiding it in his bosom, "as a reminiscence of a moment of happiness you unconsciously caused me this day, by proving to me that, in spite of misfortunes, my heart is not so dead as I fancied."

The preparations for departure were made. Don Sebastian, deprived of his servants, could not dream of continuing his journey. He decided on returning to Guadalajara, in order to obtain another escort sufficiently strong to protect his daughter from such a danger as that she had escaped by a miracle. He was, however, greatly embarrassed by Don Cornelio, whom he did not wish to abandon, and yet could not transport.

"I will take charge of this man, caballero," Don Louis then said to him. "Do not trouble yourself about him further. My friend and I are in no great haste. We will carry him to the mesón of San Juan, and not leave him till he is thoroughly cured."

Two hours later the two parties separated in front of Saccaplata's mesón, who saw them return with great terror; but the colonel thought it advisable, for Don Cornelio's sake, to appear ignorant of the part the landlord had played in the attack, to which himself and daughter had so nearly fallen victims.

Don Sebastian and Don Louis separated with a frigid bow, like men who are persuaded they will never meet again. But no one can foresee the future, and unconsciously chance was about to bring them hereafter face to face under strange circumstances, the realisation of which neither assuredly suspected at the moment.

[3] He knows not where to look; he fears or distrusts everything. If he is afraid of the anger of Heaven, why did he insult it?

[4] See the "Tiger Slayer." Same publishers.

CHAPTER I
THE NIGHT HALT

Before the discovery of the rich placers in the neighbourhood of San Francisco, California was completely wild and almost unknown. The port of San Francisco, the finest and largest in the world, destined to become very shortly the commercial *entrepôt* of the Pacific, was at that time only frequented by whalers, who, at the period when the whales retire to the shallow water, came to fish there, cut them up, and melt down their blubber.

A few Flat-head Indians wandered haphazard through the vast forests that covered the seaboard; and in this country, which trade has now seized on, and which is entering, with all sail set, into the movement of progress, wild beasts lorded it as masters.

An old officer of Charles X.'s Swiss Guard had founded a poor colony on the territory of San Francisco, and cut down trees, which he converted into planks by the aid of a few watermills.

Such was the condition in which this magnificent country languished, when suddenly the news of the discovery of rich placers in California burst on the world like a shell. Then the country, as if touched by the magic wand of some powerful enchanter, became all at once transformed. From all parts of the world adventurers flocked in, bearing with them that feverish activity and boundless audacity which ignore all difficulties, and surmount every obstacle.

At a spot where, a few days previously, gloomy and mysterious forests, old as the world, stretched out, a city was created, improvised, and within a few months counted its inhabitants by tens of thousands. The port, so long deserted, was crammed with vessels of every sort and every size, and the gold fever renewed the Saturnalia of the Spanish conquistadors of the Middle Ages.

For some time after, this country offered to the eye of the observer a sight the most hideous, the most grand, the most heart-rending, and most striking that can be imagined. All was mingled, confounded, and upturned. It was a confusion, a hurly-burly impossible to describe, where nothing existed any longer—where every tie was broken, every social idea annihilated; and in this terrible pell-mell, in this frightful race to the placers, rogues and gentlemen, soldiers and priests, diplomatists and physicians, jostled each other, all running, howling, wielding the dagger or the revolver, possessed by only one idea, instinct, or passion—that of gold. For gold these men would have sold everything—conscience, honour, probity, everything, even to themselves!

We will not enter into fuller details of this wondrous period, during which California emerged from her nothingness, to take her place, after ten years of desperate struggling, among the civilised peoples. Other pens, far more eloquent than ours, have undertaken the rude task of telling us the history of these striking incidents. We will confine ourselves to stating that, at the period of our story, gold had only just been discovered, and California was struggling against the first raging attack of *delirium tremens*.

It was about three years after the events we narrated in our prologue.

In the Sierra Nevada, upon the picturesque slopes that descend gradually to the sea, in the heart of an immense virgin forest a hundred leagues from San Francisco, between that city and Los Angeles, the heat had been stifling during the day. At sunset the sea breeze had risen, and slightly refreshed the atmosphere; but it sank again almost immediately, and the temperature had again become heavy and oppressive.

The motionless trees concealed beneath their dense foliage birds of every description, which only revealed their presence at intervals by shrill and discordant cries. Hideous alligators wallowing in the mud of the swamps, or holding on to the trunks of dead trees scattered here and there, were the only living beings that animated the landscape, which was rendered even more gloomy and mournful by the pale, uncertain, and tremulous flickering of the moonbeams that filtered with great difficulty through the rare openings in the verdurous forest dome, and sported capriciously and fantastically about the trees and branches, though unable to lessen the mysterious obscurity that reigned in the leafy covert.

A noise of horses' hoofs was heard on one of the innumerable tracks made by the wild beasts as they proceed in search of water, and two men debouched into a clearing formed by the fall of several trees that had died of old age, and whose mossy trunks were already in a state of decomposition.

These men were both dressed in the costume of hunters or wood rangers, and were armed with American rifles, long knives, and *machetes*. A *reata*, rolled up and fastened to the saddle-bow, allowed them to be recognised as partisans from the Mexican frontiers.

Both had passed middle life; but there the resemblance between them ended. At the first glance it was easy to guess that one belonged to the

Northern European race; while his comrade, on the contrary, by the olive tint of his complexion, and his angular features, offered a perfect type of the Indian aborigines of Chili, so eloquently celebrated by Ercilla, and known in South America by the name of Araucanos—a powerful, intelligent, and energetic race, the only one of all the native tribes of the New World which has managed to retain its nationality, and caused its independence to be respected to the present day.

These two men were Valentine Guillois, better known as the "Trail-hunter," and Curumilla, his silent and devoted companion ever since the day that chance so many years previously had led Valentine into Araucania. [1]

Years, while accumulating on the heads of the two men, had produced but a slight change in their external appearance. They were still quite upright, and seemed equally vigorous. A few more wrinkles had formed on the Frenchman's pensive brow, and some silvery threads were added to his locks; his features, more angular than before, had assumed those firm and distinct lines, alone produced by reflection and long contests valiantly sustained; his eye was still equally frank, but the flash was more incisive; and his face wore that melancholy impression which deceptions of every description, and great grief, stamp indelibly on the countenance of powerful men, whom the fearful storms of life have bowed, though not broken.

The Indian was still morose and concentrated. Age, which had laid even a smaller hold on his organisation than on that of his comrade, had merely increased the worthy Araucanian's habitual taciturnity, and drawn over his gloomy face a thicker veil of that stoical fatalism peculiar to the aboriginal race of America.

The two men advanced slowly side by side, apparently plunged in deep thought. At times Valentine stopped, looked cautiously around him, and then resumed his march, shaking his head dubiously. Each time that the hunter reined in his horse Curumilla imitated him, though not evidencing by the slightest sign that he took any interest in his companion's operations.

The forest grew with each step denser, the paths became narrower, and all appeared to forebode that the horses would soon be unable to advance, impeded as they were by the creepers that were intertwined into a thick trellis-work in front of them.

The two horsemen at length reached the clearing to which we have already alluded, after intense difficulty. On arriving there, Valentine stopped, and heaving a sigh of relief,—

"By Jove!" he said, "Curumilla, my good friend, I was mad to believe you and follow you so far; it is evident that we are lost."

The Indian shook his head in denial.

"Hem! I am aware that you fellows have a marvellous talent for following a trail, and that you rarely lose your way, even in a place you have never visited before. Still the darkness is so intense here, that I can hardly distinguish objects only two paces ahead of me. Come, allow that we have lost ourselves. Hang it! That may happen to anybody. I propose that we stop here and await sunrise before we renew our search, the more so because, for nearly two hours, it has been impossible to discover the slightest trace proving to us that we are still on the right road."

Curumilla, without replying, dismounted, and explored the clearing on all sides; then, at the expiration of a few minutes, he returned to his friend's side, and gave him a sign to mount again. Valentine had carefully followed his movements.

"Well," he said, checking him, "are you not convinced yet?"

"One hour more," the Indian replied, liberating himself gently, and getting into his saddle.

"Hang, it all!" Valentine said, "I confess I am growing tired of playing at hide and seek in this inextricable forest, and if you do not give me a positive proof of what you assert, I will not stir from this spot."

Curumilla bent toward him, and, showing him a small object, said,—

"Look!"

"Eh?" Valentine remarked in surprise, after carefully examining the object his comrade handed him. "What the deuce is it? Why," he added almost immediately, "I ought to have recognised it at once: it is a cigar-case, and a handsome one too. There is a cigar still in it, if I am not mistaken."

He remained for an instant in thought.

"It is true," he went on, "that I have not seen these luxurious products of civilisation for a long time; indeed, since I gave them up to lead the life of a free hunter. Where did you find it, Curumilla?"

"There," he answered, stretching out his arm.

"Good! The owner of that case cannot be far from us, so let us push on."

He pocketed the case, and the two horsemen set out once more.

After crossing the clearing, the path on which they entered began gradually to widen, and soon they noticed, by the moonbeams that lighted them at intervals, that the path had been trodden by a large number of cloven-footed animals, which had cropped the leaves and broken down the branches on both sides. These traces were still quite fresh.

"Come," Valentine said gaily, "I was wrong just now, Curumilla. We were really on the right track, and I believe we shall soon catch up the persons we have so long been seeking."

Something like a smile attempted to contract the Indian's features; but the attempt was not a happy one, and stopped at a grimace. All at once Curumilla laid his hand on his comrade's bridle, and bending forward,—

"Listen," he said.

Valentine listened attentively; but, for all that, several moments passed ere he could distinguish aught else than those confused and mysterious sounds which never expire in the desert: at length something resembling a musical note borne on the breeze gently died away on his ear. The hunter started back in surprise.

"Ah, by Jupiter!" he exclaimed, "that musician has chosen a strange time to give a concert. I am curious to see such an original a little nearer. Let us push on."

After marching for about a quarter of a mile further they began to see a fire flashing through the trees, and distinctly heard a masculine and sonorous voice singing to the accompaniment of a jarana. The hunters stopped in surprise, and listened.

"By heaven!" the Frenchman muttered, "it is the romancero of King Rodrigo, sung by an unknown voice at night in the heart of a virgin forest. Never has that powerful poetry affected me so deeply. In truth, everything here harmonises with that song, which is so thoroughly sorrowful and despairing. Whoever he may be, I must see the man who has unconsciously caused me a few moments of such gentle emotion. Were it the demon in person, I would shake his hand ere the last strains had ceased vibrating on the strings of his jarana."

And without further deliberation, Valentine, after giving Curumilla a sign to follow him, resolutely entered the circle of light. At the sound of horses' hoofs, the stranger, with a movement swift as thought, threw the guitar across his back, and leaped up with a sabre in his right hand and a revolver in the other.

"Hold!" he shouted boldly; "stop, if you please, caballero, or I shall fire."

"Pray do not do so, señor," Valentine answered, who considered it prudent to obey the order given him, "for you would run the risk of killing a friend, and they are too rare in the desert to be received, when met, by a pistol shot."

"Hum! I trust what you say is true," the other answered, still on the defensive; "still I should feel obliged by your explaining to me, in two words, who you are, and what you are seeking after the acquaintance becomes more intimate between us."

"Of course, caballero; I see no inconvenience in satisfying your wishes, especially as prudence is one of the theological virtues recommended in the regions where we now are."

"On my soul, you appear to me to be a jolly fellow! I hope we shall become friends ere long; and to prove to you that I sincerely desire it, and at the same time to arouse your confidence, I will begin by telling you who I am, which will not take long."

"Pray do so."

The stranger then thrust his revolver into his belt, took three paces forward, removed his wide-brimmed hat, whose long feather swept the ground, and saluted his new acquaintance ceremoniously.

"Señor caballero," he said with infinite grace and politeness, "my name is Don Cornelio Mendoza de Arrizabal, gentleman of the Asturias, noble as the king, and poor at this moment as Job of Bohemian memory. The few *novillos* lying around me are my property, and that of my partner, absent at this moment in search of a few strayed members of the herd, but whom I expect at any moment. These animals were purchased by us at Los Angeles, and we are taking them to San Francisco, with the purpose of selling them at the best price to the gold-seekers and other adventurers collected in that curious city."

After uttering this short speech the young man bowed again, put his hat on his head, placed the point of his sabre on his boot, and waited, foot forward, and his hand on his hip.

Valentine had listened attentively, and when he spoke of his partner a flash of joy sparkled in the hunter's eyes.

"Caballero," he answered, uncovering in his turn, "my friend and myself are two wood rangers, hunters, or trail-seekers, whichever you may please to term us. Attracted by the light of your fire, and the harmonious song that reached our ears, we came toward you for the purpose of claiming from you that hospitality which is never refused in the desert, offering to share our provisions with you, and to be hail fellows well met so long as we may remain in your agreeable company."

"You are welcome, caballeros," Don Cornelio replied nobly. "Pray consider the little we possess as your own."

The hunters bowed and dismounted.

[1] These two characters have been introduced in another work by our author, and are old friends to French readers.

CHAPTER II
FIFTEEN YEARS' SEPARATION

The reception offered the travellers by Don Cornelio was stamped with that graceful kindness and careless ease which so eminently distinguish the Spanish character. Although the adventurer's resources were extremely limited, still he gave the little he possessed with such complacency and so much good humour to his guests, that the latter knew not how to thank him for the attentions he lavished upon them.

After supping as well as they could on *tasajo* (jerked meat) and *tortillas* of maize, washed down with *pulque* and *mezcal*, they carefully wrapped themselves in their zarapés, lay down on the ground with their feet to the fire, and soon appeared to be buried in a deep sleep.

Don Cornelio took up his jarana, and leaning against a larch tree, hummed one of those interminable Spanish romances he was so fond of, in order to keep awake while awaiting his partner's return.

The bivouac where our friends now found themselves was certainly not without a degree of the picturesque. The uncertain gleams of the fire were reflected fantastically on the heads of some seven hundred and fifty novillos, lying side by side, ruminating and sleeping, while the horses were devouring their provender, stamping and neighing. The Spaniard twanged his guitar, and the two hunters slept peacefully. This scene, at once so simple and so singular, was worthy the pencil of Callot.

Two hours thus passed away, and nothing occurred to disturb the repose the encampment enjoyed, and the moon sank lower and lower on the horizon. Don Cornelio's fingers stiffened; his eyes closed; and at times, despite his efforts to keep awake, his head fell on his chest. In despair, the Spaniard at last, beaten by fatigue, was about to yield to the sleep that overpowered him, when a distant noise suddenly dispelled his somnolency, and restored him the full use of his mind and other faculties.

By degrees this noise, at first vague and indistinct, became louder; and a horseman, armed with a long goad, entered the clearing, driving before him a dozen novillos and half-savage bulls. After being helped by Don Cornelio in stockading the straying animals he brought back, the partner, who was no other than Count Louis de Prébois, dismounted and sat down to the fire with that nonchalance and careless motion produced in energetic natures, not so much by fatigue as by discouragement and moral lassitude.

"Ah!" he said, looking at the two men stretched out at the fire, and who, in spite of the noise caused by his arrival, still slept, or appeared to do so, "we have visitors, I see."

"Yes," Don Cornelio made answer, "two hunters from the great prairies. I thought I ought not to refuse them hospitality."

"You have done well, Don Cornelio: no one has a right in the desert to refuse the stranger, who asks for them courteously, the heat of his fire and a moiety of his *tasajo*."

"That was my idea."

"Now, my friend, lie down by our guests and rest yourself. This long watch after the day's toil must have fatigued you beyond measure."

"But will you not sleep a few moments, Don Louis? Rest must be more necessary to you than to myself."

"Permit me to watch," the count answered with a sad smile. "Rest was not made for me."

Don Cornelio did not press him any further. Long accustomed to his companion's character, he considered it useless to make any more objections. A few moments later, wrapped in his zarapé, and with his head on his jarana for a pillow, he slept soundly.

Don Louis threw a few handfuls of dry wood on the fire, which threatened to expire, crossed his arms on his chest, and, leaning his back against a tree, indulged in his thoughts, which were doubtlessly sorrowful and very bitter; for the tears soon fell from his eyes, and ran down his pallid cheeks, while stifled sighs exhaled from his bosom, and muttered words escaped from his lips, crushed between his teeth by sorrow.

So soon as the count, after ordering Don Cornelio to take some repose, fell down exhausted at the foot of a tree, the hunter, who appeared to be sleeping so profoundly, suddenly opened his eyes, rose, and walked gently toward him step by step.

Several hours passed away thus, Louis being still plunged in mournful thoughts, Valentine standing behind him, leaning on his rifle, and fixing on him a glance full of strange meaning.

The stars gradually expired in the depths of the sky, an opal-coloured band began slowly to stripe the horizon, the birds awoke beneath the foliage, sunrise was at hand. Don Louis let his head fall on his chest.

"Why struggle longer?" he said in a hoarse, deep voice. "What good to go farther?"

"Those are very despairing words in the mouth of a man so strong as Count Louis de Prébois," a low but firm voice whispered in his ear, with a tone of gentle and sympathising reproach.

The count shuddered as if he had received an electric shock; a convulsive tremor agitated all his limbs; and he bounded to his feet, examining with haggard eye, pale brow, and disordered features, the man who had so suddenly replied to the words pain had torn from him. The hunter had not changed his position; his eye remained obstinately fixed upon him, with an expression of melancholy, pity, and paternal kindness.

"Oh!" the count muttered in terror, as he passed his hand over his dank forehead; "it is not he—it cannot be he! Valentine, my brother!—you whom I never hoped to see again—answer, in Heaven's name, is it you?"

"'Tis I, brother," the hunter said gently, "whom Heaven brings a second time across your path when all seems once again to fail you."

"Oh!" the count said with an expression impossible to render, "for a long time I have been seeking you—for a long time I have called on you."

"Here I am."

"Yes," he continued, shaking his head mournfully, "you are here, Valentine; but now, alas! It is too late. All is dead in me henceforth—faith, hope, courage: nothing is left to me—nothing but the desire to lie in that tomb, where all my belief and all my departed happiness are buried eternally!"

Valentine remained silent for a few moments, regarding his friend with a glance at once gentle and stern. A flood of memories poured over the hunter's heart; two glistening tears escaped from his eyes, and slowly coursed down his bronzed cheeks; then, without any apparent effort, he drew the count toward him, laid his head on his wide and loyal chest, and kissed him paternally on the forehead.

"You have suffered, then, severely, my poor Louis," he said to him tenderly. "Alas, alas! I was not there to sustain and protect you; but," he added, turning to heaven a glance of bitter sadness and sublime resignation, "I too, Louis, I too, in the heart of the desert, where I sought a refuge, have endured agonising grief. Many times I felt myself strangled by despair; often and often my temples were crushed in by the pressure of the furious madness that invaded my brain; my heart was broken by the terrible anguish I endured; and yet, brother," he added in a soft voice, filled with an ineffable melodiousness, "yet I live, I struggle, and I hope," he said, so low that the count could hardly hear him.

"Oh! Blessed be the chance that brings us together again when I despaired of seeing you, Valentine."

"There is no such thing as chance, brother: it is God who prepares the accomplishment of all events. I was seeking you."

"You were seeking me over here?"

"Why not? Did you not yourself come to Mexico to find me?"

"Yes; but how did you learn the fact?"

Valentine smiled.

"There is nothing extraordinary in it. If you wish it, I will prove to you in a few words that I am much better informed than you suppose, and that I know nearly all that has happened to you since our separation at the hacienda of the Paloma."

"That is strange."

"Why so? About three months ago were you not at the Hacienda del Milagro?"

"I was."

"You left it after spending some days there on your return from a journey you had undertaken to the far west, in search of a rich auriferous placer?"

"It is true."

"During that expedition, full of strange and terrible incidents, two men accompanied you?" [1]

"Yes; a Canadian hunter and a Comanche chief."

"Very good. The hunter's name was Belhumeur, the chief's Eagle-head, I think?"

"They were."

"Do you not remember revealing to Belhumeur (a worthy and honourable hunter, by the way) the reason of the gloomy sorrow that devours you, and for what motives, mere vague suspicions though they were, you had come to Mexico in order to look for your dearest friend, from whom you had been separated so many years?"

"Yes, I remember telling him all that."

"The rest is not difficult to comprehend. I have known Belhumeur many years, and Heaven brought us together during a hunt on the Rio Colorado. One night, while seated at the fire, where our supper was roasting, after talking about a thousand indifferent things, Belhumeur, whom you had left only a few days previously, began by degrees to talk about you. At first, absorbed in my own thoughts, I paid but slight attention to his recital; but when he described to me your meeting with Count de Lhorailles in the desert, your name, uttered by Belhumeur unintentionally, made me tremble. It was then my turn to cross-question him. When I had learned everything, by making him tell the story twenty times over, my resolution was immediately formed, and two days later I set out on your track. For three months I have been following you, and have at last come up with you—this time, I hope, never to part again," he added with a stifled sigh. "Still I do not know what has occurred to you during the last three months. Tell me what you have been about. I am listening."

"Yes, I will tell you all. My object, indeed, in seeking you was to demand the fulfilment of a solemn promise."

The hunter's brow grew dark, and he frowned.

"Speak," he said; "I am listening. As for the promise to which you allude, when the moment has arrived I shall know how to fulfil it."

"The sun is rising," Louis answered with a sad smile; "I must pay the proper attention to my herd."

"I will help you. You are right; those poor brutes must not be neglected."

At this moment the gloom was dispersed as if by enchantment; the sun appeared radiant on the horizon; and thousands of birds of every variety, hidden beneath the foliage, gaily celebrated its advent by singing their matin hymn to it.

Don Cornelio and Curumilla shook off the torpor of sleep, and opened their eyes. The Indian chief rose, and walked toward Valentine with that slow and majestic step peculiar to him.

"Brother," the latter said, taking the Araucanian's hand in his own, "I was not alone in my search for you. I had near me a friend whose heart and arm never failed me, and whom I have ever found ready to help me in weal and woe."

Don Louis gazed doubtfully at the man whom the hunter pointed out to him, and who stood motionless and stoical before him. Gradually his features were expanded, his memory returned, and he affectionately offered his hand to the Indian, saying with deep emotion,—

"Curumilla, my brother!"

At this proof of memory and friendship, after the lapse of so many years—this frank and true emotion on the part of a man to whom he had already given so many marks of devotion—the crust of ice that surrounded the Indian's heart suddenly melted, his face assumed an earthy hue, and a convulsive tremor agitated all his limbs.

"Oh, my brother Louis!" he exclaimed with an accent impossible to describe.

A sob resembling a roar burst from his chest; and, ashamed of having thus betrayed his weakness, the chief turned quickly away, and hid his face in the folds of his robe.

Like all primitive and energetic natures, this man, on whom adversity had no effect, was moved like a weak child by the immense joy he experienced at seeing once again Don Louis, the man whom Valentine loved more than a brother, and whose absence he had so long lamented.

"Then you will not leave me again, brother?" Louis asked anxiously.

"No, nothing shall separate us henceforth."

"Thanks," the count answered.

"Come, come," Valentine gaily remarked, "let us attend to the cattle."

All were soon on the move in the bivouac. Don Cornelio understood nothing of what he saw. These strangers, who had arrived but a few hours ago, already so attached to his friend, talking with him like old acquaintances, produced in him a series of notions each more extravagant than the other; but Don Cornelio was a philosopher, and more than that, remarkably curious. Certain that all would end sooner or, later in a satisfactory explanation, he gaily made up his mind, and had no idea of asking any information, especially as the two helps chance had sent him could not fail to be extremely useful to him in guiding the undisciplined animals which the count and himself had burdened themselves with, and had yet so far to drive.

A person must have himself been a *vaquero* in the great American savannahs, in order to form an idea of the numberless difficulties met with in guiding novillos and untamed bulls for hundreds of leagues across virgin forests and arid plains, defending them against wild beasts which follow their track, and snap them up under your very eyes if you do not take care, and, like the roaring lion of the Gospel, wander incessantly round the herd, seeking what they may devour. At other times the animals must be defended against the raving madness, or *estampida*, caused by the want of water and the refraction of the sun, during which they rush in every direction, and gore those who try to bring them back. A man must be desperate like Don Louis, or a careless philosopher like Don Cornelio, not to recoil before the perils and difficulties of so hazardous a trade; for, among the eventualities we have enumerated, we have not mentioned the *temporales*, or tempests, which in a few minutes overthrow the face of nature, hollow out lakes, and throw up mountains; nor the *Indios bravos*, or nomadic Indians, who watch the caravans, plunder the merchandise, and murder the drivers or traders.

Valentine in vain racked his brains in order to discover why his friend, whom he had known to be so effeminate and weak, could have resolved on adopting such a mode of life. But his astonishment almost became admiration when he saw him at work, and recognised the complete metamorphosis that had been effected in him, both morally and physically, and the cold, indomitable energy which had usurped the place of the careless weakness and original irresolution of his character.

He studied him thus carefully during the whole time he was employed in restoring order among the herd, and organising everything for the day's march.

"Oh!" he said to himself, "this chosen organisation has been purified by misfortune. There remain at the bottom of that half-broken heart a few noble chords, which I will manage to set in motion when the time comes."

And for the first time since many days a feeling of hearty joy caused the trail-seeker to quiver.

[1] See "The Tiger Slåyer." Same publishers.

CHAPTER III
A SAD MISTAKE

Several days elapsed ere the two friends resumed their interrupted conversation.

They had continued their journey toward San Francisco without any incident worth noticing, owing to the skill of Valentine and Curumilla. Although this was the first time they had advanced so far from the regions they were accustomed to traverse, their sagacity made up so well for their want of knowledge that they avoided, with extreme good fortune, the dangers that menaced the success of their journey, and foresaw obstacles still remote, but which their knowledge of the desert caused them to guess, as it were, intuitively.

The two old friends observed, we may say studied, each other. After so long a separation they required to restore a community of ideas. That communion of thoughts and feelings which had existed so long between them might be eternally broken through the different media into which they had been thrown, and the circumstances that had modified their characters. Each of them rendered greater by events—having acquired the consciousness of his personal value and his intellectual power—had possibly the right no longer to admit, without previous discussion, certain theories which were formerly recognised without a contest.

Still the friendship between the two men was so lively, the confidence so entire, and the devotion so true, that, after a fortnight's travelling side by side—a fortnight during which they touched on the most varying subjects without once introducing the one they had so much interest in thoroughly discussing—they convinced themselves that they stood to each other precisely in the same position as before their separation.

Either through lassitude or deference, or perhaps the tacit recognition of his foster brother's superiority over him, during this fortnight, Don Louis, happy, perhaps, at having found once more the man who had been wont to think and act for him, had not once attempted to assume an independent position, but insensibly fell back under that moral guardianship which Valentine had so long exercised over him.

The two other persons lived on a perfectly good understanding—Don Cornelio through carelessness, perhaps, Curumilla through pride.

The Spaniard—a dear lover of liberty, happy at living in the open air without troubles or annoyances of any description—goaded his novillos, strummed his jarana, and sang the interminable *Romancero del Rey Rodrigo*, which he began again imperturbably so soon as he had finished, in spite of Valentine's repeated remarks about the silence that must be maintained in the desert, in order to avoid the ambuscades which the Indians constantly place like so many spiders' webs in the path of incautious travellers. The Spaniard listened docilely, and with a contrite air, to the hunter's remonstrances; but, so soon as they were ended, he twanged a tune, and recommenced his romancero—a philosophy which the trail-seeker, while blaming, could not refrain from admiring.

Curumilla was always the man we have seen him—prudent, foresighted, and silent—but with a double dose of each quality. With eyes ever opened and ears alert, the Araucanian chief rode from one end of the file to the other, watching so carefully over its safety that no accident occurred up to the day when we resume our narrative.

They thus descended the woody slopes of the Sierra Nevada, and entered the naked and sandy plains that stretch down to the sea, and on which, with the exception of San José and Monterey (two towns in the last throes of existence), the traveller only sees stunted trees and thorny shrubs scattered at a great distance apart.

Three days before reaching San José—a miserable *pueblo*, which serves as a gathering place for hunters and arrieros who frequent these parts; but where the population, decimated by fevers and misery, can do but little for the *forasteros* (strangers)—the caravan encamped on the banks of a stream, beneath the shelter of a few trees that had grown there by accident, and which the sea breeze shook incessantly, and covered with that fine sand which enters the eyes, nose, ears, and nothing can keep out.

The sun was plunging into the sea under the form of a huge fire-ball; there was a fresh breeze; in the distance appeared a few white sails, which, like light kingfishers fearing a tempest, were hastening to reach San Francisco; the coyotes were beginning to bark furiously on the plain; and the few birds nestled on the branches tucked their heads under their wings, and prepared to go to sleep.

The fires were lighted, the animals penned, and after supper each hastened to repair, by a few hours' sleep, the fatigue of a long day's journey beneath a burning sky.

"Sleep!" Louis said. "I will keep the first watch—the idler's watch," he added with a smile.

"I will take the second, then," Valentine said.

"No, I will take that," Curumilla objected. "An Indian's eyes see clearly in the night."

"Hum!" the hunter remarked; "and yet I fancy my eyes are not so bad either."

Curumilla, without further reply, placed his finger on his lips.

"Good!" the hunter said; "as you wish it, keep watch in my place, chief. When you are tired, however, be sure and wake me."

The Indian bowed. The three men wrapped themselves in their zarapés, and lay on the ground, Don Louis alone remaining awake.

It was a magnificent night: the sky, of a deep azure, was studded with an infinity of stars that sparkled like diamonds; the moon poured forth its tremulous and pallid beams; the atmosphere, wondrously pure and transparent, allowed the country to be surveyed for an enormous distance; the evening breeze had risen, and deliciously refreshed the air; the earth exhaled acrid and balmy perfumes; the waves died away amorously, and with mysterious murmurs, on the beach; and in the distance might be indistinctly traced the outlines of the coyotes which prowled about, howling mournfully, for they scented the novillos.

Louis, seduced by this splendid evening, and yielding to that prairie languor which conquers the strongest minds, was indulging in a gentle reverie. He had attained that stage of mental somnolency which is not waking, and yet not sleeping. He was enjoying the magic pictures his fancy conjured up, when he was suddenly roused from this charming sensation by a hand pressing heavily on his shoulder, while a voice muttered in his ear the single word,—

"Prudence."

Louis, suddenly recalled to a consciousness of the present, opened his half-closed eyes, and turned sharply round. Curumilla was leaning over him, and repeated his warning, with a sign of terrible meaning. The count seized his rifle, which rested near him.

"What is the matter?" he asked in a low voice.

"Come, but keep in the shade," Curumilla replied in the same tone.

Louis obeyed the hint, whose importance he recognised. Lying down on the ground, he glided gently in the direction indicated by the Indian.

He soon found himself sheltered behind a thicket, where he saw Don Cornelio and Valentine in ambush, with their bodies bent forward, and looking anxiously into the darkness.

"Good heavens, friends!" the count said, "what is the meaning of this? The profoundest silence prevails around us. All appears tranquil. Why this alarm?"

"Curumilla noticed this evening, before our halt, traces of Yaqui Indians. You know, brother, that these demons are the most daring robbers in the world. It is plain that they are after our beasts."

"But what makes you suppose that? These traces, whose existence I do not deny, may belong to travellers as well as to vagabonds. Nothing up to the present makes us suppose that these fellows intend attacking us, and we have not even seen them."

A sinister smile contracted the chief's thin lips, and, touching the count's arm with his finger, while at the same time lifting his own robe, he showed him a bleeding scalp hanging from his belt.

"Oh, oh!" Don Louis said, "have those demons ventured so near us, then?"

"Yes; and had it not been for Curumilla, whose eye is never closed, and mind ever on the watch, our animals would probably have been carried off more than an hour ago."

"Thanks for his vigilance, then," the count said with an expression of annoyance, which he could not entirely conceal; "but you know the Indians, comrades: so soon as they find they are detected, they are no longer to be feared. I believe that, after the lesson they have received, we are now in safety, and we need not trouble ourselves about them more."

"No, brother, you are mistaken. Look at your novillos; they are restless. At each instant they raise their heads, and do not eat their food in comfort. God has given animals an instinct of self-preservation which never deceives them. Believe me, they fear a danger, and scent enemies not far from them."

"It is possible, indeed. Let us watch, then."

The four men remained thus silent and attentive. An hour almost passed away, and nothing happened to confirm their suspicions. Still the bulls pressed more closely together. They had left off eating, and their restlessness increased instead of diminishing.

Suddenly Curumilla stretched out his arm in a north-eastern direction, and after laconically whispering, "Do not stir," he gave Valentine his rifle to hold, and before his friends had time to guess the direction he had taken, he disappeared in the gloom. The three hunters exchanged a silent glance, and cocked their rifles, so as to be ready for any event.

There cannot be a more painful position than that of the brave man who, in a strange country and on a dark night, is obliged to stand on guard against a danger whose extent he cannot calculate. Affected by the silent majesty of solitude, he creates phantasms a hundredfold more terrible than the actual danger, and feels his courage fly away piecemeal beneath the harsh pressure of waiting for something unseen.

Such was the situation in which our three friends now were; and yet they were three lion hearts, accustomed for many years to Indian warfare, and whom no peril, however great it might have been, would have been able to affect beneath the warm beams of the sun; but, during the darkness, imagination creates such horrible phantoms, that, if we may be allowed to employ a trivial comparison, we might say that people are not so much afraid of the danger itself as of the fear of that danger.

The three men had remained in this awkward situation for some time; when suddenly a fearful yell rose in the air, followed by the fall of a body to the ground, and the flight of several men, whose black outlines stood out on the horizon. The adventurers fired at random, and rushed rapidly in the direction where they heard the struggle, which seemed still going on.

At the moment they arrived, Curumilla, whom they recognised, had his right knee pressed into the chest of a man he held down under him, while his left hand compressed his throat, and reduced him to the most perfect state of powerlessness.

"Wah!" the Araucanian said, turning to his comrades with a look of inexpressible ferocity, "a chief!"

"Good prize," Valentine said. "Thrust your knife into the scoundrel's chest, and there's an end of him."

Curumilla raised his knife, whose blade sent forth a bluish flash.

"A moment," Don Louis exclaimed. "Let us see first who he is; we shall still be able to kill him if we think fit."

Valentine shrugged his shoulders.

"Let the chief settle that business," he said; "he understands it better than we do. When you have one of those vipers under your heel you must crush him, lest he may sting you presently."

"No," the count remarked resolutely, "I will never consent to see a man murdered before me. That poor wretch has acted in accordance with his nature; let us act in accordance with ours, then. Curumilla, I implore you, allow your prisoner to rise, but watch him, so that he cannot escape."

"You are wrong, brother," the implacable hunter replied; "you do not know these demons so well as I do. Still act as you please; but you will eventually see that you have committed a folly."

The count made no reply, but only gave Curumilla another sign to do as he ordered. The Araucanian obeyed with repugnance. Still he helped his half-strangled prisoner to rise, and while carefully watching him, led him to the fire, where the hunters had already preceded him.

The count took a rapid glance at the Indian. He was a man of Herculean stature, powerfully built, and still young, with haughty, gloomy, and cruel features; in a word, though he was a handsome rather than an ugly man in appearance, there was an expression of roguery, baseness, and ferocity about him, which in no way pleaded in his favour. He wore a species of hunting shirt, without sleeves, of striped calico, drawn in round the waist by a large girdle of untanned deer hide; breeches of the same stuff as the shirt hung down to his knees; and the lower part of his legs was protected from stings by leather gaiters fastened to the knee and ankle. He wore on his feet moccasins artistically worked, and adorned behind by several wolf tails—a mark of distinction only allowed to renowned warriors. His plaited hair was raised on either side his head, while behind it fell to his waist, and was decorated with plumes of every possible colour. Round his neck hung several medals, among which was one rather larger than the rest, representing General Jackson, ex-President of the American Union. His face was painted with four different colours—blue, black, white, and red.

So soon as he found himself in the presence of the hunters seated round the fire, he crossed his arms on his chest, raised his head haughtily, and waited stoically till they thought proper to address him.

"Who are you?" Don Louis asked him in Spanish.

"Mixcoatzin (the Serpent of the Cloud)."

"Hum!" Valentine muttered to himself, "the scoundrel is well named. I never saw such a hangdog face as his before."

"What did Mixcoatzin want in my camp?"

"Does not the *Yori* know?" the Indian said imperturbably. "Mixcoatzin is a chief among the Yaquis."

"You wished to steal my cattle, I suppose?"

"The Yaquis are not robbers; all that is on their land belongs to them. The palefaces need only return to their home on the other side of the great salt lake."

"If I condemn you to death what will you say?"

"Nothing; it is the law of war. The paleface will see how a Yaqui chief endures pain."

"You allow, then, that you deserve death?"

"No; the paleface is the stronger—he is the master."

"If I let you go what will you think?"

The Indian shrugged his shoulders.

"The paleface is not a fool," he said.

"But suppose I do act in that way?"

"I shall say that the paleface is afraid."

"Afraid of what?"

"Of the vengeance of the warriors of my nation."

It was Don Louis' turn to shrug his shoulders.

"Then," he proceeded, "if I restored you your liberty you would feel no gratitude?"

"Why should I be grateful? A warrior should kill his enemy when he holds him. If he does not do so he is a coward."

The hunters could not refrain from a start of surprise at the enunciation of this singular theory. Don Louis rose.

"Listen," he said. "I do not fear you, and I will give you a proof of it."

And, with a movement quick as thought, he seized the long tail that hung down the chiefs back, and cut it off with his knife.

"Now," he added, buffeting him with the tress he had cut off, "be off, villain: you are free. I despise you too much to inflict on you any other punishment than that you have undergone. Return to your tribe, and tell your friends how the whites avenge themselves on enemies so contemptible as yourself, and those that resemble you."

At the deadly insult he received the Indian's face became hideous; he suffered a momentary stupor caused by shame and anger; but by a supernatural effort he suddenly overcame his feelings, seized Don Louis' arm, and thrusting his face into the Frenchman's,—

"Mixcoatzin is a powerful chief," he hissed. "Let the Yori remember his name, for he will meet him again."

And, bounding like a tiger, he dashed into the plain, where he at once disappeared.

"Stop!" Don Louis shouted to his friends, who were rushing in pursuit; "Let him escape. What do I care for such a wretch's hatred? He can do nothing to me."

The hunters reluctantly took their seats again by the fire.

"Hum!" Louis added, "I have perhaps committed a folly."

Valentine looked at him.

"Worse than a folly, brother," he said; "a sad mistake. Take care of that man: one day or other he will revenge himself on you."

"Possibly," the count said carelessly; "but when did you begin to fear the Indians so greatly, brother?"

"From the day I first learned to know them," the hunter said coldly. "You have offered that man an insult which demands blood; be assured that he will make you repent of it."

"I care little."

After these few words the hunters resumed their interrupted sleep, and the rest of the night passed without any fresh incident.

At sunrise the adventurers continued their journey; and by night, after a day of incredible fatigue through the burning sands of the savannah, they at length reached the *pueblo* or *lugar* of San José, where the inhabitants received them with shouts of joy, persuaded as they were that the strangers would not leave without supplying them with a few of those objects of primary necessity which they have themselves no means of procuring.

San José is the last caravan halt before reaching San Francisco. The travellers had made a journey of more than one hundred and eighty leagues in less than three weeks, through difficulties and dangers without end—a speed hitherto unexampled.

CHAPTER IV
EXPLANATIONS

The hunters placed their animals in a vast corral; then they sought a shelter for themselves in a mesón, the landlord of which, a perfect likeness of the worthy Knight of La Mancha, received them to the best of his ability. After the rough journey they had made, it was a great delight to the adventurers to rest their heads once again beneath a roof, and be, for a few hours at least, lodged in a manner almost civilised.

Don Louis and Valentine occupied the same cuarto, while Curumilla and Don Cornelio selected that exactly facing theirs. So soon as these provisional arrangements were made, and supper enjoyed in common, all retired to rest.

Before lying down on the *cuadro*, covered with an oxhide, intended for his bed, Don Louis walked up to Valentine, who, lying back in a *butaca* (easy chair), was smoking a cigarette, and idly watching the blue smoke ascend in spirals.

"What are you thinking about?" he asked him, as he leant familiarly on the back of the butaca.

"About you," Valentine replied, turning to him with a smile.

"About me?"

"Yes. What other anxiety can I have at present, save to see you happy?"

The count looked down on the ground and sighed.

"It is impossible," he said.

Valentine looked at him.

"Impossible!" he repeated. "Oh, oh! Have we reached that point? Come, let us have an explanation, once for all."

"You are right; the hour has arrived: let us have a hearty explanation."

The count drew up a butaca, sat down opposite Valentine, took a cigar from the case his foster brother handed him, and lit it. The hunter followed all his movements attentively. When he saw him comfortably installed, he said, —

"Speak."

"Alas! My life has nothing very interesting in it; it has resembled that of all adventurers. At one time rich, at another poor, I have wandered about, traversing Mexico in every direction, dragging after me the memory of my lost happiness, like the galley slaves cannon ball. For a moment I imagined that a future might still exist for me, and that I might at least regain my rank in the world, if I did not secure again a position like that I had lost I started for San Francisco, that weird Eldorado, whose marvels the hundred-mouthed rumour was narrating. There I found myself mixed up with a crowd of greedy and unbridled adventurers, whose life was one continued orgy, and whose sole passion was gold. I saw there, within a few months, the most prodigious metamorphoses. I saw the most scandalous fortunes spring up and collapse again, and plunging resolutely into this gulf, I demanded from chance my share of feverish joys and intoxicating emotions; but I lacked faith, and nothing succeeded with me. I tried every profession, ever pursued by that implacable fatality which was determined to crush me. I had great difficulty in saving myself from a death by hunger. In turn hunter, porter, Heaven knows what, my efforts availed nothing in that Babel, where the condemned of civilisation jostled each other, who, all marked with the indelible seal of Dante's reprobates, piled ruin on ruin to form themselves a pedestal of ingots, which was immediately overthrown by another. Disgusted with this mingled life of blood, filth, rags, and gold, I set off, resolved to become a drover. A noble profession, is it not, for a Count de Prébois, whose ancestors made three crusades?" he added, with a bitter laugh. "But I knew generals ostlers, marquises waiters; hence I, who had never been anything, could, without any great degradation, become a trader in cattle. And then I had another object in the choice of my profession. Ever since my arrival in North America I have been looking for you: I hoped to find you again some day. For the first time fortune has smiled on me, you see, as I have succeeded in meeting with you. That is all I had to say to you. Now you know as much about my life as I do; so ask me no more."

After these words, uttered in a sharp voice, the count threw himself back on his butaca, relit his cigar, crossed his arms on his chest, and seemed determined not to add a word. Valentine looked at him for a long time with the most concentrated attention, at times tossing his head, and frowning with evident dissatisfaction. At length he resolved to renew the conversation.

"Hum!" he said, "I now know your whole life, I grant it. There is nothing very extraordinary about it in a country like that where we are. It in no way departs from the common law. You would do very wrong to complain."

"I do not complain," the count exclaimed quickly; "I merely assert a fact."

"Of course," Valentine said; "and yet, in all you have told me, one point remains obscure to me."

"Which?"

"You told me all you wished to do—that is well; but leaving out of the question the fraternal friendship that attaches us, and which, however powerful it may be, cannot to my mind account for your settled determination to find me again, you have not told me for what purpose you sought me so obstinately."

The count sprang up, and his eye flashed.

"Have you not guessed it, Valentine?"

"No!"

The count let his head fall, and for a few moments the conversation was again interrupted.

"You are right, Valentine: better finish at once, and never return to the subject again; besides, you know as well as I what I wish to say," the count replied, with the accent of a man whose mind is made up.

"Perhaps so," the hunter said laconically.

"Come, come, I am not an ass; and on the morning of that day when you asked a shelter at my bivouac, you understood me at the first word I let fall."

"It is possible," Valentine said imperturbably; "still, as I have no pretence to the art of divination, be good enough to explain yourself clearly and categorically."

"You insist on it?"

The hunter bowed his assent.

"Well, be it so," the count went on; "you are still the same man you were fifteen years ago."

"Are we not referring to that very period now?" Valentine said with a smile.

"Ah!" the count exclaimed, striking the arm of his butaca, "you see that you understood me."

"Did I say the contrary?"

"Why, then, do you demand——?"

"Because it must be so," the hunter said dryly.

"Be at rest, for I will repeat your own words."

"I am listening."

"You remember, I suppose, a cold winter night, in the bedroom of my house at Paris?"

"December 31st, 1834, at eleven in the evening," Valentine remarked.

"Yes; the rain lashed the window panes, the wind whistled in the long passages. I was awaiting your coming. You arrived. Then, as now, I was face to face with ruin. I wished to die: you prevented me."

"It is true. Did I do wrong?"

"Perhaps," the count said in a hollow voice; "but these are the words you made use of."

"Allow me to repeat them myself; for, in spite of the fifteen years that have elapsed, Louis, that scene is as present to my mind as if it took place yesterday. After proving to you that you did wrong to despair," Valentine said in a solemn voice, "that all was not lost, I replied to a final objection you raised, 'Be easy, Louis, be easy. If I have not fulfilled my promise in two years, I will hand you the pistols myself, and then—' 'Then?' you asked. 'Then,' I added, 'you shall not kill yourself alone.' 'I accept,' you answered. Those were the words that passed between us on that night, which decided your future and made a man of you. Is it not so? Have I forgotten the slightest detail? Answer."

"No, you have forgotten nothing, Valentine."

"Well?"

"Well, now that I have faithfully fulfilled the promise I made you, I come to claim of you the complete execution of our compact."

"I do not comprehend you."

"What! You do not comprehend me?" the count said, bounding from his butaca.

"No," Valentine answered coldly. "Did I not keep my promise? Ah, Louis, since you insist on it, by heavens!" he added, growing animated in his turn, "let us reckon up accounts. I ask nothing better. What do you mean by talking to me of fulfilling an agreement? Have I not fulfilled my engagements? Did I not find for you that woman you despaired of ever seeing again? Did you not marry her? Did you not enjoy with her ten years of perfect happiness? By what right do you complain of the fatality that pursues you? By what right do you curse your destiny, ungrateful man!

Whose happiness lasted ten years—ten ages in this earth? Look around you. Show me a man who, throughout his whole life, can reckon one year of that happiness you rail at, and then I will pity you, will weep with you, and, if it must be, help you to die. Oh! All men are the same—weak in the presence of joy as in grief, forgetting, in a few hours of adversity, years of happiness. And so, after fifteen years, you have returned to the same point. Insensate! Do you know, you who speak in that way, what it is to pass a whole existence of suffering and horrible agony: to feel hour by hour, minute by minute, your heart lacerated, and that without hope, and yet smile and seem gay—in a word, live? Have you for a single day endured that atrocious suffering, you who speak so deliberately about dying?"

Gradually, while speaking, Valentine had grown animated, his features were contracted, and his eyes flashed flames. Louis gazed on his friend without comprehending him, but startled at the state of exaltation in which he saw him.

"Valentine," he exclaimed, "Valentine, in heaven's name, calm yourself!"

"Ah!" the hunter continued, with a ghastly laugh, "you suffer, you say— you are unhappy; and yet listen. That woman you loved, whom I found for you again, whom I enabled you to marry—well, it was not love I felt for her, but idolatry. To be able to tell her so I would joyfully have parted with my blood drop by drop; and yet I, to whom you have just told your grief, I placed you in each other's arms. I smiled—do you understand me?—smiled on your love, and without a murmur, a word, to reveal that passion which gnawed my heart, I fled into the desert, alone with my love. Face to face with it I suffered for fifteen years. Oh, my God, my God! The wound is as painful now as on the first day. Tell me, Louis, now that you know all— for we are frank with each other—what are your sufferings compared with mine? By what right would you die?"

"Oh, pardon me, pardon me, Valentine!" Louis exclaimed, as he rushed into his arms. "Oh! You are right; I am very ungrateful to you."

"No," Valentine answered sadly, as he returned his embrace; "no, Louis, you are a man; you have followed the common law. I cannot and ought not to be angry with you. Pardon me, on the contrary, for allowing myself to be carried away so far as to reveal to you the secret which I had sworn to bury eternally in my heart. Alas! We have all our cross to bear in this world, and mine has been rude. God doubtlessly decreed it so, because I am strong," he added, with an attempt at a smile. "But, to return to yourself, it is true that youth has fled far from us, with its gay perspective and smiling illusions; life has no longer anything to offer us, save the painful trials of a ripe age. I am as wearied of existence as yourself; it weighs equally on me as on you. You see, my friend, I am fully of your opinion. I will not only not prevent you from dying, but I wish to accomplish my promise fully by accompanying you into the tomb."

"You, Valentine! O no! It is impossible."

"Why so? Is not our position the same? Have we not both suffered equally? An implacable creditor, you have asked me to honour my signature. Very good; but on one condition."

Louis was too well acquainted with his foster brother's firm and resolute character to try and combat his will.

"What is it?" he asked simply.

"I shall choose the mode of death."

"Be it so."

"Oh, pardon me, Louis! I shall not propose an ordinary suicide, so I must have your word of honour before I explain myself more fully."

"I give it you."

"Good! There are two difficult things for a man to do in this world— arranging his life, and arranging his death. The man who kills himself coldly by blowing out his brains in his room, after writing to his friends to announce his suicide, is either a coward or a madman. That is not the sort of suicide I wish; it means nothing, it proves nothing, and is of no service. But there is a manner of suicide which I have ever dreamed of, because it is noble and great: it is that of the man who, unable or unwilling to do more with a life he despises, sacrifices it for his fellow men, with no other object than that of being useful to them, and falls after accomplishing his task."

"I believe I understand you, Valentine."

"Perhaps so; but let me finish. We are in the country best prepared for such a design. Already several attempts—all unsuccessful, however—have been made, especially by the Count de Lhorailles in his colony of Guetzalli. Sonora, which is the richest country in the world, is in the last throes, under the brutalising and unintelligent system of the Mexican government. Well, let us restore life to this country; let us galvanise it, summon to our aid the French emigrants in California, and come here to give liberty to a people whose energetic character will comprehend us. What do we risk in the event of non-success? Death! Why, that is exactly what we desire. At any rate, when we have fallen, we shall sleep in a shroud of glory as martyrs, bearing with us the regrets and sympathies of all. Instead of killing ourselves like cowards, we shall have died in the breach like heroes. Is not that martyrdom the noblest, the most sublime of all?

"Yes, Valentine, you are right—always right Oh, men like ourselves can only die in that fashion!"

"Good!" Valentine exclaimed; "you have understood me."

"Not only have I understood you, brother, but I guessed your meaning before."

"How so?"

"When I met the Count de Lhorailles for the last time in the desert, I was returning with Belhumeur and an Indian chief from visiting a placer of incalculable value which that Indian had discovered, and the ownership of which he gave to Belhumeur, who, in his turn, handed it over to me. On my return, I proceeded to Mexico, where I entered into negotiations with several notable persons; among others, the French *chargé d'affaires*. You of course know how slow everything is to succeed in this unhappy country. Still, owing to the rich samples I had the precaution to bring with me, and, above all, the powerful protection of certain persons, I succeeded in founding a company, of which I was appointed chief, with the right of levying a French company, armed and disciplined, in order to take possession of the placer, and work it on behalf of the company."

"What then?"

"Well, I returned to San Francisco, and made a few arrangements; but I needed two things—first, patience, and next, money to enlist my men and purchase the necessary stores; and—shall I confess it to you?—what I most needed was the desire to succeed. But you, Valentine, have caused that desire to spring up in me; your presence has restored all my energy, and though I know not how I shall remove all the obstacles that oppose the execution of my plan, I shall do so, I swear it to you."

"What were you doing in Sonora, then?"

"I can hardly explain it to you. My speculation in cattle was more a flight than anything else. I was disgusted with everything, and tried to make an end of it, no matter how."

"Now it is my turn. Tomorrow, at sunrise, you will start. You will proceed at full speed to San Francisco. Your excursion in Sonora was only an exploring tour. You will employ any pretext you like, in a word, and set to work earnestly forming your company. During that time I will sell your herd, and arrange so as to procure you the funds you require. Trouble yourself about nothing, but push ahead boldly."

"But how will you manage it? The sum I need is large."

"That does not concern you: let me arrange matters in my way; At the appointed hour I will furnish you with more than you want, so it is settled. You will start at sunrise?"

"I will do so; but when and where shall I see you again?"

"Ah! That is true. On the twenty-fifth day from this, at sunset, I will enter your room."

"But I do not know myself yet where I shall lodge."

"Do not let that trouble you; I shall find out."

"So, then, at sunset of the twenty-fifth day?"

"Yes, I will arrive with the treasure ships," Valentine replied with a laugh.

"Thanks, brother; you are my good genius. If my life has had a few blemishes, you are preparing me a glorious death to expiate them."

"Pity yourself, pray! I am going to make of you a Francisco Pizarro and an Almagro."

The two men shook hands affectionately, while exchanging a sorrowful smile. After a few more unimportant remarks, they threw themselves on their beds, where they soon fell asleep, overpowered as they were by fatigue.

CHAPTER V
THE CONSEQUENCES OP A LOVE SONG

During the conversation between the foster brothers, certain events we must describe to the reader occurred in the cuarto to which Curumilla and Don Cornelio had retired.

On entering the room, Curumilla, instead of lying down on the cuadro intended for him, laid his zarapé on the tiled flooring, stretched himself out upon it, and immediately closed his eyes. Don Cornelio, on the contrary, after hanging the lamp to a nail in the wall, trimmed up the smoking wick with the point of his knife, sat down on the side of the bed, with his legs hanging down, and then began in a sonorous voice the romance of King Rodrigo.

At this slightly unseasonable music Curumilla half opened one eye, though without protesting in any other way against this unwonted disturbance of his rest. Don Cornelio may or may not have noticed the Indian's silent protest; but in either case he took no heed of it, but went on singing, raising his voice to the highest compass of which it was capable.

"Wah!" the chief said, raising his bead.

"I was certain," Don Cornelio remarked with a friendly smile, "that the music would please you."

And he redoubled his flourishes.

The Araucanian rose, went up to the singer, and touched him gently on the shoulder.

"We must sleep," he said in his guttural voice, and with an ill-tempered grimace.

"Bah, chief! Music makes a man forget sleep. Just listen.

"'Oh, si yo naciera ciego!
Oh, tú sin beldad nacieras!
Maldito sea el punto—'" [1]

The Indian seemed to listen with sustained attention, his body bent well forward, and his eyes obstinately fixed on the singer. Don Cornelio felicitated himself internally on the effect he fancied he had produced on this primitive native, when suddenly Curumilla, seizing him by the hips, squeezed him in his nervous hands at in iron pincers, and lifting him with as much ease as if he had been but a child, carried him, spite of his resistance, into the patio, and seated him on the side of the wall.

"Wah!" he said, "music is good here."

And, without adding another word, he turned his back on the Spaniard, walked into his cuarto, laid himself on his zarapé, and went to sleep immediately.

At first Don Cornelio was quite confounded by this sudden attack, and knew not if he ought to laugh or feel vexed at the simple way in which his companion had got rid of his company; but Don Cornelio was a philosopher, gifted with an admirable character. What had happened to him seemed so droll that he burst into an Homeric laugh, which lasted several minutes.

"No matter," he said, when he had at length regained his seriousness, "the adventure is curious, and I shall laugh at it for many a long day. After all, the fellow was not entirely in the wrong. I am famously situated here to sing and play my jarana as long as I think proper; at any rate I shall run no risk of disturbing the sleepers, as I am quite alone."

And after this consolation, which he administered to himself to satisfy his somewhat offended pride, he prepared to continue his serenade.

The night was clear and serene; the sky was studded with a profusion of stars, in the midst of which sparkled the dazzling southern cross; a slight breeze, laden with the perfumes of the desert, gently refreshed the air; the deepest silence brooded over San José; for, in the retired Mexican pueblos, everybody returns home at an early hour. Everybody appeared asleep, too, in the mesón, although at a few windows the weak and dying light of the candles gleamed behind the cotton curtains.

Thus Don Cornelio, unconsciously yielding to the influences of this magnificent evening, omitted the first four verses of the romancero, and after a skilful prelude, struck up the sublime description of night:—

"A l'escaso resplendor,
De cualque luciente estrella,
Que en el medroso silencio,
Tristamente centellea." [2]

And he continued thus with eyes uplifted to heaven, and brow glowing with enthusiasm to the end of the romance; that is to say, until he had sung the ninety-six verses of which this touching piece of poetry is composed.

The Mexicans, children of the Andalusians, the musicians and dancers *par excellence,* have not degenerated in this respect from their forefathers; on the contrary, they have, if that be possible, exaggerated these two passions, to which they sacrifice everything.

When Don Cornelio began singing, the patio, as we have, already remarked, was completely deserted; but gradually, as the musician became more animated, doors opened in every corner of the yard, men and women appeared, advanced gently to the singer, and formed a circle round him; so that after the final strophe he found himself surrounded by a group of enthusiastic hearers, who applauded him frenziedly.

Don Cornelio rose from the wall on which he was seated, lifted his hat, and saluted his audience gracefully.

"Come," he said to himself, "this will be something for that Indian, who appreciates music so slightly, to reflect upon."

"*Capa de Dios!*" an arriero said, "that is what I call singing."

"Poor Señor Don Rodrigo, how he must have suffered!" a young criada exclaimed in short petticoats, and with a flashing eye.

"And that perfidious *picaro* of a Count Julian, who introduced the Moors into a Catholic country!" the landlord said with an angry gesture.

"God be praised!" the audience said in chorus; "Let us hope that he is roasting in the lowest pit."

Don Cornelio was at the pinnacle of jubilation. Never before had he obtained such a success. All his hearers thanked him for the pleasure he had caused them, with those noisy demonstrations and cries of joy which distinguish southern races. The Spaniard did not know whom to listen to, or on which side to turn. The shouts assumed such a character of enthusiasm, that the singer began to fear that he would be unable to get rid of his frenzied audience the whole long night.

Fortunately for him, at the moment when, half willingly, half perforce, he was preparing, on the general request, to recommence his romance, there was a movement in the crowd; it parted to the right and left, and left a passage for a tall and pretty girl, who, with a well-turned leg confined in silk stockings with gold clocks, her *rebozo* coquettishly drawn over her head, and her hair buried beneath a profusion of jasmine flowers, placed herself resolutely before the singer, and said with a graceful smile, which allowed her double row of pearly teeth to be seen, —

"Are you not, caballero, a noble hidalgo of Spain, of the name of Don Cornelio?"

We must do Don Cornelio the justice to allow that he was so dazzled by this delicious apparition that he remained for some seconds with gaping mouth, unable to find a word.

The girl stamped her foot impatiently.

"Have you been suddenly turned into stone?" she asked, with a slightly mocking accent.

"Heaven forbid, señorita!" he at length stammered.

"Then be good enough to answer the question I asked you."

"Nothing easier, señorita. I am indeed Don Cornelio Mendoza de Arrizabal, and have the honour to be a Spanish gentleman."

"That is what I call plain speaking," she said, with a slight pout. "If it be so, caballero, I must ask you to follow me."

"To the end of the world," the young man exclaimed impetuously. "I should never travel in pleasanter company."

"I thank you for the compliment, caballero, but I do not intend to take you so far. I only wish to conduct you to my mistress, who desires to see you and speak with you for an instant."

"*Rayo del cielo!* If the mistress be only as pretty as the maid, I shall not regret the trip if it last a week."

The girl smiled again.

"My mistress is staying in this inn, only a few steps off."

"All the worse, all the worse! I should have preferred a journey of several leagues before meeting her."

"A truce to gallantry. Are you willing to follow me?"

"At once, señorita."

And throwing his jarana on his back, and bowing for the last time to the audience, who opened a passage for him respectfully,—

"I am at your orders," he said.

"Come, then."

The girl turned away and hurried off rapidly, the Spaniard following close at her heels.

Don Cornelio, like all the adventurers whom a hazardous life in Europe had cast on the American shores, nourished in his heart a secret hope of re-establishing, by a rich marriage, his fortunes, which were more than compromised. Several instances, though rare, we allow, of marriages contracted in this romantic fashion, had imbedded this idea deeply in the Spaniard's somewhat windy brain.

He was young, noble, handsome—at least he thought so; hence he possessed all needed for success. It is true that, until this moment, fortune had never deigned to smile on him; no young girl seemed to care for his assassinating glances, or respond to his interested advances. But this ill success had in no way rebuffed him, and what happened at this moment seemed to justify his schemes, by offering him, at the moment he least expected it, that occasion he had so long awaited.

Only one thing saddened his brow, and clouded the internal joy he experienced, and that was the seedy condition of his attire, sadly ill-treated by the brambles, and torn by the sharp points of the rocks, during his long journey in Sonora. But with that characteristic fatuity innate in the Spaniards, he consoled himself by the reflection that his personal advantages would amply compensate for the seedy condition of his dress, and that the lady who had sent for him, if she felt any tender interest in him, would attach but slight value to a new cloak or a faded cloak. It was with these conquering feelings that Don Cornelio arrived behind the *camarista* at the door of a cuarto, before which she stopped.

"It is here," she said, turning round to him.

"Very good," he said, drawing himself up. "We will enter whenever you please."

She smiled cunningly with a twinkle of her black eyes, and turned the key in the lock. The door opened.

"Señorita," the waiting-maid said, "I have brought you the gentleman."

"Let him come in, Violanta," a sweet voice answered.

The girl stepped aside to make room for Don Cornelio, who walked in, twisting his moustache with a conquering air.

The room in which he found himself was small, and rather better furnished than the other cuartos in the hostelry, probably owing to the indispensable articles the temporary occupier of the room had the precaution to bring with her. Several pink candles burned in silver chandeliers, and on a sofa lay a lovely young girl of sixteen to seventeen years of age, buried in muslin, like a hummingbird in a nest of roses, who bent on the Spanish gentleman two large black eyes sparkling with humour, maliciousness, and curiosity.

In spite of the immense dose of self-love with which he was cuirassed, and the intimate conviction he had of his own merits, Don Cornelio stopped in considerable embarrassment on the threshold, and bowed profoundly, without daring to advance into the interior of this cuarto, which appeared to him a sanctuary.

By a charming sign the young woman invited him to draw nearer, and pointed out a butaca, about two paces from the sofa on which she was reclining. The young man hesitated; but the camarista, laughing like a madcap, pushed him by the shoulders and compelled him to sit down.

Still the position of our two actors, opposite each other, was rather singular. Don Cornelio, a prey to the most powerful embarrassment he ever experienced, twisted the brim of his beaver in his hands, as he cast investigating glances cautiously around; while the girl, no less confused, timidly looked down, and seemed at present almost to regret the inconsiderate step she had let herself be led to take.

Still, as in all difficult circumstances of life, women possess a will of initiative greater than that of men, because they make a strength of their weakness, and know at once how to approach the most awkward questions, it was the lady who first regained her coolness and commenced the conversation.

"Do you recognise me, Don Cornelio?" she asked him in a deliberate tone, which made the Spaniard quiver.

"Alas, señorita!" he replied, trying to gain time, "where could I have had the happiness of ever seeing you? I have only lived up to the present in an *inferno*."

"Let us speak seriously," she said with an almost imperceptible frown. "Look me well in the face, caballero, and answer me frankly: do you recognise me—yes or no?"

Don Cornelio timidly raised his eyes, obeyed the order he had received in so peremptory a fashion, and after a few seconds,—

"No, señorita," he said with a suppressed sigh, "I do not recognise you; I do not believe that I ever had the happiness of meeting you before today."

"You are mistaken," she replied.

"I! O no! It is impossible."

"Do not swear, Don Cornelio; I will prove to you the truth of what I assert."

The young man shook his head incredulously.

"When a man has had once the happiness of seeing you—" he murmured.

She interrupted him sharply.

"You do not know what you say, and your gallantry is misplaced. Before contradicting me you would do better by listening to what I have to say to you."

Don Cornelio protested.

"I repeat," she said distinctly, "that you are mad. For two days you travelled in the company of my father and myself."

"I!"

"Yes, you."

"Oh!"

"It is just three years ago. At that period I was only a child, scarce fourteen: there is, consequently, nothing extraordinary in your having forgotten me. At that period you sang your inevitable romance of Don Rodrigo, of which I will say no harm, however," she added, with an enchanting smile, "because I recognised you by that song. My father, now governor and political chief of Sonora, was at that time only a colonel."

The Spaniard struck his forehead.

"I remember," he exclaimed. "You were going from Guadalajara to Tepic, when I had the pleasure of meeting you in the middle of the night."

"Yes."

"That is it. Let me see, your father's name is Don Sebastian Guerrero, and yours—"

"Well, and mine?" she said, with a pretty challenging pout.

"Yours, señorita," he said gallantly, "is Doña Angela. What other name could you bear?"

"Come," she said, clapping her dainty hands together with a ringing laugh, "I am glad to see that you have a better memory than I believed."

"Oh!" he muttered reproachfully.

"We had a rather disagreeable adventure, if I remember right, with certain bandits?" she continued.

"Extremely disagreeable, for I was half killed."

"That is true; I remember something of the sort. Were you not rescued by a hunter, a wood ranger? I can hardly remember."

"A noble gentleman, señorita," Don Cornelio replied with fire, "to whom I owe my life."

"Ah!" she said carelessly, "that is possible. The man helped you, nursed you, and then you parted?"

"Not exactly."

"What!" she said, with some agitation, "you continued to live together?"

"Yes."

"Always?"

"Yes."

"But now?" she said, with a certain hesitation in her voice.

"I repeat to you, señorita, that we have not separated."

"Indeed! Is he here?"

"Yes."

"In this hostelry?"

"On the other side of the yard."

"Ah!" she murmured, letting her head fall on her breast.

"What's the matter now?" the Spaniard asked himself.

And not interrupting the sudden reverie into which the young lady had fallen, he waited respectfully until it pleased her to renew the conversation.

[1] Oh, if I had been born blind, or if you had been born ugly! Accursed be the day and hour—

[2] By the feeble light of some clear star, which, in the midst of the gloomy silence, mournfully twinkles.

CHAPTER VI
DELILAH

The position of our two characters toward each other was somewhat singular. Both appeared to be watching each other, and trying to discover the flaw in the armour; but in this struggle of a man against a woman, the latter must inevitably prove the conqueror.

Don Cornelio had possibly a rather exaggerated opinion of himself. This was what ruined him, and delivered him bound hand and foot over to his dangerous adversary.

Doña Angela, resting coquettishly on her elbow, with her chin on the palm of her dainty hand, fixed on him two eyes sparkling with maliciousness, so that the Spaniard, as it were, fascinated by the brilliancy of this irresistible glance, had not even the will to turn his head, and liberate himself from the deceptive charm that fascinated him.

"Violanta," the girl said, in a voice soft and pure as the song of the *centzontle*, the American nightingale, "have you no refreshments to offer this caballero?"

"Oh, certainly," said the crafty camarista, with a look sufficient to tempt St. Anthony; and she rose quickly to obey her mistress's directions.

Don Cornelio, flattered in his heart by this politeness, which he was far from expecting, thought it necessary to break out in excuses; but Doña Angela cut him short by herself saying,—

"You will forgive me, caballero, for receiving you so poorly, but I did not expect to have the honour of your visit in this wretched pueblo."

Naturally enough, Don Cornelio, infatuated with the advantages he fancied he possessed, regarded this remark as a compliment.

Angela maliciously bit her rosy lips, and continued, with a bow,—

"But now that I have been so fortunate as to meet again with an old friend, for I hope you will permit me to give you that appellation——"

"Oh, señorita!" the young man said with a movement of joy.

"I flatter myself that I shall have the pleasure of enjoying your company more frequently."

"Señorita, believe me that I shall be too happy."

"I know your gallantry, Don Cornelio," she interrupted him with a smile. "I am aware that you will seize every opportunity to offer me your homage."

"Heaven is my witness, señorita. Unfortunately, adverse fate will possibly ordain differently."

"Why so?"

"You are only passing through this wretched town."

"Yes. My father is proceeding to Tepic, where his new position as governor of the province demands his residence."

"That is true. You see, then, madam, that it is almost impossible for us ever to meet again."

"Do you think so?" she asked.

"Alas! I am atrociously afraid of it."

"Why so?" she said, bending her body forward in curiosity.

"Because, according to every probability, tomorrow, at sunrise, we shall take diametrically opposite routes, señorita."

"Oh, that is not possible!"

"Unfortunately it is too true."

"Explain this enigma to me."

"I would it were one; but a child can read it."

"I do not at all understand you?"

"I will explain myself more clearly."

"Go on."

"When you and your father, madam, start tomorrow for Tepic, my friends and myself will set out for San Francisco."

"San Francisco!"

"Alas! Yes."

"What need have you to go there?"

"I! None."

"Well, then?"

Don Cornelio behaved like most men when in a state of embarrassment; that is to say, he scratched his head. At length he said, —

"I cannot leave my friends."

"What friends?"

"Those in whose company I am."

"Then they want to go to San Francisco?"

"Yes."

"What to do?"

"Ah! That is it," the Spaniard replied, more and more embarrassed by the obligation of confessing the trade in which he was engaged, and which he fancied must lower him to an extraordinary degree in the eyes of the young lady whose heart he fancied he had touched.

"I am waiting," she said with a slight frown of her arched brows.

Don Cornelio, driven into his last retrenchments, determined to make a clean breast of it.

"You must know," he said in a honeyed voice, "that my friends are hunters."

"Ah!" she remarked.

"Yes."

"Well, what then?"

"Why, then, why, they hunt, I suppose," he continued, discountenanced by the lady's singular tone.

"That is probable," she said, with a little silvery laugh. "And what do they hunt?"

"Well, pretty nearly all sorts of animals."

"Specify."

"Wild bulls, for instance."

"Very good; we will say, then, that they hunt wild bulls?"

"Yes."

"Why those animals more than others?"

"I will tell you."

"I shall feel delighted."

Don Cornelio bowed.

"You must know that at San Francisco—"

"San Francisco again?"

"Alas! Yes."

"Very good: proceed."

"Oxen, bullocks, and generally all animals that serve for food, are extremely dear."

"Ah!"

"O dear, yes! You understand that people in that country pay great attention to finding gold, and very little to seeking food."

"Quite correct."

"So my friend reasoned thus."

"Which friend?"

"The hunter, Don Louis."

"Don Louis?"

"Yes, the man who three years back, when the bandits attacked you, arrived so opportunely, and whom I have never quitted since."

Doña Angela experienced such a startling emotion that her face suddenly turned pale. Don Cornelio, busied with his story, did not perceive the effect the accidental mention of that name produced, but continued, —

"'Very good, then,' he said to himself. 'Bulls obtain fabulous prices in California; in Mexico they may be had for almost nothing. Let us go and buy or lasso them in Mexico.'"

"So then?"

"Well, we set out."

"You were in California at that time?"

"At San Francisco, with Don Louis."

"And now?"

"We have a magnificent herd of novillos, which we have driven a long distance, and which we hope to dispose of at a large profit at San Francisco."

"I hope so."

"Thank you, madam; the more so as we had an enormous difficulty in procuring them."

"But all that does not teach me why you cannot separate from your friends."

"At any rate not until we have sold the bullocks. You understand, señorita, that acting otherwise would be ungentlemanly."

"That is true; but why insist on selling your bulls nowhere save at San Francisco?"

"We do not at all insist on that."

"Then, supposing you found a good price here, you would dispose of them?"

"I see nothing to prevent it."

Doña Angela gave a start of joy, which Don Cornelio naturally interpreted to his own advantage.

"That might be arranged," she said.

"You think so?"

"Yes, if you are not too craving."

"You need not apprehend that, señorita."

"My father possesses a hacienda a few leagues from this town. I know that he intends to re-form his *ganado*, and he stopped here today in order to have an interview with his *mayordomo*."

"Oh! That is a providential chance."

"Is it not?"

"It is really. Has the mayordomo arrived?"

"Not yet: we do not expect him till tomorrow. I fancy that a day's delay will do you no injury."

"Not the slightest."

"Well, then, if you consent, we will settle this affair while we are together; that is to say," she added, "you will tell me the prices, that I may inform my father."

"Ah!" he said, with a certain hesitation, "I can, unfortunately, say nothing on that head."

"Why so? Are you not the owner of the herd?"

"Pardon me."

"Well, what then?" she interrupted, looking at him with fixed attention.

"That is to say, I am not sole owner."

"You have partners?"

"Yes, I have one."

"And that partner— —?"

"Stay, madam, I prefer being frank with you, and telling you clearly how matters stand."

"I am listening, caballero."

"I am owner without being so."

"I do not understand you at all."

"It is very simple, however, as you will see."

"I am all anxiety."

"Just imagine that Don Louis, after curing me of my wounds, felt that loyal and open friendship for me which has no counterpart in town life. Not only would he not consent to my leaving him, but aware that, owing to reverses too long to repeat to you, I was almost penniless, he insisted on my becoming a sharer in all the enterprises he thought proper to undertake; so that, without the outlay of a penny, I hold one half the property. Hence, as you will see, I can do nothing until I have first taken his instructions."

"That is only just, it seems to me."

"And to me too, madam; and that is the reason why, in spite of the lively desire I entertain to settle the business with you at once, I find it impossible to do so."

Doña Angela seemed to reflect for a moment, then went on with a palpitation of the heart and a tremor in her voice, which she could not conceal, in spite of all her efforts: —

"After all, the matter is perfectly simple, and may be arranged very easily."

"I ask nothing better; still I confess, to my shame, that I do not see what means I should employ."

"It is a trifle, tomorrow, before the mayordomo's arrival, I will speak with my father: he will, I doubt not, be delighted to render a service to the man who saved our lives. You will tell your friend, he will come to an arrangement with my father, and all will be settled."

"Indeed, madam, I did not think of that. All can be arranged in that way."

"Unless your friend—Don Louis, I think you called him——?"

"Yes, madam, Don Louis. He is a gentleman belonging to one of the noblest and oldest families in France."

"Ah! All the better. Unless, I say, he should not consent to deal with my father."

"And why should he not, señorita?"

"Oh! I do not know; but on our first meeting, after saving my father's life and mine, that caballero behaved so singularly toward us that I fear— —"

"You are wrong, madam, to suppose that Don Louis could refuse an offer so advantageous as that you make him; besides, I will talk with him, and am certain to bring him over to my views."

"O dear me!" she said negligently, "I have but a very slight interest in all this. I should not like the proposal to cause you the slightest annoyance with your partner. I am only looking after your interests in the affair, Don Cornelio."

"I am convinced of it, madam, and thank you humbly," he replied, with a low bow.

"I only know you. Your partner, though he rendered me a great service, is but a stranger to me, especially after the peremptory manner in which he declined my father's advances and offers of service."

"You are perfectly right, señorita. Believe me that I attach full value to the delicacy of your conduct."

"Still," she continued, in an insinuating and slightly malicious voice, "I confess to you that I should not be sorry to find myself once more face to face with that strange man, were it only to convince myself that the opinion I formed of him was wrong."

"Don Louis, madam," the Spaniard answered complacently, "is a true caballero, kind, noble, and generous, ever ready to help with purse or sword those who claim his assistance. Since I have had the honour of living in his society I have had many opportunities of appreciating the greatness of his character."

"I am happy to hear what you tell me, señor, for I confess that this caballero left a very bad impression on me, doubtlessly through the rough manner in which he parted from us."

"That bad impression was unjust, madam. As for the roughness with which you reproach him alas! It is only melancholy."

"What!" she exclaimed quickly, while a rosy tinge suddenly invaded her forehead, "melancholy, do you say? Is the gentleman unhappy?"

"Who is not so?" Don Cornelio asked with a sigh.

"Perhaps, though, you are mistaken."

"Alas! No, madam. Don Louis has been the victim of frightful disasters: judge for yourself. He had a wife he adored, who had presented him with several charming children. One night the Indians surprised his hacienda, fired it, massacred his wife, his children, his whole family, in a word, and himself only escaped by a miracle."

"Oh, that is horrible!" she exclaimed, as she buried her face in her hands. "Poor man! Now I heartily pardon what appeared singularity in his manners. Alas! The society of his fellow men must weigh upon him."

"Yes, madam, it doubtlessly does so; for the grief he endures is of that nature which cannot be consoled. And yet, when he knows of a misfortune to alleviate, or any good deed to do, he forgets himself only to think of those he wishes to aid."

"Yes, you are right, caballero; that man has a noble heart."

"Alas, madam! I should ever remain below the truth in what I might tell you of him. You must live his life, be constantly by his side, in order to understand and appreciate him at his full value."

There were a few moments of silence. The night was drawing on; the candles were beginning to dim; the camarista, who had but a very slight interest in this conversation, had laid her head against the back of her butaca; her eyes were closed, and she was enjoying that catlike sleep peculiar to women and the feline race, and which does not prevent them being constantly on the watch.

"Tell me, Don Cornelio," Doña Angela continued with a smile, "have you never spoken with Don Louis about our meeting during the long period that has since elapsed?"

"Never, madam."

"Ah!"

"Once, and only once, I remember that I tried to bring the conversation round to that subject by some rather direct allusions."

"Well?"

"Don Louis, who, till then, had seemed to listen kindly to my observations, suddenly requested me, in very distinct language, never to return to that subject, remarking that he had only acted in accordance with his duty; that he would do the same again; and that it was not worth while talking about, the less so as chance would, in all probability, never again bring him into contact with the persons to whom he had been so fortunate as to render this slight service."

The young lady frowned.

"I thank you," she said in a slightly affected voice, "I thank you, Don Cornelio, for the kindness with which you have treated the whims of a woman you did not know."

"Oh, madam!" he exclaimed in protest; "for a long time I have been your most humble slave."

"I know your gallantry, but will not abuse it longer. Be assured that I shall keep our long conversation in pleasant memory. Be kind enough not to forget the proposals I wish to make to Don Louis."

"Tomorrow, madam, at the hour you think most suitable, my friend and myself will have the honour to present ourselves to the general."

"Do not derange yourselves, caballero; a criado will warn you when my father is ready to receive you. Farewell!"

"Farewell!" he replied, bowing respectfully to the young lady, who dismissed him with a gracious smile.

The Spaniard went out with joy in his heart.

"Oh!" Doña Angela murmured, so soon as she was alone, "I love him!"

Whom was she speaking of?

CHAPTER VII
A RETROSPECT

Before carrying our story further we must give the reader certain details about the family and antecedents of Don Sebastian Guerrero, who is destined to play a great part in our narrative.

The family of Don Sebastian was rich; he descended in a straight line from one of the early kings of Mexico, and pure Aztec blood flowed in his veins. Like several other great Mexican families, his ancestors had not been dispossessed by the conquerors, to whom they rendered important services; but they were obliged to add a Spanish name to the Mexican one, which sounded harshly in Castilian ears.

Still the Guerrero family boasted loudly of its Aztec origin, and if it seemed ostensibly devoted to Spain, it secretly maintained the hope of seeing Mexico one day regain her liberty.

Thus, when the heroic Hidalgo, the humble curate of the little village of Dolores, suddenly raised the standard of revolt against the oppressors of his country, Don Eustaquio Guerrero, though married but a short time previously to a woman he adored, and father of a son hardly six years of age, was one of the first to respond to the appeal of the insurgents, and join Hidalgo at the head of four hundred resolute men raised on his own enormous estates.

The Mexican revolution was a singular one; for nearly all the promoters and heroes were priests—the only country in the world where the clergy have openly taken the initiative in progress, and thus displayed profound sympathy for the liberty of the people.

Don Eustaquio Guerrero was in turn companion of those modest heroes whom disdainful history has almost forgotten, and whose names were, Hidalgo, Morelos, Hermenegildo Galeana, Allende, Abasolo, Aldama, Valerio Trujano, Torres, Rayon, Sotomayor, Manuel Mier-y-Teran, and many others whose names have escaped me; and who, after fighting gloriously for the liberty of their country, now repose in their bloody tombs, protected by that glorious nimbus which Heaven places round the brow of martyrs, whatever be the cause they have defended, so long as that cause is just.

More fortunate than the majority of his brave comrades in arms, who were destined to fall one after the other, some as victims to Spanish barbarity, others conquered by treachery, Don Eustaquio escaped as if by a miracle from the innumerable dangers of this war, which lasted ten years, and at length witnessed the complete expulsion of the Spaniards and the proclamation of independence.

The brave soldier, prematurely aged, covered with wounds, and disgusted by the ingratitude of his fellow countrymen, who, scarce free, began attacking each other, and inaugurated that fatal era of *pronunciamientos*, the list of which is already so long, and will only be closed by the ruin of the country, and the loss of its nationality, retired, gloomy and sad, to his Hacienda del Palmar, situated in the province of Valladolid, and sought, in the company of his wife and son, to recover some sparks of that happiness he had formerly enjoyed when he was but an obscure citizen.

But this supreme consolation was denied him; his wife died in his arms scarce two years after their reunion, attacked by an unknown disease, which dragged her to the grave in a few weeks.

After the death of the woman he loved with all the strength of his soul, Don Eustaquio, crushed by sorrow, only dragged on a wretched existence, which terminated exactly one year after his wife's death. Her name was the last word that wandered on his pallid lips as he drew his parting breath.

Don Sebastian, who was scarce twenty years of age, was left an orphan. Alone, without relatives or friends, the young man shut himself up in his hacienda, where he silently bewailed the two beings he had lost, and on whom he had concentrated all his affections.

Don Sebastian would probably have remained for many years in retirement, without seeing the world, or caring how it went on—leading the careless, idle, and brutalising life of those great land-holders whom no idea of progress or amelioration impels to trouble themselves about their estates, timid and fearful, like all men who live alone, spending his days in hunting and sleeping—had not chance, or rather his lucky star, brought to Palmar an old partisan chief who had long fought by the side of Don Eustaquio, and who, happening to pass a few leagues from the place, felt old reminiscences aroused in him, and determined to press the hand of his old comrade, whose death he was not aware of.

The name of this man was Don Isidro Vargas. He was of lofty stature, his shoulders were wide, his limbs athletic, and his features imprinted with an uncommon energy; in a word, he presented in his person the type of that powerful and devoted race which is daily dying out in Mexico, and of which, ere long, not a specimen will be left.

The unexpected arrival of this guest, whose heavy spurs and long steel-scabbarded sabre re-echoed noisily on the tiled floors of the hacienda, brought life into the mansion which had been so long devoted to silence and the gloomy tranquillity of the cloister.

Like all old soldiers, Captain Don Isidro had a rough voice and sharp way of speaking; his manners were brusque, but his character was gay, and gifted with a rare equanimity of temper.

When he entered the house Don Sebastian was out hunting, and the hacienda seemed uninhabited. The captain at first found enormous difficulty in meeting with anyone to address. At length, by careful search, he detected a peon half asleep under a verandah, who gave some sort of answer to the questions asked him. By great patience and questions made with that craft peculiar to the Mexicans, the captain succeeded in obtaining some valuable information.

The death of Don Eustaquio only astonished the worthy *soldado* slightly; he expected it, indeed, from the moment he learnt the death of the señora, for whom he knew his old comrade professed so deep a love; but on learning the idle life Don Sebastian had led since his father's death, the captain burst out in a furious passion, and swore by all the saints in the Spanish calendar (and they are tolerably numerous), that this state of things should not last much longer.

The captain had known the young man when he was but a child. Many times he had dandled him on his knee, and thus, with his ideas of honour and generosity, he thought himself obliged, as an old friend of his father, to remove the son from the slothful existence he led.

Consequently the old soldier installed himself authoritatively in the hacienda, and firmly awaited the return of the man he had been accustomed to regard for a long time almost in the light of a son.

The day passed peacefully. The Indian peons, long accustomed to profess the greatest respect for embroidered hats and jingling sabres, left him free to act as he pleased—a liberty the old soldier did not at all abuse, for he contented himself with ordering an immense vase full of an infusion of tamarinds, which he placed on a table, up to which he drew a butaca, and amused himself with smoking an enormous quantity of husk cigarettes, which he made as he wanted them, with that dexterity alone possessed by the Spanish race.

At about *oración* time, or six in the evening, the captain, who had fallen quietly asleep, was aroused by a great noise, mingled with shouts, barking, and the neighing of horses, which he heard outside.

"Ah, ah!" he said, turning up his moustache, "I fancy the *muchacho* has at last arrived."

It was, indeed, Don Sebastian returning from the chase.

The old partisan, who was sitting opposite a window, was enabled to examine his friend's son at his ease, without being perceived in his turn. He could not repress a smile of satisfaction at the sight of the vigorous young man, with his haughty features bearing the imprint of boldness, wildness, and timidity, and his well-built limbs.

"What a pity," he muttered to himself, "if such a fine fellow were to be expended here without profit to himself or to others! It will not be my fault if I do not succeed in rousing the boy from the state of lethargy into which he is plunged. I owe that to the memory of his poor father."

While making these reflections, as he heard the clanking of spurs in the room before that in which he was, he fell back on his butaca, and put on again his usual look of indifference. Don Sebastian entered. He had not seen the captain for several years. The greeting he gave him, though slightly awkward and embarrassed, was, however, affectionate. After the first compliments they sat down face to face.

"Well, muchacho," the captain said, suddenly plunging *in medias res,* "you did not expect a visit from me, I fancy?"

"I confess, captain, that I was far from supposing that you would come. To what fortunate accident do I owe your presence in my house?"

"I will tell you presently, muchacho. For the present we will talk about other matters, if you have no objection."

"At your ease, captain; I do not wish to displease you in any way."

"We will see that presently, *cuerpo de Dios!* And in the first place, to speak frankly, I will tell you that I did not come to see you, but your worthy father, my brave general. *Voto a brios!* The news of his death quite upset me, and I am not myself again yet."

"I am very grateful, captain, for the kindly memory in which you hold my father."

"*Capa de Cristo!*" the captain said, who, among other habits more or less excellent, possessed to an eminent degree that of seasoning each of his phrases with an oath, at times somewhat unorthodox, "of course I hold in kind memory the man by whose side I fought for ten years, and to whom I owe it that I am what I am. Yes, I do remember him, and I hope soon, *canarios!* To prove it to his son."

"I thank you, captain, though I do not perceive in what way you can give me this proof."

"Good, good!" he said, gnawing his moustache. "I know how to do it, and that is enough. Everything will come at its right season."

"As you please, my old friend. At any rate, you will be kind enough to remember that you are at home here, and that the longer you stay the greater pleasure you will afford me."

"Good, muchacho! I expected that from you. I will avail myself of the hospitality so gracefully offered, but will not abuse it."

"An old comrade in arms of my father's cannot do that in his house, captain, and you less than anyone else. But," he added, seeing a peon enter, "here is a servant come to announce that the dinner is served. I confess to you that, as I have been hunting all day, I am now dying of hunger: if you will follow me we will sit down to the table and renew our acquaintance glass in hand."

"I ask nothing better, *rayo de Dios!*" the captain said as he rose. "Though I have not been hunting, I think I shall do honour to the repast."

And without further talking they passed into a dining room, where a sumptuously and abundantly-served table awaited them.

According to a patriarchal custom, which, unfortunately, like all good things, is beginning to die out, at Palmar the master and servants took their meals together. This custom, which had existed in the family since the conquest, Don Sebastian kept up—in the first place, through respect for his father's memory, and secondly, because the servants at the hacienda were devoted to their master, and to some extent supplied the place of a family.

The evening passed away, without any incident worthy of remark, in chatting about war and the chase. Captain Don Isidro Vargas was an old soldier, as cunning as a monk. Too clever to assail the young man's ideas straightforwardly, he resolved to study him for some time, in order to discover the weak points of his character, and see how he must attack him in order to drag him out of that slothful and purposeless life he led in this forgotten province. Thus several days were passed in hunting and other amusements, and the captain never once alluded to the subject he had at heart. At times he might make a covert allusion to the active life of the capital, the opportunities of securing a fine position which a man of

Don Sebastian's age could not fail to find at Mexico, if he would take the trouble to go there, and many other insinuations of the same nature; but the young man let them pass without making the slightest observation, or even appearing to understand them.

"Patience!" the captain muttered. "I shall eventually find the flaw in his cuirass; and if I do not succeed, I must be preciously clumsy."

And he recommenced his covert attacks, not allowing the young man's impassive indifference to rebuff him.

Don Sebastian performed his duties as master of the house with thoroughly Mexican grace, amenity, and sumptuousness; that is, he invented every sort of amusement which he thought would be most suited to the worthy captain's tastes. The latter let him do so with the utmost coolness, and conscientiously enjoyed the pleasures the young man procured him, charmed in his heart by the activity he displayed in pleasing him, and more and more persuaded that, if he succeeded in arousing in him the feelings which he supposed were slumbering in his mind, it would be easy to convert him to his own ideas, and make him abandon the absorbing life of a *campesino*.

More than once, during the few days they spent in hunting in the magnificent plains that surrounded the hacienda, accident enabled the captain to admire the skill with which the young man managed his steed, and his superiority in all those exercises which demand strength, activity, and, above all, skill.

On one occasion especially, at the moment the hunters galloped in pursuit of a magnificent stag they had put up, they found themselves suddenly face to face with a cougouar, which threatened to dispute their progress. The cougouar is the American lion. It has no mane. Like all the other carnivora of the New World it cares little about attacking a man, and it is only when reduced to the last extremity that it turns upon him; but then it fights with a courage and energy that frequently render its approach extremely dangerous.

On the occasion to which we allude the cougouar seemed resolved to await its enemies boldly. The captain, but little accustomed to find himself face to face with such enemies, experienced that internal tremor which assails the bravest man when he finds himself exposed to a serious danger. Still, as the old soldier was notoriously brave, he soon recovered from this involuntary emotion, and cocked his gun, while watching the crouching animal, which fixed its glaring eyes on him.

"Do not fire, captain," Don Sebastian said with a perfectly calm voice; "you are not used to this chase, and, without wishing it, might injure the skin, which you see is magnificent, and that would be a pity."

Don Sebastian thereupon let his gun fall, took a pistol from his holster, and spurring his horse at the same time that he checked it, made it rear. The animal rose, and stood almost on its hind legs; the cougouar suddenly bounded forward with a terrible roar; the young man dug his knees into his horse, which bounded on one side, while Don Sebastian pulled the trigger. The monster rolled on the ground in convulsive agony.

"*Cuerpo de Cristo!*" the captain shouted; "why, you've killed it on the spot! No matter, muchacho; you played for a heavy stake."

"Bah!" the other said as he dismounted; "it is not so difficult as you fancy; it only requires practice."

"Hum! It must require practice to shoot such an animal on the wing. The ball has entered its eye."

"Yes, we generally shoot them there, so as not to spoil the skin."

"Ah, very good! To tell you the truth, though, I, who am by no means a bad shot, should not like to try the experiment."

"You are calumniating yourself."

"Very possibly."

"Poor Pepe, my tigrero, will lose by that a reward of ten piastres—all the worse for him. Shall we return to the hacienda, and send someone to bring the brute in?"

"With all my heart."

They went back.

"Hum!" the captain said to himself as they galloped on, "I must have a definitive explanation with him this very evening."

CHAPTER VIII
A MEXICAN'S PROGRESS

The Hispano-Americans usually drink nothing with their meals: it is only when the *dulces*, or cakes and sweetmeats, have been eaten, and each guest has swallowed the glass of water intended to facilitate digestion, that the liquors are put on the table, and the Catalonian *refino* begins to circulate; then the *puros* and *pajillos* are lighted, and the conversation, always rather stiff during the meal, becomes more intimate and friendly, owing to the absence of the inferior guests, who then retire, leaving the master of the house and his guests at perfect liberty.

The captain had judiciously chosen this moment to commence his attack. Not that he hoped to have a better chance with the young man at the termination of the meal—for the sobriety of the Southern Americans is proverbial—but because at that moment Don Sebastian, being freed from all cares, must more easily yield to the influence the captain fancied he could exercise over him.

The captain poured some refino into a large glass, which he filled with water, lit a puro, leant his elbows on the table, and looked fixedly at the young man.

"Muchacho," he said to him abruptly, "does the life you lead in the desert possess a great charm for you?"

Surprised at this question, which he was far from expecting, Don Sebastian hesitated ere he replied.

"Yes," the captain said, emptying his glass, "do you amuse yourself greatly here? Answer me frankly."

"On my word, captain, as I never knew any other existence than that I am leading at this moment, I cannot answer your question thoroughly: it is certain that I feel myself hipped at times."

The captain struck his tongue against his palate with evident satisfaction.

"Ah, ah!" he said, "I am glad to hear you speak so."

"Why?"

"Because I hope you will easily accept the proposition I am about to make to you."

"You!"

"Who else, then, if not I?"

"Speak!" the young man said with a careless air; "I am listening."

The captain threw away his cigar, gave vent to two or three sonorous *hums*, and at length said in a sharp voice,—

"Sebastian, my dear fellow! Do you think that, if your worthy father could return to this world, he would be well pleased to see you thus idly wasting the precious hours of your youth?"

"I do not at all understand your meaning, captain."

"That is possible. I never pretended to be a great orator, and today less than at any other period of my long career. I will, however, try to explain myself so clearly that, if you do not understand me, *caray!* It is because you will not."

"Go on; I am listening."

"Your father, muchacho, whose history you probably do not know, was at once a brave soldier and a good officer. He was one of the founders of our liberty, and his name is a symbol of loyalty and devotion to every Mexican. For ten years your father fought the enemies of his country on every battlefield, enduring, though rich and a gentleman, hunger and thirst, heat and cold, gaily and without complaining; and yet, had he wished it, he might have led a luxurious and thoroughly easy life. You loved your father?"

"Alas, captain! Can I ever be consoled for his loss?"

"You will be consoled. You have many things to learn yet, and that among others. Poor boy! There is nothing eternal in the world—neither joy, nor sorrow, nor pleasure. But let us return to what I was saying. Were your father permitted to quit the abode of the just, where he is doubtlessly sojourning, and return for a few moments to earth, he would speak to you as I am now doing; he would ask an account of the useless indolence in which you spend your youth, thinking no more of your country, which you can and ought to serve, than if you lived in the heart of a desert. Did your father endure so many sacrifices in order to create such an existence—tell me, muchacho?"

The worthy captain, who had probably never preached so much in his life, stopped, awaiting a reply to the question he had asked; but this reply did not come. The young man, with his arms crossed on his chest, his body thrown back, and his eyes obstinately fixed on the ground, seemed plunged in deep thought. The captain continued after a lengthened delay,—

"We," he said, "demolished; you young men must rebuild. No one at the present day has the right to deprive the Republic of his services. Each must, under penalty of being considered a bad citizen, carry his stone to the social edifice, and you more than anyone else, muchacho—you, the son of one of the most celebrated heroes of the War of Independence. Your country calls you—it claims you: you can no longer remain deaf to its voice. What are you doing here among your dogs and horses, wasting ingloriously your courage, dissipating your energy without profit to anyone, and growing daily more brutalised in a disgraceful solitude? *Cuerpo de Cristo!* I can understand that a man may love his father, and even weep for him—for that is the duty of a good son, and your father certainly deserves the sacred recollection you give him—but to make of that grief a pretext to caress and satisfy your egotism, that is worse than a bad action—it is cowardice!"

At this word the young man's tawny eye flashed lightning.

"Captain!" he shouted, as he struck the table with his clenched fist.

"*Rayo de Dios!*" the old soldier continued boldly, "the word is spoken, and I will not withdraw it: your father, if he hear me, must approve me. Now, muchacho, I have emptied my heart; I have spoken frankly and loyally, as it was my duty to do. I owed it to myself to fulfil this painful duty. If you do not understand the feeling that dictated the rough words I uttered, all the worse for you; it is because your heart is dead to every generous impulse, and you are incapable of feeling how much I must have loved you to find the courage to speak to you in that way. Now do as you think proper; I shall not have to reproach myself for having hidden the truth from you. It is late. Good night, muchacho. I will go to bed, for I start early tomorrow. Reflect on what I have said to you. The night is a good counsellor, if you will listen in good faith to the voices that chatter round your pillow in the darkness."

And the captain emptied his glass and rose. Don Sebastian imitated him, took a step toward him, and laid his hand on his shoulder.

"One moment," he said to him.

"What do you want?"

"Listen to me in your turn," the young man said in a gloomy voice. "You have been harsh with me, captain. Those truths you have told me you might perhaps have expressed in milder language, in consideration of my age, and the solitude and isolation in which I have hitherto lived. Still I am not angry at your rude frankness; on the contrary, I am grateful to you for it, for I know that you love me, and the interest you take in me alone urged you to be so severe. You say that you depart tomorrow?"

"Yes."

"Where do you intend going?"

"To Mexico."

"Very good, captain; you will not go alone. I shall accompany you."

The old soldier looked at the young man for a moment tenderly; then pressing with feverish energy the hand held out to him,—

"It is well, muchacho," he said to him with great emotion. "I was not mistaken in you; you are a brave lad, and, *caray!* I am satisfied with you."

The two men left Palmar together the next morning, and rode toward Mexico, which city they reached after a ten days' journey. But during those ten days, spent *tête-à-tête* with the captain, the young man's ideas were completely modified, and a perfect change came over his aspirations.

General Guerrero's son belonged unconsciously to that numerous class of men who are utterly ignorant of themselves, and pass their lives in indolence until the moment when, an object being suddenly offered them, their imagination is inflamed, their ambition is aroused, and they become as eager in the chase as they had been previously negligent and indifferent as to their future.

Captain Don Isidro Vargas heartily praised the intelligence with which the young man he emphatically called his pupil understood the lessons he gave him as to his behaviour in the world.

Don Sebastian experienced no difficulty—thanks to his name, and the reputation his father so justly enjoyed—in obtaining his grade as lieutenant in the army. This step was, for the young man, the first rung of the ladder, which he prepared to climb as rapidly as possible.

It was fine work at that day, in Mexico, for an intelligent man to fish in troubled waters; and, unfortunately, we are obliged to confess that, in spite of the long years that have passed since the proclamation of its independence, nothing is as yet changed in that unhappy country, where anarchy has been systematised.

If ever a country could do without an army, it was Mexico after the recognition of her liberty and the entire expulsion of the Spaniards, owing to her isolation in the midst of peaceful nations, and the security of her frontiers, which no enemy menaced. Unhappily, the war of independence had lasted ten years. During that long period the peaceful and gentle population of that country, held in guardianship by its oppressors, had become transformed. A warlike ardour had seized on all classes of society, and a species of martial fever had aroused in every brain a love of arms.

Hence that naturally came about which all sensible people expected; that is to say, when the army had no longer enemies before it to combat, the troops turned their arms against their fellow citizens, vexing and tyrannising over them at their pleasure.

The government, instead of disbanding this turbulent army, or at any rate reducing it to a *minimum* by only keeping up the depôts of the various corps, considered it far more advantageous to lean on it, and organise a military oligarchy, which pressed heavily on the country. This deplorable system has plunged this unhappy country into disastrous complications, against which it struggles in vain, and has dug the abyss in which its nationality will sooner or later be swallowed up.

The army, then, after the war, assumed an influence which it has ever since retained, and which increased in proportion as the men placed at the head of the government more fully understood that it alone could maintain them in power or overthrow them at its good pleasure. The army, therefore, made revolutions that its leaders might become powerful. From the lowest *alférez* up to the general of division, all the officers look to troubles for promotion—the alférez to become lieutenant, the colonel to exchange his red scarf for the green one of the brigadier general, and the general of division to become President of the Republic.

Hence pronunciamientos are continual; for every officer wearied of a subaltern grade, and who aspires to a higher rank, pronounces himself; that is to say, aided by a nucleus of malcontents like himself, which is never wanting, he revolts by refusing obedience to the government, and that the more easily because, whether conqueror or conquered, the rank he has thus appropriated always remains his.

The military career is, therefore, a perfect steeplechase. We know a certain general, whose name we could write here in full if we wished, who attained the presidency by stepping from pronunciamiento to pronunciamiento without ever having smelt fire, or knowing the first movement of platoon drill—an ignorance which is not at all extraordinary in a country where one of our sergeant conductors would be superior to the most renowned generals.

Don Sebastian judged his position with the infallible eye of an ambitious man; and suddenly attacked by a fever of immense activity, he resolved to profit cleverly by the general anarchy to gain a position. He clambered up the first steps at full speed and became a full colonel with startling rapidity. On reaching that position he married, in order to secure himself, and to give him that solidity he desired for the great game he intended to play, and which, in his mind, only ended with the presidential chair.

Already very rich, his marriage increased his fortune, which he sought to augment, however, by every possible scheme; for he was aware what the cost of a successful pronunciamiento was, and he did not mean to suffer a defeat.

As if everything was destined to favour this man in all he undertook, his wife, a dear and charming woman, whose love and devotion he never comprehended, died after a short illness, and left him father of a girl as charming and amiable as herself—that lovely Angela whom we have already met several times in the course of our narrative.

Don Sebastian could have married again if he liked; but by his first marriage he had obtained what he wanted, and preferred to remain free. At the period we have now reached he had attained general's rank, and secured the appointment of political governor of the state of Sonora, the first stepping-stone for his ambitious projects.

Colossally rich, he was interested in all the great industrial enterprises, and a shareholder in most of the mining operations. It was for the object of watching these operations more closely, that he had asked for the government of Sonora, a new country, almost unknown, where he hoped to fish more easily in troubled waters, owing to its distance from the capital, and the slight surveillance he had to fear from the government, in which he had, moreover, all-powerful influences.

In a word, General Guerrero was one of those gloomy personages who, under a most fascinating exterior, the most affable manners, and most seductive smiles, conceal the most perverse instincts, the coldest ferocity, and the most rotten soul.

Still this man had in his heart one feeling which, by its intensity, expiated many faults.

He loved his daughter.

He loved her passionately, without calculation or afterthought; yet this paternal love had something terrible about it: he loved his daughter as the jaguar or the panther loves its cubs, with fury and jealousy.

Doña Angela, though she had never tried to sound her father's impenetrable heart, had still divined the uncontrolled power she exercised over this haughty nature which crushed everything, but became suddenly weak and almost timid in her presence. The charming maid employed her power despotically, but ever with the intention of doing a good deed, as, for instance, to commute the sentence of a prisoner or succour the unfortunate; in a word, to render lighter the yoke of iron under which the general, with his feline manners, crushed his subordinates.

Thus the girl was as much adored by all those who approached her as the general was feared and hated. God had doubtlessly wished, in His ineffable goodness, to place an angel by the side of a demon, so that the wounds inflicted by the latter might be cured by the former.

Now that we have described these two persons to the best of our ability, whose characters will be more fully developed in the course of our story, we will resume our narrative at the point where we interrupted it.

CHAPTER IX
THE NEXT DAY

The sky was just beginning to be tinted with shades of opal—a few stars still shone feebly here and there in the gloomy depths of the sky. It was about half past three in the morning.

Within the *locanda* men and animals were sleeping that calm sleep which precedes sunrise. Not a sound, save at intervals the barking of a dog baying at the moon, broke the silence that brooded over the pueblo of San José.

The door of the cuarto in which the foster brothers rested was cautiously opened, a thin thread of light found its way through the orifice, and Valentine and the count came out. Don Louis had no reason for departing unseen; he had no motives for hiding himself. If he took so many precautions, it was only through a fear of disturbing the sleep of the other lodgers, who had not such good reasons as himself for rising so early, and whom, consequently, it was unnecessary to arouse.

On arriving in the patio Don Louis prepared his horse's trappings, while Valentine led the animal from the corral, carefully rubbed it down, and gave it water. When all was in order Valentine opened the gate, the two men shook hands for the last time, and Don Louis entered the gloom of the only street of the pueblo, where he soon disappeared, amid the barking of the masterless dogs aroused by his passing, and who rushed after him howling furiously, and snapping at his horse's legs.

Valentino remained for a moment motionless and thoughtful, listening mechanically to the decreasing sound of the hoofs on the hardened ground.

"Perhaps I ought not to have put him on that path," he muttered. "Who knows what awaits him at the other end?" A stifled sigh broke from his bosom. "Bah!" he added a moment after, "all roads do not lead to the same point—death! Why let such foolish forebodings have any effect over me? Live and learn."

The worthy hunter, somewhat comforted by these philosophic reflections, re-entered the patio, and set to work shutting the outer door, before throwing himself for an hour or two on his cuadro. While engaged in this occupation, he heard the sound of approaching footsteps behind him: he turned his head, and recognised Don Cornelio.

"Ah, ah, my dear friend!" he said gaily, offering him his hand, which the other pressed affectionately; "You are up very early."

"Eh?" the Spaniard answered with a laugh. "I think it a good joke for you to make that remark to me."

"Why so?"

"Because, if I have risen so early, it appears as if you had not been to bed at all."

Valentine began laughing.

"By Jove! You are right. The fact is that, with the exception of yourself and myself, it is certain that everybody is asleep in the pueblo; and now that this door is closed again, with your permission, I will go and do the same for an hour or two."

"What! You are going to bed again?"

"Certainly."

"What to do?"

"Why, to sleep, I suppose."

"Pardon me, but I did not mean that."

"I suppose not."

"And you know what I wish to say to you?"

"I! Not the least in the world. But, as you are a man far too intelligent to spend in walking about the time you might pass far more agreeably in sleeping, I presume that you have certain weighty reasons for being here now."

"That is true, on my word."

"You see!"

"Yes; but I did not wish exactly to speak with you."

"Whom with, then?"

"With Don Louis."

"Hum! And you cannot tell it to me?"

"O yes, I can; but I think it would be better to speak with him myself."

"Confuse the thing!"

Don Cornelio gave that shrug of the shoulders which in all countries and languages signifies the same thing; that is, that the shrugger declines all responsibility.

"And," Valentine continued, "what you have to communicate to Don Louis is probably very important?"

"Very."

"Hang it all, that is annoying; for it is impossible for you to speak with him."

"Bah! How so?"

"Because there is an obstacle."

"For me?"

"For you and for everybody else."

"Oh, oh! And what is that obstacle, Don Valentine, if you please?"

"Oh, I do not want to make any mystery of it; I am more vexed than yourself at what has happened; but the obstacle is very simply that Don Louis has gone away."

"Gone! Don Louis!" the other said in amazement.

"Yes."

"How was that—without speaking to anybody? Gone off at a venture?"

"Not exactly. There were urgent reasons to speed his departure; and see, I was engaged in shutting the gate after him when you arrived. A moment earlier and you would have met him."

"How unlucky!"

"It is; but what would you do? After all, the misfortune is not so great as it may seem to you at the first blush. We shall see him again in a few days."

"You are sure of it?"

"Quite; for it is arranged between us. So soon as I have succeeded in selling the herd, we shall go and join our friend again. So take patience, Don Cornelio; the separation will not be long. Console yourself with that thought, and good night."

Valentine turned and walked a few steps, but the Spaniard stopped him.

"What do you want now?"

"Only one word."

"Make haste, for I am dropping with sleep."

"Pardon me, but you made a remark this moment which struck me greatly."

"Ah! What was it?"

"You said that Don Louis had commissioned you to sell the herd."

"Yes, I did. What then?"

"That was the very subject I wished to speak with him about."

"Bah!"

"Yes, I have found a purchaser."

"What! For the whole herd?"

"Yes, in a lump."

"Stay, stay!" Valentine said, fixing his piercing eyes upon him; "that would singularly simplify matters."

"Would it not?"

"Where on earth have you dug up this strange purchaser since last night?"

"There is nothing at all strange about him, I assure you. I found him here."

"Here, in this locanda?"

"On my word, yes."

"I really beg your pardon," Valentine said. "I am too well acquainted with the gravity of your character to suppose that you have any intention of deceiving me—"

"Oh!"

"But all this is so extraordinary—"

"I am as much astonished as yourself at it."

"Really!"

"The more so because I did not know that Don Louis wished to sell the herd here, and consequently the proposition does not emanate from me."

"That is true. So you have been offered—"

"To take the whole herd off my hands this very day—yes."

"That is strange. Tell me all about it, my dear friend. What a pity that Don Louis has started!"

"Is it not?"

"Well, you said, then—"

"Permit me, if you have no objection, we will proceed to your cuarto, where we can converse much more agreeably than here."

"You are right, especially as people are beginning to get up in the house."

In fact, the servants of the hostelry and the muleteers were already stirring, and walking round our two friends, whom they examined curiously, while attending to their own business. Valentine and Don Cornelio left the patio, and proceeded to the hunter's cuarto. So soon as they had installed themselves Valentine said,—

"Now I am all attention. Speak, my good fellow. I confess I am anxious to hear the solution of this riddle."

Don Cornelio was aware of the friendship existing between Don Louis and Valentine; hence he had not the slightest difficulty in telling the hunter what had happened to him that night in the minutest details.

"Is that all?" Valentine said, who had listened with the greatest attention.

"Yes; and now what do you think of it?"

"Hum!" the hunter said thoughtfully, "if I must give you my opinion, it appears to me rather less clear now than an hour ago."

"Nonsense!"

"That is my opinion. Still we must not neglect this opportunity which presents itself so famously to get rid of our cattle advantageously."

"That is what I think."

"Very good; then do not stir. Above all, do not say a syllable about Don Louis' departure."

"Do you think so?"

"That is important."

"As you please."

"Then supposing you are summoned?"

"I will go."

"No, we will both go; that will be more proper. Is that understood?"

"Perfectly."

"Then good night; I am going to sleep a little. If there is anything new wake me up."

"All right."

And Don Cornelio withdrew.

Valentine was not at all inclined to sleep; but he wished to be alone, that he might reflect on what he had just heard. He perfectly understood that the young lady had been playing with the Spaniard like a cat with a mouse, feigning an interest in him which she did not at all feel. But what was her object in all this? Did she love Don Louis? Had the maiden retained in her heart the remembrance of what had happened to the child? Had gratitude unconsciously changed in her into love with growing years?

This was what the hunter could not fathom. Valentine had never been very expert in the matter of women; their hearts were to him as a dead letter, an unknown tongue, in which he could not read a word. The life he had constantly led in the desert, ever contending either with Indians or with wild beasts, had not been at all favourable to the study of the feminine heart; and besides, the deep love of his early youth—a love the memory of which still palpitated in his heart—had prevented him paying the slightest attention to the few women chance had at times thrown in his way, and who had only appeared to him weak, defenceless creatures, whom it was his duty to defend.

Thus the worthy hunter was now considerably bothered, and knew not what to do in order to read the young lady's intentions. It was evident to him that Doña Angela had a secret object she desired to gain, and that the purchase of the novillos was only a pretext to draw nearer to Don Louis. But what was that object? Why did she wish to see his friend? That was what he vainly sought, and was unable to discover.

"After all," he muttered to himself, while going over the chaos of thoughts that jostled each other in his brain, "it is perhaps better that she should not see Louis. Who knows what might be the result of such an interview? The lady's father is governor of Sonora, and we must be most careful not to get into any trouble with him. Who knows whether we may not need him hereafter? It is strange, I do not know where I have heard his name before; but I am certain I do not hear it today for the first time. Guerrero—Don Sebastian Guerrero. Under what circumstances can that name have been pronounced in my presence?"

The hunter had reached this point in his monologue when the door opened gently, and a man entered. It was Curumilla. Valentine started with joy on seeing him.

"You are welcome, chief," he said.

The Araucanian pressed his hand, and sat down silently by his side.

"Well, chief," Valentine continued, "you are awake. Have you been taking a turn in the pueblo?"

The Indian smiled disdainfully.

"No," he said.

An idea crossed the hunter's mind.

"My brother should go down into the patio," he said. "It seems there are other travellers beside us: he should see them."

"Curumilla has seen them."

"Ah!"

"He knows them."

Valentine made a sign of astonishment.

"What! You know them?" he exclaimed.

"Only the man. Curumilla is a chief: his memory is long."

"Ah, ah!" the hunter went on. "Is it possible that I shall obtain in this way the information I have been racking my brains to find?"

The Indian smiled and shook his head.

"Who is the man, chief? Is he a friend?"

"He is an enemy."

"An enemy, by Jupiter! I was certain I had heard his name before."

"Let my brother listen," the chief went on. "Curumilla has seen the paleface: he will kill him."

"Hum! Do not go to work so fast, chief. In the first place tell me who he is; then we shall see what we have to do. Unfortunately we are not here on the prairies: the death of that individual, whoever he may be, might cost us dear."

"The palefaces are women," the Indian replied disdainfully.

"That is possible, chief; but prudent. Tomorrow is not passed, as you gentlemen say, and every man gains his point who knows how to wait. For the present let us be shy; we are not the stronger."

Curumilla shrugged his shoulders. It was plain that the worthy Indian was not a friend to temporising measures; still he did not raise the slightest objection.

"Come, chief, tell me who he is, and under what circumstances we had a quarrel with him."

The Indian rose and stood right in front of Valentine.

"Does not my brother remember?" he asked.

"No."

"Wah! The conspiracy of the Paso del Norte, when Curumilla killed Dog-face."

"Oh!" Valentine exclaimed, striking his forehead, "I have it; it is the general who commanded the Mexican troops, and to whom Don Miguel de Zarate surrendered."

"Yes."

"Well, he was a brave and honest soldier in those days; he kept his word to our friend nobly. I cannot be angry with him."

"He is a traitor."

"From your point of view, chief, possibly so, but not from mine. It is true; I perfectly remember him now. Poor General Ibañez often spoke to me about him: he was not fond of him either. It is a strange coincidence. Good! Fear nothing, chief; I will watch. Whether friend or foe, this man has never seen me—he knows not who I am; hence I have a great advantage over him. Thanks, chief!"

"Is my brother satisfied?"

"You have rendered me an immense service, chief; so you can judge whether I am satisfied."

Curumilla smiled.

"Wah!" he said, "all the better."

"Yes, chief, all the better, and let us breakfast. I feel a ferocious appetite ever since, thanks to you, I have been able to see my way a little more clearly."

Curumilla and Don Cornelio had prepared their frugal meal in their cuarto, consisting of red haricot beans with pepper, a few *varas* of dried meat, and maize tortillas, the whole washed down with aloe pulque of the first quality, and a few *tragos* of excellent Catalonian refino.

The three friends ate with good appetite, and were preparing to light their cigars, the obligato termination of every American meal, when they heard a discreet tap at the door, which was only leaned to.

"Come in," Valentine said.

A criado appeared, and after bowing courteously to all present, said,—

"My master, his Excellency General Don Sebastian Guerrero, presents his civilities to the caballeros here assembled, and desires that Señor Don Cornelio and Señor Don Louis will favour him with a moment's interview, if their occupations will permit of it."

"Tell his Excellency," Valentine answered, "that we shall have the honour of obeying his orders."

The servant bowed and retired.

"Why, you know, señor," Don Cornelio then said, "that Don Louis is absent."

"No matter: am I not here?"

"That is true, but—"

"Leave me alone," the hunter quickly interrupted him; "I will answer for everything."

"Very good; do as you think proper."

"Trust to me. How can it concern this man whether he deals with Don Louis or anyone else, so long as the ganado is young, vigorous, and cheap?"

"That is true; it must be a matter of indifference to him."

"Come on: you will see that I shall settle this affair satisfactorily."

And he went out, followed by Don Cornelio, who, however, did not seem completely satisfied.

CHAPTER X
IN WHICH THE SALE OF THE
HERD IS DISCUSSED

What Doña Angela had told Don Cornelio was true: her father was really expecting his mayordomo that morning, in order to consult with him about certain improvements he wished to introduce at one of his haciendas, and also about buying cattle to re-stock his prairies, which had been devastated during the last periodical incursion which the Apache and Comanche Indians are in the habit of making upon the Mexican territory.

Still, Doña Angela, like the true Creole she was, had never hitherto troubled herself about her father's domestic affairs, having too much to do in thinking of her toilet and pleasures. Hence she did not know how to bring the conversation gently round to that point, without allowing the interest she took in it to be suspected. But the most simple-minded woman becomes crafty when her interest is at stake. After the Spaniard had withdrawn the girl remained pensive for a few moments; but then a smile played on her rosy lips, she patted her dainty little hands gleefully together, and fell asleep murmuring softly, —

"I have found it."

The Mexicans are early risers, that they may enjoy the freshness of the morning hours. At half past seven Doña Angela opened her eyes, and devoutly paid her matin orisons to the Virgin; then, aided by Violanta, her clever camarista, she proceeded to the charming mystery of her toilet.

Her sleep had been as peaceful as that of a bird: hence she was calm, and gloriously lovely. At the moment that Violanta put in the last pin, intended to hold the long and thick tresses of her magnificent hair, a knock was heard at the door. It was the general.

Don Sebastian was dressed in the rich costume of the Sonorian country gentry; but his masculine and sharply-cut features, his haughty glance, his long moustaches, but, above all, his decided walk, allowed him to be recognised for a soldier at the first glance, in spite of the dress he had assumed. It had been the general's custom for many long years to come thus every morning, and wish his daughter good day: his child's frank and simple smile sent a gentle ray of sunshine into his heart, whose reflection aided him during the rest of the day in supporting the inseparable cares of power.

Violanta hastened to open, and the general walked in. Doña Angela cunningly watched the expression of his face, and she bounded with delight on fancying she saw that he was pleased in spite of the severe appearance he sought to give his features. Don Sebastian kissed his daughter affectionately, and sat down on a butaca which Violanta drew forward for him.

"Oh, my child!" he said, "how fresh and radiant you are this morning! It is easy to see that you have passed an excellent night."

"At any rate, papa," she said with a little pout, "if it was not so, it was not my fault, I assure you; for I was greatly inclined to sleep when I retired last night."

"What do you mean? Was your sleep disturbed?"

"Yes, several times."

"*Caramba!* Dear little one, it was the same with me. Some scamp persisted in strumming the most melancholy airs on the guitar, that would have frightened the cats themselves, and kept me awake all night Deuce take the musician and his silly instrument!"

"It was not that, papa. I scarcely heard the man of whom you are speaking."

"What was it, then? I was not aware of any other noises last night but that."

"I cannot explain to you positively what I heard; but Violanta was also aroused several times like myself."

"Is that true, little one?" the general asked, turning to the camarista, apparently busy at the moment in arranging the cuarto.

"Oh, señor general," she exclaimed, clasping her hands, "it was a fearful noise—a noise to wake the dead!"

"What the deuce could it be?"

"I do not know," she replied, assuming her most innocent air.

"Did it last long?"

"All the night," she said, trumping what her mistress had alleged.

"Hum! But it must have resembled something, I suppose?"

"Certainly, papa; but I do not know with what to compare it."

"And you, little wench, cannot you make a guess?"

"I fancy I know."

"Ah! Well, then, tell us at once, instead of leaving us in the dark."

"I will, Excellency. This morning, taking advantage of my lady's sleeping, I went down very gently to try and discover the cause of the noise that kept us awake all night."

"And you found it?"

"I think I did."

"Very good: go on."

"It seems that hunters arrived here yesterday with a large herd of novillos, toros, &c., which they are taking, I believe, to California. It was these animals which, by stamping and roaring, prevented us sleeping, for their corral adjoins this house."

"And how did you learn all this?"

"Oh! Very easily, Excellency. Accident willed it that I should address one of the owners of the herd."

"Listen to that! Accident was very kind."

Violanta blushed. The general did not notice it, but continued, "Are you sure they were not vaqueros belonging to some hacienda?"

"O no, Excellency; they are hunters."

"Good; and they want to sell their *ganado*?"

"The man I spoke with said so."

"I suppose he asks a high price?"

"I do not know."

"That is true. Well, my child," he added, rising and turning to his daughter, "so soon as you are ready we will breakfast, and perhaps I will deliver you from the horrible noise of these animals."

The general kissed his daughter once again, and left the room. So soon as he was gone the two girls began laughing like little madcaps.

We must allow that both had played their part to perfection, and though he little suspected it, had, in a few moments, led the general to do exactly what they wanted, while leaving him persuaded that he was merely acting from his own impulse.

A few minutes later Doña Angela joined her father in the cuarto, which was employed as dining room. The mayordomo had arrived, and the general only awaited his daughter's presence to begin the meal. This mayordomo, already known to the reader, was no other than Don Isidro Vargas, who had accepted this situation as a retiring pension.

The Mexican haciendas, especially in Sonora, are often eight to ten leagues in extent. To watch so large a tract of country, on which immense bands of wild horses and numerous herds of cattle pasture at liberty, a young, robust, and active man is generally selected, who is called in that country a *hombre de a caballo*. In truth, the profession of a mayordomo is excessively severe: he must constantly be on horseback, galloping day and night, in heat or cold, doing everything and looking after everything himself, and obliging the peons to work, who are the idlest fellows in existence, and the biggest thieves imaginable.

Don Isidro was no longer young. At the period when we bring him again on the stage he was nearly seventy; but this long, thin man, on whose bones a yellow skin, dry as parchment, seemed to be glued, was as upright and vigorous as if he were but thirty: age had gained no power over his body, which was solely composed of muscles and nerves. Thus, by his continual vigilance, his indefatigable ardour, and his uncommon energy, he was the terror of the poor fellows whom their evil destiny had placed under his orders, and who fully believed that their mayordomo had made a compact with the demon, so closely did he watch them, and so thoroughly was he acquainted with their slightest actions.

The mayordomo had retained his *botas vaqueras*, and his spurs with enormous rowels, which compel the wearer to walk tiptoe. His zarapé and hat of vicuna skin were negligently thrown on a butaca in a corner, and at his left side hung a sheathless machete, passed through an iron ring.

So soon as he perceived the young lady he walked up to her, wished her good day, and embraced her affectionately. The captain knew Doña Angela from the day of her birth, and loved her as his daughter. She, for her part, entertained a great friendship for the old soldier, with whom she had played when a child, and whom she still liked to tease, to which the worthy mayordomo lent himself with the best grace in the world.

They sat down to table; but that expression is somewhat pretentious when applied to a Mexican breakfast.

We have already frequently remarked that the Spanish Americans are the most sober people in the world. The least thing suffices them. Thus the breakfast in question was only composed of a small cup of that excellent chocolate which the Spaniards alone know how to make, of a few maize tortillas, and a large glass of water. This meal, if it be one, is common to all classes of society in Mexico.

The party sat down to table, then, Doña Angela said the benedicite and the chocolate was served. The conversation, at the outset, was completely in the hands of the general and the captain, and turned exclusively on what had happened at the hacienda since the general's last visit; then it gradually veered round to the subject of the ganado.

"By the way," Don Sebastian said, "have you recovered any of the cattle those demons of Apaches took from us in their last attack?"

"Not a head, general, *Válgame Dios!* You might as well pursue the wind and the tempest as try to catch up those red devils."

"Then we have lost—"

"All that was within their reach; that is to say, about 2500 head."

"That is hard; and how have you repaired the loss?"

"Up to the present I have only succeeded in collecting 1500 head; and if you remember, it was on this very subject that you gave me the meeting here."

"I remember the fact perfectly; still I do not exactly see what we can do, except buy other cattle."

"Hang it! That is the only way we have of completing our herds."

"Have you any in view?"

"At this moment?"

"Yes."

"No, indeed, I have not, for the ganado is growing beyond all price. The discovery of gold in California has caused an enormous number of adventurers from every country to flock there. You know what the *gringos* are; they must have meat. These miserable heretics are such gluttons that they could not do without it; and thus they have devoured all the ganado they could find in their neighbourhood, and are now obliged to fetch it for nearly two hundred leagues. You can understand that such a thing sends prices up enormously."

"That is annoying."

"And yet, general, only an instant agone, while placing my horse in the corral. I saw the most magnificent herd of novillos that can be imagined. It is evident that the poor animals have travelled at least one hundred leagues, for they appear so fatigued."

Doña Angela gave a sly glance at her camarista, who was standing behind her.

"I have heard of them," the general said carelessly; "they are on the road to San Francisco, I believe."

"What did I say not a moment ago?" the captain exclaimed, striking his fist on the table. "*Caray!* If those confounded gringos are let alone, they will have devoured all our cattle before ten years have passed."

"Can we not try to purchase these?"

"It would be an excellent business for us, even if we paid dearly; but their owners will not be inclined to sell."

"Who knows? I fancy, on the contrary, that they are willing to get rid of them."

"*Rayo de Dios!* Buy them, then."

"Yes; but at what price?"

"It is certain that cattle are growing scarcer and scarcer: offer them for each head bought here the price it would fetch at San Francisco."

"Hum! And how is the market down there?"

"About eighteen piastres."

"Oh, oh! That is to say, for six hundred head—"

"Ten thousand eight hundred piastres: offer the even money."

"That is dear."

"What would you have? You will have to do it."

"That is true; but it is hard."

The general reflected for a moment, and then turned to his daughter.

"Angela," he said, "what is the name of the hunter who owns the herd?"

The young lady started.

"Why do you ask me, papa?" she replied, with feigned astonishment; "I really do not know what you mean. I am entirely ignorant whether there is a herd in this hostelry."

"That is true," the general said, recollecting. "Where the deuce is my head gone? It was your camarista, I believe, who spoke to one of the fellows."

"Yes, papa."

"Pardon me. Come, Violanta, my child, can you tell me this man's name?"

The girl approached with downcast eyes, and twisting the hem of her fine muslin apron between her fingers with an embarrassed air. It was evident she was trying all she knew to blush. The general awaited her answer for several minutes, but then lost patience.

"Come, you little fool," he exclaimed, "will you make up your mind to speak, yes or no? People would fancy I was asking you a question unfit for a maiden to answer."

"I do not say that, general," she replied hesitatingly.

"Enough of that mock modesty. What is the name of the owner of this ganado?"

"There are two, general."

"What are their names, then?"

"One is a Spaniard, the other a Frenchman, Excellency."

"What do I care what country the scamps belong to? I only want to know their names."

"One is called Don Cornelio."

"And the other?"

"Don Louis."

"But they have other names beside those?"

Violanta exchanged a rapid glance with her mistress.

"I do not know them," she said.

"Hum!" the general remarked sarcastically, "you only know people, it appears, by their baptismal names. That's worth knowing."

This time the girl really blushed, and retired in great confusion. Don Sebastian made a sign to a peon who was standing respectfully a few paces off.

"Gregorio," he said, "go and present the compliments of General Don Sebastian Guerrero to the Señores Don Louis and Don Cornelio, and beg them to honour him with a visit. You understand me?"

The peon bowed and went out.

"We must be polite with these people," the general observed. "Now that the discovery of the Californian placers has overthrown all classes of society, who knows with whom we may have to deal?"

And he accompanied this remark by a sarcastic laugh, in which the captain, as the worthy Mexican he was, noisily joined.

We will observe parenthetically that General Guerrero, like the majority of his countrymen, professed the most inveterate hatred for Europeans, a hatred which nothing justified, unless it was that superiority which the Creoles are obliged to recognise in the Europeans—a superiority which they submit to unwillingly, but before which they are forced to bow their heads.

Several minutes elapsed, and then the peon returned.

"Well?" the general asked him.

"Excellency," the peon answered respectfully, "the caballeros will have the honour of waiting on you. They are following me."

"Very good. Put a bottle of Catalonian refino and glasses on the table. I know from experience that these gentry have no partiality for pure water."

After this new jest the general rolled a *papelito*, lighted it, and waited. Within five minutes the sound of footsteps was heard in the corridor; the door opened, and two men appeared.

"It is not he!" Doña Angela murmured in a low voice, for her eyes were anxiously fixed on the door.

The two men were Valentine and Don Cornelio.

CHAPTER XI
A COMMERCIAL TRANSACTION

We have mentioned in a previous chapter the object for which Valentine presented himself in his friend's place. He wished to try and discover for what reason Doña Angela desired so ardently to see Louis again. As for Don Cornelio, he was intimately persuaded that his personal merits had done it all, and that the young lady's sole wish was to have another interview with himself.

On the other hand, the hunter, warned by Curumilla, was not sorry to see the man with whom he had been indirectly connected at another period of his life—a connection which might at any moment become more intimate, owing to the general's new position and Don Louis' projects.

The two strangers presented themselves boldly; their manner was respectful, without arrogance or excessive humility; such, in a word, as might be expected from men long tried by the innumerable hazards of an adventurous life.

The general probably expected to see men of low habits and vulgar features. At the sight of the two men, whose masculine and honest faces struck him, he started imperceptibly, rose, saluted them courteously, and invited them to sit down on chairs he ordered to be placed for them.

Doña Angela knew not what to think after Don Cornelio's positive statement. The absence of Don Louis, and the substitution for him of a man she did not know, appeared inexplicable. Still, without exactly understanding her feelings, she guessed, under this substitution, a mystery which she sought in vain to fathom. Violanta was as confused and astonished as her mistress: the captain alone remained indifferent to what passed. The old soldier, profiting cleverly by the fact of the bottle of refino having been placed on the table, had poured out a large glass of aguardiente, which he swallowed in small doses, while patiently waiting till the general thought proper to open the ball.

When the hunters had at length taken their seats, after repeated pressing, the general took the word.

"You will pardon me, gentlemen, for having disturbed you by compelling you to come here, when it should have been my place to go to your cuarto, as it is I who wish to speak with you."

"General," Valentine answered with a respectful bow, "my friend and myself would have been in despair had we caused you the least annoyance. Pray believe that we shall always be happy to obey your orders, whatever they may be."

After this mutual interchange of compliments the speakers bowed again. No people in the world carry to such an extent as the Mexican the feline gentleness of manner, if we may be permitted to employ the expression.

"Which of you two gentlemen," the general continued gracefully, "is Señor Don Cornelio?"

"It is I, caballero," the Spaniard answered with a bow.

"In that case," Don Sebastian went on, turning to the hunter with an amiable smile, "this caballero is Don Louis?"

"Pardon me, general," the Frenchman answered distinctly, "my name is Valentine."

The general started.

"What?" he said in surprise. "And where, then, is Señor Don Louis?"

"It is impossible for him to obey your orders."

"Why so?"

"Because," Valentine continued, casting a side glance at the young lady, who, though she appeared to be very busily talking with her camarista, did not lose a word that was said, "because, general, Don Louis, unaware that he should have the honour of being received by your Excellency this morning, started at sunrise for San Francisco."

Doña Angela turned pale as death, and was on the point of fainting at this news; still she overcame the emotion she experienced, and became apparently calm. She wished to learn all. This emotion, though so transitory, had not escaped Valentine's observation. The general nearly turned his back on his daughter: hence it was impossible for him to see anything that passed.

"That is annoying," he answered.

"I am in despair, general."

"His absence will doubtlessly be of short duration?"

"He will not return."

Valentine pronounced these words dryly. The emotion Doña Angela experienced was so lively that she could not check a slight cry of pain.

"What is the matter, niña?" her father asked her, turning sharply. "What is the meaning of that cry?"

"I cut myself," she answered with the most innocent air possible.

"Oh, oh!" her father said in alarm; "it is not dangerous?"

"No; a mere scratch. I was a goose to be frightened. Forgive me, papa."

The general asked no further questions, but continued his conversation with the Frenchman.

"I am vexed at this *contretemps*," he said, "for I wished to consult with your friend on very important business."

"No matter; I am here. My friend, on starting, gave me full power to act in his name. You can speak, general; that is to say, if you do not consider me unworthy of your confidence."

"Such a supposition would be an insult, sir."

Valentine bowed.

"Well, caballero," the general continued, "the affair I wished to discuss with your friend is certainly important; but if your full powers extend to commercial transactions, I do not see why I should not treat with you as well as with him."

"Speak openly, then, general, for I am Don Louis' partner."

"This is the affair in two words—"

"Pardon me," Doña Angela suddenly said, with a little air of resolution, which even imposed on the general himself; "before you begin talking about trade, I should like to ask this gentleman a few questions."

The general turned in surprise, and bent an inquiring glance on his daughter.

"What can you have to ask this caballero?" he said.

"You will soon know, my dear papa," she replied with a slight tone of sarcasm, "if you will permit me to ask him two or three questions."

"Speak, then, you little madcap," the general exclaimed with a shrug of his shoulders; "speak, and make a finish as soon as you can."

"Thank you, papa. Your permission is, perhaps, not very graciously granted, but I shall not bear you malice on that account."

"As you permit it, general, I am at the lady's orders."

"In the first place, sir, promise me one thing."

"What is it, señorita?"

"That you will answer frankly and honestly all the questions I may ask you."

"What is the meaning of this folly, Angela?" the general said impatiently. "Is this the moment or the place? Is it befitting for—?"

"Papa," the young lady boldly interrupted him, "you gave me permission to speak."

"Granted; but not in the way you seemed inclined to do so."

"Have a little patience, papa."

"Bah!" the captain said, interposing, "let her speak as she likes. Go on, my child—go on."

"I am waiting this gentleman's answer," she said.

"I make you the promise you ask, señorita," Valentine answered.

"I hold your word. What is your friend's name, sir?"

"Which one, señorita?".

"The one whose place you have taken."

"His name is Count Louis de Prébois Crancé."

"He is a Frenchman?"

"Born at Paris."

"You have known him a long time?"

"Since his birth, señorita. My mother was his nurse."

"Ah!" she said with pleasure; "then you are really his friend?"

"I am his foster brother."

"He has no secrets from you?"

"None, I fancy."

"Good!"

"Come, come," the general exclaimed, "this is becoming intolerable. What is the meaning of this interrogatory to which you subject the caballero, and to which he has the goodness to yield so complacently? Confound it, niña! I beg the señor's pardon in your name; for your conduct toward him is most improper."

"What is there improper in it, papa? My intentions are good, and I am certain that you will agree with me when you learn why I asked the caballero these simple questions, which, however, appear to you so extraordinary."

"Well, go on. What is the reason?"

"This. Three years back, during your journey from Guadalajara to Tepic, were you not attacked by salteadores at the spot called the Mal Paso?"

"Yes; but what has that in common, I ask—?"

"Wait," she said gaily. "Two men came to your assistance?"

"Yes, and I am not ashamed to confess that, without them, I should probably have not only been robbed, but murdered by the bandits. Unfortunately these men obstinately refused to tell me their names. All my researches up to the present have been fruitless. I have been unable to find them again, and show them my gratitude, which I assure you vexes me extremely."

"Yes, papa, I know that you have often in my presence regretted your inability to find the courageous man to whom you owe your life, as well as I do, who was but a child at the time."

The young lady uttered these words with an emotion that affected all her hearers.

"Unfortunately," the general said a moment later, "three years have elapsed since that adventure. Who knows what has become of that man?"

"I do, papa."

"You, Angela!" he exclaimed in surprise. "It is impossible."

"My father, the questions I addressed to the gentleman, and which he answered so kindly, had only one object; to acquire a certainty by corroborating through the answers I received certain information I had obtained elsewhere."

"So that—?"

"The man who saved your life is the Count Don Louis, who started this very morning for San Francisco."

"Oh!" the general said in great agitation, "it is impossible. You are mistaken, my child."

"Pardon me, general, but my friend has frequently told me the story in its amplest details," Valentine observed. "Why seek to hide longer a thing you now know?"

"And to remove all doubts, if any remain, which I hardly suppose, papa, in the presence of this caballero's loyal assurance, look at this man," she added, pointing to the Spaniard. "Do you not recognise Don Cornelio, our old travelling companion, who constantly sang to his jarana the romance of El Rey Rodrigo?"

The general examined the young man attentively.

"It is true," he said presently; "I now recognise this caballero, whom I left wounded, at his own request, in the hands of my generous liberator."

"Whom I have not left since," Don Cornelio affirmed.

"Ah!" the general said. "But why this obstinacy on Don Louis' part to keep his secret? Did he fancy that gratitude was too heavy a burden for me to bear?"

"Do not think such a thing of my friend," Valentine exclaimed quickly. "Don Louis believed, and still believes, that the service he rendered you was too trifling to have such great importance attached to it."

"*Caspita!* When he saved my honour! But now that I know him he shall not escape me longer. I will find him sooner or later, and prove to him that we Mexicans have a memory as long for good as for ill. I am his debtor, and, by heavens! I will pay him my debt."

"That is good, papa," the young lady exclaimed, as she threw herself into his arms.

"Enough, little madcap, enough. Confusion! You are stifling me. But tell me, little rogue, I believe that in all this you have been playing me a nice little trick."

"Oh, father!" she answered with a blush.

"Would you, miss, have the goodness to explain to me how you obtained all this information? I confess that it puzzles me considerably, and I should like to know."

Doña Angela, began laughing to conceal her embarrassment; but suddenly making up her mind with that decision which marked her character,—

"I will tell you, if you promise not to scold me too severely," she said.

"Go on; we will see afterwards."

"I told you a story this morning, papa," she said, letting her eyes fall.

"I suspect it: go on."

"If you frown in that way, and put on your naughty air, I warn you that I shall not say a word."

"And you will be right, niña," the captain supported her.

The general smiled.

"Come," he said, "you are taking her part, are you?"

"*Caspita!* I should think so."

"Come, come, be at your ease; I will not be angry, the more so because I suspect that the pretty baggage behind you, with her cunning looks, has something to do with the plot," he said, looking at Violanta, who could not keep her countenance.

"You have guessed it, papa. I slept splendidly last night: nothing disturbed my slumbers."

"Just listen to that, the little deceiver!"

"Last evening, however, I heard the sound of a jarana accompanying the Romance del Rey Rodrigo. I remembered our old travelling companion who never sang anything else. I know not how it was, but I persuaded myself that he was the singer, and so I sent Violanta to invite him to my room. Then—"

"Then he told you all?"

"Yes, papa. As I knew the desire you felt to know your liberator, I wished to surprise you by letting you find him at the moment you least expected. Unfortunately chance has thwarted all my plans, and destroyed my combinations."

"That was right, niña, for it will teach you not to have any secrets from your father. But console yourself, my child; we will find him again, and then he must allow us to express our gratitude to him, which time, far from lessening, has only heightened."

The young lady, without saying anything further, returned pensively to her seat. The general turned to Valentine.

"It is now our turn, caballero. You are the owner of the herd of cattle?"

"Yes, general; but I am not the only one."

"Who are your partners?"

"Don Louis and the caballero here present."

"Very good. Do you wish to dispose of your cattle advantageously?"

"It is my intention."

"How many head have you?"

"Seven hundred and seventy."

"And you are taking them—?"

"To San Francisco."

"*Caramba!* That is a tough job."

"We purpose hiring peons to drive the animals."

"But if you could find a purchaser here?"

"I should prefer it."

"Well, I want cattle: most of mine have been stolen by the Apaches—those infernal plunderers! If you consent we will strike a bargain. Your herd suits me. My mayordomo has seen it, and I will buy it in the lump."

"I wish nothing better."

"We say seven hundred and seventy head, I think?"

"Yes."

"At twenty-five piastres apiece: that makes 19,250 piastres, if I am not mistaken. Does that suit you?"

"No, general," Valentine replied firmly.

Don Sebastian looked at him in amazement.

"Why so?" he said.

"Because I should rob you."

"Hum! That is my business."

"That is possible, general; but it is not mine."

"What do you mean?"

"I mean that cattle are sold, one with the other, at eighteen piastres in San Francisco, and I cannot sell them for twenty-five here."

"Nonsense! I fancy I know the value of ganado as well as any man; and I offer you the price your herd is worth."

"No, general, it is not worth it, and you know it as well as I do," the hunter objected resolutely. "I thank you for your generosity, but I cannot accept it: my friend would be angry with me for making such a bargain."

"Then you refuse?"

"I do."

"It is perfectly novel for a merchant to refuse to gain a profit on his wares."

"Pardon me, general, I do not refuse an honest profit; but I will not rob you, that is all."

"On my word, you are the first man I ever knew to look at trade in that light."

"Probably, general, because you have never had dealings with a Frenchman."

"I must yield. What do you ask for the beasts?"

"Nineteen piastres per head, which, I assure you, will give me a very handsome profit."

"Be it so. That makes—?"

"Fourteen thousand six hundred and thirty piastres."

"Very good. If that will suit you, I will give you an order for that sum on Messrs. Torribi, Dellaporta, and Co., at Guaymas."

"That will do admirably."

"You hear, captain, the herd is ours?"

"Good! This night it will start for the hacienda."

"When do you propose leaving, señores?"

"As soon as our business is settled here, general. We are anxious to rejoin our friend."

"In an hour the bill of exchange will be ready."

Valentine bowed.

"Still," the general continued, "you will be good enough to tell Don Louis that I regard myself as his debtor, and if ever he come to Sonora I will prove it."

"Possibly he may soon arrive," the hunter replied, with a side glance at Doña Angela, who blushed.

"I hope so; and now, gentlemen, I am at your service. If I can be of any use to you, remember that you can always apply to me."

"Receive my thanks, general."

After exchanging a few more words they parted. In passing Doña Angela, Valentine bowed respectfully.

"Don Louis still has your reliquary," he muttered in so low a voice that she guessed the words rather than heard them.

"Thank you," she answered; "you are kind."

"She loves Louis," Valentine said to himself as he returned to the cuarto, accompanied by Don Cornelio.

"The man is a fool to refuse a profit of 5000 piastres," the general said to Don Isidro so soon as he found himself alone with him.

"Perhaps so," the latter replied thoughtfully; "but I fancy he is an enemy."

The general shrugged his shoulders contemptuously, not deigning to attach the slightest importance to this insinuation.

The same evening Valentine and his two companions left San José, and proceeded toward Guaymas, without seeing Doña Angela or the general again.

CHAPTER XII
CONVERSATION

During the few thousand years since the world on which we vegetate issued from the hands of the Creator, many revolutions have taken place, many extraordinary facts have been accomplished. How many nations have succeeded each other, rising and falling in turn, disappearing without even leaving a trace, after traversing history like dazzling meteors, and then going out eternally in the night of ages!

But of all the strange facts of which the memory has been preserved, none in our opinion can be compared with what we have seen accomplished under our own eyes, with extraordinary audacity and success, during about three-quarters of a century.

Adventurers bursting from every quarter of the globe—some impelled by the fanaticism of religious faith, others by a spirit of adventure, others again, and the large majority, urged on by wretchedness—after landing as pilgrims on the American shores, asking shelter from the poor and innocent inhabitants of those hospitable countries, and purchasing for a song fertile estates, gradually congregated, expelled the first possessors of the soil, founded cities and ports, built arsenals, and one day shaking off the yoke of the mother country under whose ægis they had timidly sought shelter, constituted themselves an independent state, and founded that colossus, with feet of clay, body of gold, and head of mud, which is called the United States of America.

Humble at the outset, this poor Republic, singing in a loud voice the words, "Liberty and Fraternity!"—words whose noble and grand significance it never comprehended—displaying a rigid tolerance, an exaggerated virtue and puritanism, stepped insidiously into the councils of the European powers, climbed cunningly up to the thrones of sovereigns, and, beneath the mask of disinterestedness, gained acceptance from all. Suddenly, when the favourable moment arrived, the United States rose and assumed a haughty posture. They who had laid down in their Act of Independence that they would never consent to any aggrandisement, said in a domineering voice to Europe, surprised and almost terrified by such audacity, "This quarter of the globe is ours. We are a powerful nation. You must henceforth settle with us."

Unfortunately for themselves, in uttering these proud words, the Northern Americans did not believe them. On the one hand they were perfectly aware of their weakness; and, on the other, they knew very well that a multitude of individuals collected from all sides, without any tie of family or language among them, cannot form a people—that, is to say, a nation—in one century, not even in two.

Still, to be just and impartial to the United States, we must allow that their inhabitants possess to a supreme degree that feverish ardour which, if well directed, produces great results.

It is evident that these bold adventurers are accomplishing, though they little suspect it, a providential mission. What it is no one can say, themselves least of all. These men who stifle on the frontiers, which their population, though daily increasing, cannot fill; who aspire continually to leap over the barriers which other nations oppose to them; who only dream of the unknown, and are perpetually gazing at the distant horizon—these men, in whose ear a secret voice constantly murmurs, as to the Jew of the legend, "Onward, onward!"—these men are destined, ere long, to play a grand, glorious, and noble part in modern civilisation, if the profound egotism that undermines, and the thirst for gold which devours them, does not kill in them those regenerating virtues with which they are unconsciously endowed; and if, forgetting the spirit of conquest and desire for further aggrandisement, they draw more closely together the ties between the several states, and practise among themselves that liberty and fraternity of which they talk so jactantly abroad, but know so little at home.

No people equals the Americans in the art of founding towns. In a few days, on the spot where a virgin forest full of mystery and shadow stood, they lay out streets, build houses, light gas; and in the midst of these streets and squares, created as if by enchantment, the forest trees are not yet dead, and a few forgotten oaks flourish with a melancholy air.

It is true that many of these towns, improvised for the exigencies of the moment, are frequently deserted as rapidly as they were built; for the North American is the true nomadic race. Nothing attaches it to the soil: convenience alone can keep it at any given spot. It has none of those heart affections, none of those memories of childhood or youth, which induce us often to endure suffering in a place rather than quit it for others where we should be comparatively much better off. In a word, the American has no *home*, that word so endearing to Europeans. To him the most agreeable and comfortable abode is that where he can pile dollar on dollar with the greatest facility.

San Francisco, that city which now counts more than 60,000 inhabitants, and in which all the refinements of luxury can be found, is an evident proof of the marvellous facility with which the Americans improvise towns. We can remember bartering, scarce fifteen years back, with Flat-head Indians, beneath the shade of secular trees, on sites where splendid edifices now rise. We have fished alone in this immense bay, the finest in the world, which is at present almost too small to hold the innumerable vessels that follow each other in rapid succession.

At the period of our story San Francisco was not yet a city in the true acceptation of the word. It was a conglomeration of huts and clumsy cabins built of wood, and which afforded some sort of shelter to the adventurers of every nation whom the gold fever cast on its shores, and who only stopped there long enough to prepare for proceeding to the mines, or throw into the bottomless abysses of the gambling houses the nuggets they had collected with so much difficulty and suffering.

The police were almost non-existing: the stronger man made the law. The knife and revolver were the *última ratio*, and lorded it over this heterogeneous population, composed of the worst specimens the five parts of the globe could throw up.

A population incessantly renewed, never the same, lived in this Hades, a prey to that constant and fatal intoxication which the sight of that terrible metal called gold produces in even the strongest-minded men.

Still, at the period of which we are writing, the first fury of the race to the placers had somewhat cooled down. Owing to the impulse given by a few resolute men, gifted with lofty intellects and generous hearts, the normal life was beginning to be gradually organised; the bandits no longer daringly held the top of the causeway, honest men could at length breathe and raise their heads, all foreboded better days, and the dawn of an era of order, peace, and tranquillity had arrived.

About two months after the events we narrated in our preceding chapter we will lead the reader to a charming house built a little out of the throng, as if the inhabitants had sought to isolate themselves as much as possible; and after introducing him into a room modestly furnished with a few common chairs and a table, on which lay a large map of Mexico, we will listen to the conversation of the two men who were leaning over this map.

One of them is already well known to us, for he is the Count Louis; the other was a man of middle age, with a fine and intelligent face, whose eye sparkled with boldness and frankness; his manners were also very elegant. He appeared to be a Frenchman; at least he was talking in that language. At the moment we joined them the two gentlemen were inserting black-headed pins into certain districts of the map spread out before them.

"I am perfectly of your opinion, my dear count," the stranger said as he rose: "that road is the most direct, and at the same time the safest."

"Is it not?" Louis answered.

"Without any doubt. But tell me—you are quite resolved to disembark at Guaymas?"

"That is the most favourable point."

"I ask you that question, my dear countryman, because I have written to our representative in that town."

"Well?" the count said quickly, rising in his turn.

"All goes well; at least he tells me so in his letter."

"He has answered you?"

"Courier for courier. The Mexican authorities will see your arrival with the greatest pleasure; a barrack will be prepared for your men, and the principal posts of the town intrusted to them. You are expected with the most lively impatience."

"All the better, for I confess to you that I feared much annoyance in that quarter: the Mexicans have such a singular character, that one never knows how to deal with them."

"What you say is perfectly true, my friend; but remember that your position is an exceptional one, and can in no possible manner cause umbrage to the authorities of the town. You are the owner of a placer of incalculable richness, situated in a country where you will have continually to apprehend attacks from the Indians; you will, therefore, only pass through Guaymas."

"Literally so; for I declare to you that I shall set out with the least possible delay for the mine."

"Another thing, too: most of the men whose hatred or envy you might have occasion to fear are shareholders in the company you represent. If they show you any ill will, or try to impede your operations, they will carry on the war at their own expense, and naturally will be the first punished."

"That is true."

"And then you have no political object: your conduct is clearly laid down. Your desire is to find gold."

"Yes, and to insure a happy and independent position for the brave men who accompany me."

"What more noble task could you undertake?"

"So you are satisfied, sir?"

"I could not be more so, my dear count. Everything smiles on you: the company is definitively formed at Mexico."

"I knew that before. During my stay in that city I drew up the plans and prepared everything; besides, I believe I can reckon on the friends we have there."

"I believe so too. Did not the President of the Republic himself seem to adopt your views?"

"Enthusiastically."

"Very good. Now, in Sonora, the governor, with whom you will have alone to deal, is one of our largest shareholders, so you have nothing to fear in that quarter."

"Tell me, sir, do you know our representative at Guaymas?"

At this question a cloud passed over the stranger's forehead.

"Not personally," he answered, after a certain degree of hesitation.

"Then you can give me no information about him? You understand that it is important for me to know the character of the man with whom I shall doubtlessly enter into permanent relations, and from whom I shall be compelled to ask protection in certain difficult circumstances, such as may occur at any moment."

"That is true, my dear count. As you observe, you know not in what position accident may place you; it is, therefore, necessary that I should instruct you, so listen to me."

"I am giving you the most earnest attention."

"Guaymas, as you are very well aware, is of very slight importance to our nation in a commercial point of view. During the whole year not a dozen ships bearing our flag put in there. The French Government, therefore, considered it useless to send a French agent to that town, and acted like most of the powers—it selected one of the most respectable merchants in Guaymas, and made him its representative."

"Ah, ah!" the count said thoughtfully; "then our consular agent in that port is not a Frenchman?"

"No; he is a Mexican. It is unlucky for you; for I will not hide from you that our countrymen have several times complained of not obtaining from him that protection which it is his duty to give them. It seems, too, that this man is wonderfully greedy for gain."

"As far as that is concerned I do not alarm myself at all."

"The rest need not trouble you either. The Mexicans generally are not bad. They are children—that is all. You will easily master this man by talking to him firmly, and not yielding an inch of what you consider your right."

"Trust to me for doing that."

"There is nothing else to be done."

"Thanks for this precious information, which I shall profit by, be assured, at the proper time and place. What is his name?"

"Don Antonio Mendez Pavo; but, before your departure, I will give you a letter for him, which I am sure will prevent your having any vexatious disputes with the fellow."

"I accept with great pleasure."

"And now another point."

"Go on."

"Are your enlistments completed?"

"Nearly so; I only need ten more men at the most."

"You are organising your expedition in a military manner?"

"I wished to avoid it, but that is impossible, owing to the Indian tribes through which we must pass, and with whom we shall have doubtlessly a tussle."

"You may expect it."

"So you see, my dear sir, I take my precautions in consequence."

"You act wisely. What will be the strength of your company?"

"Two hundred and fifty to three hundred men at the outside."

"You are right: a larger force would arouse the susceptibility of the Mexicans, and perhaps cause them alarm as to the purity and loyalty of your intentions."

"That is what I wish to avoid at any price."

"Are your men French?"

"All. I do not wish to have any men with me on whose devotion I cannot calculate. I should be afraid, by mixing strangers among my fellows, that I might relax those family ties so necessary for the success of an expedition like mine, and which can be easily established among men all belonging to the same nation."

"That is extremely logical."

"And then," the count went on, "I only enlist old soldiers or sailors, all men accustomed to military discipline, and who are familiar with the use of arms."

"Then your organisation is terminated?"

"Nearly so, as I told you."

"All the better. In spite of the pleasure I feel in your delightful society, I should like to see you at work already."

"Thank you, but that will not be long first: the vessel is chartered, and if nothing happen to derange my plans, I shall say good-by to you within a week. You know that, in an affair like this, speed is the great point."

"Success depends, above all, on celerity and decision."

"I shall be deficient in neither, be assured."

"Above all, do not forget to take with you two or three men you can trust, and who are thoroughly acquainted with the country you are about explore."

"I have with me two wood rangers, from whom the desert has no secrets."

"You can trust in them?"

"As in myself."

"Bravo! I feel a presentiment that we shall succeed."

"Heaven grant it! For my part, I will do all to deserve it."

The stranger took his hat.

"Ah, ah! I have been here a long time, and forget that people may be waiting for me at the office. I must leave you, my dear count."

"Already?"

"Needs must. Shall I see you this evening?"

"I cannot promise. You know that I am not my own master either, especially at this moment."

"That is true; still try to come."

"I will."

"That's right. Good-by till I see you again."

The two men shook hands affectionately, and the stranger departed.

So soon as he was alone the count bent again over the map, which he studied carefully: it was not till night had completely set in that he gave up his task.

"How is it," he said to himself thoughtfully, "that Valentine has not yet arrived? He should have been here."

As he finished this monologue he heard a rap at the door.

CHAPTER XIII
PREPARATIONS

The period at which our story happens was a happy time for desperate enterprises and filibustering expeditions.

In fact, the political commotions that had overthrown Europe some time previously had brought to the surface, and set in motion, a great number of those unprincipled men, whose sole object is to secure from the revolutions that desolate their country very lucrative, if not very honourable, positions, and for whom anarchy is the sole safety valve.

But, after the first convulsions inseparable from a revolution, when the popular effervescence began gradually to cool down, and the overflowing waters returned to their bed—in a word, when society, wearied of paltry struggles sustained for no avowable motives, and merely kept up to satisfy the disgraceful ambition of a few men of no value, understood that the re-establishment of order was the sole path of salvation, all those individuals who had for a season played a part more or less important found themselves cast on the pavement of the towns without resources; for, with that improvidence inherent in their natures, squandering day by day the favours which blind fortune had lavished on them, they had kept nothing for bad times, convinced as they were that the state of things they had produced would last for ever.

For a few months they struggled, not courageously, but obstinately, against adversity, seeking by every means to recapture the prey which they had so foolishly allowed to slip from their grasp. But they were soon compelled to allow that times had changed, that their hour was past, and that the ground which had hitherto maintained them was sinking hourly beneath their feet, and threatened to swallow them up.

Their position was becoming critical. It was impossible for them to resume their humble and peaceful avocations, and return to that nothingness from which a mad caprice of chance had drawn them. The idea did not even occur to them. They had tasted luxury and honour; they could not and would not work again: pride and sloth imperiously forbade it.

Cincinnatus has never found an imitator in history, and that is the reason why his memory has been so preciously kept up by all to the present day.

The men of whom we are speaking were far from being like Cincinnatus, though they in so far resembled the Roman Dictator that they claimed to govern nations.

What was to be done?

Fortunately Providence, whose ways are incomprehensible, watched over them.

The discovery of the rich placers of California, the news of which had been almost stifled under the blow of the terrible European political commotions, suddenly returned to the surface, and in a short time assumed a considerable extension. The most extravagant stories circulated about the incalculable riches that lay almost on the ground in the soil of the new Eldorado. Then all the vagabond imaginations began to ferment. All eyes were fixed on America, and the birds of prey that wanted a booty in Europe rushed with a loud cry of joy toward that unknown land, where they fancied they should find in a few days all the joys with which they had been gorged, and which they hoped this time to satisfy.

Unfortunately, in California, as elsewhere, the first condition for acquiring wealth is incessant, permanent, and regular labour.

On landing in America numerous poignant deceptions awaited the adventurers. The mines, indeed, existed—they were rich; but the gold they contained could only be extracted with great difficulty, great fatigue, and, above all, great expense—three impossibilities which our gold-seekers could not overcome.

Many perished either of want, or of a violent death through pot-house quarrels, or through the change of climate, to which they had not the time to grow accustomed. Those who survived, wan and ragged, displayed their starving faces in all the bad places of San Francisco, ready to do anything for the smallest sum of money that would lull their wolfish appetite.

In the meanwhile the first adventurers had been succeeded by others, and still they flocked in. The few, privileged by fortune, who returned to Europe rich in a few months, had naturally aroused the cupidity of the numberless pariahs of civilisation; and San Francisco, that country blessed by Heaven, whose climate is so fine and soil so fertile, threatened to become a vast and mournful cemetery.

At this time it happened that a few enterprising men, seeing their illusions fading away, and perceiving that the gold they coveted so ardently constantly fled before them while they were unable to catch it, turned their glances in another direction, and, despairing of growing rich in the mines, resolved to seize, sword and revolver in hand, those riches which it was impossible for them to acquire otherwise; that is to say, they resuscitated for their own behoof the filibustering expeditions of the sixteenth and seventeenth centuries.

Thus was a new path opened to emerge from the frightful wretchedness in which they languished, and the adventurers eagerly entered upon it. Filibustering enterprises sprang up on all sides with as much regularity as if they had been perfectly respectable financial operations; and the plethora of San Francisco began, to the great relief of the peaceful population, to be diverted on the surrounding countries.

The count had, therefore, arrived at a propitious moment to put in execution the plan he meditated. He belonged to one of the oldest and noblest families in France. He enjoyed, and that justly, a spotless reputation in California; moreover, he was very strict in the selection of the men he enlisted; finally, he offered an honourable scope for their ambition, which is very flattering to men who have nothing to lose. Nothing more was needed to excite the emulation of all the ragamuffins, and urge them to place themselves under his orders.

Among the adventurers were many really estimable persons, who in no way merited the sad fate they were undergoing, and who, seduced by the unknown, had been attracted to California by the fallacious promises of European speculators, and had been the victims of the scoundrels who induced them to emigrate. These men endured their sufferings nobly, awaiting with the patience of well-tempered hearts the opportunity to take their revenge and regain that position which a moment of mad intoxication and credulous simplicity had made them forfeit.

The Count, with that infallible glance he possessed, and the knowledge of mankind which lengthened misfortune had enabled him to acquire, had picked out the best men from the crowd that daily invaded his house so soon as his intention became known, and assured himself of the co-operation of devoted comrades of tried courage, who, regarding the count's enterprise as the sole means of emerging from their frightful position, attached themselves to him with a firm resolve to do or die.

Hence we will assert here that of all the expeditions formed at that period in California, the only really honourable one which contained the elements of success was that led by Count Louis de Prébois Crancé.

We do not go beyond the mark when we say that the count was adored by his comrades. These rude adventurers, so harshly tried by destiny, had guessed, with the ineffable perspicacity of men who have suffered greatly, the inexhaustible kindness, perfect loyalty, and vast intelligence locked up in the heart of their chief, and how much tender solicitude and friendship for them were concealed beneath his mournful countenance and the imposing severity of his liquid blue eye. Thus it was not merely respect he inspired them with, but veneration and devotion, extending almost to fanaticism.

An expedition like that the count was preparing was no easy thing to organise, especially with the scanty resources he had at his disposal; for he only obtained vague promises from his partners, and was forced to seek in himself the means for satisfying all.

The rich placer which Belhumeur and Eagle-head pointed out to him had been worked in the time of the Spanish monarchy; but since the declaration of independence, carelessness and disorder having taken the place of the energy displayed by the Castilians, the Indians soon expelled the miners: the placer had, therefore, been temporarily abandoned. Then gradually the Apaches and Comanches, growing bolder as they perceived the weakness of the white men, advanced and recaptured vast territories, on which they established themselves permanently, knowing that the Mexicans would never attempt to drive them out. In this way the placer to which we allude, formerly situated in the possessions of New Spain, was now surrounded by Indian territory, and to reach it it was necessary to wage a mortal contest with the two most dangerous nations of the desert, the Apaches and Comanches, who would under no pretext suffer the invasion of their frontiers by the whites, but would defend their ground inch by inch against them.

The Mexican government had only authorised the formation of the mining company founded by the count on the express condition that the miners, organised as a military force, should pursue the Indians, attack them whenever they came up with them, and definitively expel them from the territory they had usurped since the proclamation of independence. The count had accepted a rough and almost impossible mission: any other in his place would have backed out and refused to accept such terms. But Count Louis was a man in a thousand, gifted with a rare energy, which obstacles only rendered greater. And then, personally, what did he care for the issue of the affair? It was not wealth, but death, he sought; still he did not wish to fall till he had given his comrades that wealth he had promised them, and rescued them from the stings of adverse fortune.

He accepted the conditions, then, but not blindly, ambitiously, or egotistically. He accepted them as a man of heart, who sacrifices himself for an idea, and for the general happiness; and who, while recognising the almost insurmountable difficulties that oppose the success of his noble projects, hopes to succeed in overcoming them by his courage, perseverance, and abnegation.

The energy, patience, and intelligence which the count had displayed during the two months since his parting with Valentine, no one but himself could have told. One of the clauses in his contract with the suspicious and shifting Mexican government obliged him not to take more than three hundred men with him. The President of the Republic, General Arista, doubtlessly feared the invasion and conquest of Mexico by the French, had they been four hundred in number.

These wretched conditions are so ridiculous, that they would be incredible were they not rigorously true. We could, if we pleased, write down here the words uttered in the Senate of Mexico, in which this fear of invasion is distinctly expressed.

The count, in order to dissipate all doubts on this head, and, above all, not to arouse suspicions, decided on only taking two hundred and sixty men instead of three hundred.

But this company, destined to traverse a country swarming with obstinate enemies, compelled during the journey to fight perhaps several times a day, constrained in this desolate country to supply its own wants (for it had no help to expect anywhere), must receive a powerful organisation.

This was what the count thought of first.

Those persons who have never worn that heavy harness called a military tunic cannot form even a distant idea of the thousand difficulties of detail which arise at every step in the complete organisation of a company, so that the service may be done properly, and the soldier not suffer needlessly.

The count was obliged to improvise. He had never served, and was not at all aware of the nature of such a task as his; but he was a gentleman and a Frenchman, two reasons for inventing what a man is ignorant of when war is the subject. The military genius is so innate in the French nation, that we may say every man is a soldier. At any rate, Louis proved it in an undeniable manner.

Obliged to foresee everything, and provide for all eventualities, he undertook everything; and, on seeing the nature of his arrangements, his men, all old soldiers and connoisseurs in such matters, were convinced that their chief had been long engaged in military affairs.

He made a regular army of his company; that is to say, he had infantry, cavalry, and artillery. In order that the discipline might be strictly maintained the infantry were divided into sections, commanded by tried men selected by himself. A few sailors, accustomed to handle guns, were appointed to serve a small mountain howitzer, which the count carried with him, more for the purpose of terrifying the Indians than in the hope that it would ever prove of use to him.

Lastly, some forty picked men, most of them old Chasseurs d'Afrique, formed the cavalry, and were placed under the orders of an officer for whom the count felt a peculiar esteem, whom he had known a long time, and in whose ability he placed entire confidence.

But what we have described was nothing when compared with what still remained to be done—purchasing arms, provisions, the necessary tools for working the mine, ammunition, and, above all, means of transport.

The count was not discouraged. He improvised a commissariat, and alone—alone we repeat; for he had refused the offer of large American bankers, who at length, recognising his value, had proposed to take an interest in his enterprise—with his scanty resources, he had done everything, organised everything, and now only awaited his foster brother's arrival, in order to pay the balance of his accounts, ship his company, and set sail.

Now that we have fully explained these matters to our reader, which are so important to a proper understanding of what follows, we will resume our narrative at the point where we were compelled to break it off.

CHAPTER XIV
VALENTINE'S RETURN

As we have already said, the count sprang up on hearing a rap at the door of his house.

"Who can come at this hour," he muttered. "I expect nobody."

And he went to the door and opened it. Three men entered, wrapped closely in their cloaks. The darkness in the room prevented Don Louis recognising their features, which were, besides, half hidden by the brims of their sombreros.

"Good evening, gentlemen," he said to them. "Who are you, and what would you with me?"

"Oh, oh!" one of the newcomers said with a laugh. "By Jupiter! That is a very dry reception."

Don Louis started at the sound of this voice, which he recognised at once.

"Valentine!" he exclaimed with emotion.

"By Jove!" the other said gaily, as he threw off his cloak, "I suppose you thought I was dead?"

"And do you not recognise me, Señor Don Louis?" the second person said, also throwing off his cloak.

"Don Cornelio, my friend, you are welcome."

"That's right," Valentine went on; "we are beginning to understand one another at last—that is fortunate. Were you going out?"

"Yes, but for no urgent matter."

"I do not disturb you, then?"

"On the contrary, sit down and let us talk."

"All right."

"Have you supped?"

"Not yet; and you?"

"Nor I either. That is capital—we will sup here together. In that way we can say what we like, and not fear listeners, unless you prefer going to the hotel."

"St! Deuce take me if I care about it. Let us sup here, my boy; it will be better in every way."

"That is what I thought. Let me give some orders, and I shall be at your service."

Louis went out.

"Ouf!" Valentine said, stretching himself in an easy chair, "I am beginning to get tired. How do you feel, Don Cornelio?"

"I!" the latter replied with a sigh. "I can move neither arm nor leg; I walk about like a somnambulist."

"Nonsense! Such a stout fellow as you."

"Stout as you please—do you know we have not been to bed or to sleep for seven nights?"

"Do you think so?" the Frenchman said carelessly.

"*Capa de Dios!* Do I think so? I am sure of it. The proof of it is, that in those seven days we rode three hundred leagues, and killed ten horses."

"On my word, that is true."

"So you see——"

"Well, what do you conclude from that?"

"Why, that you were in a hurry."

"And yet, in spite of all our diligence, my friend thinks that we have been too slow."

"Then I must say he is not reasonable. But are we going to leave the chief kicking his heels at the door?"

"Good gracious! I never thought of him," Valentine said as he rose.

And he walked toward the door.

At the same moment Curumilla appeared at one end of the room, while Don Louis came in at the other, at the head of several servants. Louis placed the candlesticks he held in his hand on the table, and turning to his friend,—

"Where are you going?" he asked him.

"To look for Curumilla, whom I left in charge of the horses; but there he is!"

"Do not trouble yourself about the horses; I have given orders as to them."

"To supper, then, for I am dying of hunger; my comrades and myself have eaten nothing for sixteen hours."

The four men sat down to the table, which had been copiously covered with dishes of every description. The meal began: the guests ate for a long time without exchanging a word. The newcomers had an imperious necessity to recruit their strength. At length, when the edge was slightly taken off his appetite, Valentine poured out some drink, and addressing his foster brother, began the conversation.

"Why, Louis, do you know that you are not difficult to find in this deuce of a city? Your reputation appears to be enormous."

"How so?" Louis said with a smile.

"By Jove! Everybody knows your address: they only call you the general. I did not need to ask many questions to find this house—everybody offered to guide me. It seems as if affairs are going on well, eh?"

The count smiled softly; but, before replying, he made the servants a sign to leave the room, and when the door was closed upon them,—

"All goes on very well," he said; "but now that you have arrived it will go on better still."

"Ah, ah! You think so?" Valentine said, sipping like an amateur the Bordeaux in his glass.

"I hope so."

"Well, you are not mistaken, brother; I hope so too."

Louis gave a start of joy.

"You have been a long time in coming," he said.

"Do you think so?"

"If you knew how impatiently I expected you."

"I suppose so; but believe me, my friend, when you have heard all I have done, only one thing will astonish you—that I am here already."

"What do you mean?"

"Patience! Tell me first what you have been doing during our separation. But one word first—have you beds for us?"

"Yes."

"Well, then, as supper is over, through pity for Don Cornelio, who is asleep in that easy chair, let him be taken to a bed, where he can repose at his ease: he needs it, I assure you."

"The fact is," the Spaniard stammered, "that my eyes *will* close, in spite of all my efforts to keep them open."

Louis had risen. On a signal he gave, a servant took charge of Don Cornelio, and led him away. Curumilla had lighted his calumet, and was smoking silently.

"Now for us two," Valentine said.

"But the chief," Louis observed: "does he not wish to rest?"

"Do not trouble yourself about him—he is made of iron; but if by any accident sleep comes upon him, you need not be alarmed—he will stretch himself in a corner of this room."

"Very good. Now, then, listen to me."

"I am all attention."

Louis gave his friend a detailed account of all he had done since his return to San Francisco. The narrative was long, for the count had much to tell. Valentine listened with the closest attention, not interrupting him once. The night was far advanced when Louis at length ended his report. Curumilla was still smoking.

When the count stopped there was a moment's silence, and then Valentine took the word.

"You have done miracles. You have accomplished impossibilities."

"Then you are satisfied with me?"

"I admire you. You have displayed in all this business incredible energy and intelligence. Now let us arrive at the financial question."

"Yes, that is the serious point at this moment. Unfortunately it will not be so easy to settle as the others."

"Who knows? Then you owe a deal of money?"

"An enormous sum."

"Oh, oh!"

"Why, you understand I had everything to buy."

"That is right; and you possessed?"

"As you know, nothing."

"Hum, hum! The account is clear. Then you owe for everything?"

"Nearly so."

"Are your accounts in order?"

"Of course, as I only waited for you to start."

"Let us have a look at them."

Louis opened a drawer, from which he took several papers covered with figures. He spread them out on the table with a stifled sigh.

"Why do you sigh?" Valentine asked him.

"Because I am anxious."

"Anxious about what?"

"Why, hang it! About paying them."

Valentine smiled.

"Nonsense!" he said, "let us look all the same."

The count bent over the papers.

"What are you doing?" Valentine said.

"I am calculating."

"What is the good? Tell me the totals only—that will be quicker."

"You are right: 17,533 piastres, 6 reals."

"Good!" Valentine commenced writing the amount in pencil on a piece of waste paper. "Next."

"Twenty-one thousand two hundred and seven piastres, five reals."

"Very good: go on."

"Twelve thousand eight hundred and twenty-three piastres."

"No reals?"

"No."

"Go on."

"Seven thousand six hundred and seventy-five piastres, six reals."

"Six reals. Very good. What next?"

"That is all."

"What! No more?"

"Is not that enough?"

"I do not mean that; but, from the way you spoke, I expected a formidable amount."

"Is not this so?"

"Not so very. Come, let us add it up."

"That is very easy. Here it is: total, 59,239 piastres, 7 reals."

"Seven reals. The total is correct. Have you not a few small debts beside?"

"Of course, I have a few personal matters to pay; and then I should not like to start empty-handed."

"That would be awkward; so that, as far as I can see you will want about eighty or one hundred thousand piastres to be perfectly clear?"

"Oh! Then I should have more than I require."

"It is better to have too much than not enough."

"That is true; but where to find such a sum?"

"Let me tell you a story."

"Eh?" Louis said in surprise. "Are you jesting, brother?"

"I never jest in serious matters. Listen to my story, I am convinced that it will interest you."

Louis could not suppress a movement of ill temper. He fell back in his chair, and crossed his arms.

"Speak," he said, "I am listening."

"Patience!" Valentine said, with a smile.

The count tossed his head.

"I am beginning," the hunter went on. "You remember in what way we parted at the *venta* of San José?"

"Perfectly."

"The next day I sold the herd in a lump. Another time, I will explain to you in what way; and I shall have certain explanations to ask of you. For the present, suffice it for you to know that I made an excellent deal, and sold it for 14,630 piastres."

"A famous sum! Unfortunately, we are still far from our reckoning."

"Patience! Then the bargain was a good one."

"Excellent: I should not have got such a price here."

"All the better; at Guaymas I took a bill on Wilson and Baker. Do you know them?"

"Very well; it is a substantial house."

"Good! Then tomorrow we will cash it. After selling the herd, I left San José with my two friends, not knowing, I confess, how to procure the money I had promised you, and of which you had such pressing need."

"A need I still have," Louis observed.

"Agreed," Valentine continued; "after galloping about for a long time, without knowing exactly where we were going, I resolved to ask my companions' advice. Of course Don Cornelio could suggest nothing. He contented himself with strumming a melancholy air on his guitar: you know that is his resource in embarrassing circumstances. You have known Curumilla as long as I have: the worthy chief only speaks when he is compelled; but when he opens his mouth, he speaks gold, and this time it really occurred."

While saying this, Valentine could not refrain from smiling. Louis turned to the chief, to whom he offered his hand, which the other pressed with a grimace of pleasure. The hunter continued, —

"From the descriptions you had given me, I knew pretty nearly the position of the mine of which you had become proprietor. Curumilla offered to take us there. 'We shall be very unlucky,' he said, 'we who know the desert so well, if we do not succeed in foiling the Indians and reaching the mine. Once there, we will take as much native gold as we want to satisfy our friend's wants.' As the advice was good, I resolved to follow it."

"What!" Louis shouted, rising hurriedly, "you did that, brother?"

"Of course I did."

"But you ran a risk of assassination at every step."

"I knew it; but I knew also that you must have a large sum."

"Oh, brother, brother!" Louis exclaimed, in great emotion, "so much devotion, while I was accusing you."

"You did not know what I was doing; you were right."

"Oh! I shall never forgive myself."

"Nonsense! Did we not swear once for all, to be entirely devoted to each other?"

"That is true. Oh! You have nobly kept your oath everywhere and ever, brother."

"And have you not done the same? Besides, this time the idea does not belong to me; I only followed the chief's advice."

"Oh, he is like you; you dare not say anything to him, or he would be vexed."

Curumilla laid down his calumet for an instant; and, approaching the count, laid his hand on his shoulder, and looking at him with an expression impossible to describe, while touching the Frenchman's chest and his own in turn, —

"Koutenepi," he said, in a quivering voice, "Louis, Curumilla — three brothers, one heart."

And he sat down again.

There was a long pause. The two white men were admiring the devotion and admiration of this brave Indian, who only lived for and through them, and asked themselves in their hearts, if, in spite of the warm friendship they bore him, they were really worthy of so profound an attachment.

"In short," Valentine went on at last, "no sooner said than done. I will not describe to you the incidents of our journey, for that would occupy too much precious time. Suffice it for you to know that, thanks to our lengthened prairie experience, after surmounting innumerable obstacles, and almost falling into the clutches of the redskins a hundred times, we at length reached the mine. Oh, brother, I know not the riches of the Californian placers, but I doubt whether they can be compared to the one of which you are now owner."

"Ah!" Louis exclaimed; "it is true then, it is rich?"

"Brother, its riches are incalculable; the native gold is found on the surface. Even I, whose, I will not say disinterestedness, but whose indifference for gold you know, was dazzled, so dazzled, that for some moments I could not imagine what I saw was real. I asked myself was I awake, or if I was not dreaming."

While Valentine spoke thus, Louis walked up and down the room, wiping away the perspiration that stood on his forehead.

"Oh!" he exclaimed, much agitated; "now I shall succeed, no matter what may happen."

"Do not defy chance, brother," Valentine replied sorrowfully.

"Do not fancy, brother, that these immense riches turn me mad. No, no; what do I care for self? I am thinking of the poor fellows I have attached to my fortunes; those who have placed confidence in me, and who will be happy through me. No, I do not defy chance; I thank Providence."

He sat down again, poured out a glass of water, which he swallowed at a draught, and passing his hand over his brow,—

"Go on, now," he said; "I am calm."

"I have not much more to add. I had taken with me three bât horses; I loaded them. I put gold, too, in my *alforjas*, in Curumilla's, and in Don Cornelio's. That worthy gentleman was perfectly mad: he bounded like a wild colt, and strummed his guitar furiously. He would not leave the placer, but insisted on awaiting our return there, alone. I was almost obliged to employ force to carry him off, so greatly had the sight of that gold fascinated him. In conclusion, you asked me for 80,000 piastres. Here are bills for 150,000 on Wilson and Baker. Add the price of the herd sold at San José, and you have a sum of 164,000 piastres, which is a very pretty lump of money in my opinion. What do you say?"

He then drew the bills from his breast, and handed them to his foster brother. Louis was confounded. He could not find words to reply.

"Ah!" Valentine added carelessly, "I forgot. As I supposed you would not be sorry to have a specimen of your placer, to show your partners, I brought you this."

He handed him a lump of gold, about as large as a man's fist. Louis took it mechanically, laid on the table, and looked at it for an instant with a fixed and haggard eye; then two tears coursed down his pallid cheeks, and a sob burst from his chest. He stretched out his arms; and, seizing Valentine and Curumilla, drew them to him, and embraced them passionately, murmuring,—

"Brothers, brothers! Thanks not only for myself, but for our poor countrymen, whom your sublime devotion has saved from wretchedness, perhaps from crime!"

CHAPTER XV
THE DEPARTURE

French emigration, in America or elsewhere, has rarely, or, to speak more truthfully, has never succeeded.

Whence does this result? The Frenchman is brave to rashness, intelligent, and laborious. He laughs and sings continually, supporting with the greatest philosophy the rudest blows of fortune, and carelessly confiding in the future. All that is true. But the Frenchman is no coloniser; that is to say, under all circumstances, he remains a Frenchman, and does not wish to be anything else.

The French emigrant, when he quits his country, retains always, not only the desire, but the intention of seeing it again some day. All his efforts tend to acquire the necessary sum to return to the village or town where he was born. No matter whether chance deserts him, he ever regards himself as a traveller and not as a sojourner; whatever be the position he may achieve, his eyes are incessantly fixed on France, the only country, in his opinion, where men can live and die happily.

Infatuated by his nationality, never willing to make the slightest concession to the habits, creeds, and manners of the people, with whom he is temporarily obliged to live, esteeming them as far beneath himself in intelligence and civilisation, the Frenchman passes through foreign nations with a sardonic smile on his lips, and a mocking glance—shrugging his shoulders in contempt at all that he sees, without trying to explain it, and preferring a sarcasm to a good lesson. Hence it generally happens that the Frenchman is not only not loved; but in spite of his open, frank, and merry character, is almost detested, by foreigners.

At San Francisco, the French emigrants—being without any socialities, and composed of individuals of every description, who shunned or tried to injure each other, instead of affording mutual aid—were, we are forced to confess, very slightly esteemed by the Americans, those colonisers *par excellence*. A few energetic men had contrived individually to make the French name respected.

Count de Prébois' expedition was consequently, in every respect, a blessing for his unhappy countrymen: in the first place by delivering them from the frightful want that held them in its iron clutches; and secondly by elevating them in their own eyes, and in those of the adventurers of every country whom the *mineral yellow fever* had attracted to these parts.

The count's enterprise had the result of rendering the French colony, at first so despised, highly respectable; and the Americans now began to feel secretly jealous of it. The enlistment of the French company to work the rich placers of Apacheria, was the important event of the day; it was spoken of everywhere. A number of adventurers burnt to take part in the expedition, and employed every means to gain acceptance.

But, as we have said, the count had laid down in this respect a line of conduct from which he would not deviate: the principal condition of enlistment was the fact of being a Frenchman; thus any number of poor fellows was rejected by the count, and many a violent enmity did he collect on his head, but the count cared little for all the disturbance; he continued his work imperturbably. Thus, as we have said, when Valentine arrived at San Francisco, the company was almost complete, and composed of picked men.

The hunter heard the news from his friend's lips, with the greatest satisfaction.

"Come," he said; "you have lost no time."

"Have I?"

"By Jove! To form a mining company, and collect a body of men in less than two months, is no trifle. I congratulate you with all my heart."

"Thank you. Still, without you nothing would have been effected; for mark the fact, Valentine, that although I have the richest capitalists and highest men in Mexico as shareholders in the *Atravida*, not one of them would have advanced me an ochavo to pay the expenses of the organisation, which I was bound to settle alone."

"That is a clever arrangement, brother. You have to deal with cunning shareholders."

"All the better. I will soon prove to them that they did wrong in not giving me all that confidence I deserve."

"I like that way of revenging yourself. But tell me— —"

"What?"

"Have you influential men among your shareholders?"

"What do you mean by influential?"

"Why, men whose political position offers you a certain guarantee against the annoyances which will be inevitably created down there, to prevent the success of your enterprise, and prepare its failure."

"I fear nothing of the sort."

"All the better."

"Judge for yourself. I have among my shareholders the French envoy at Mexico, the French consul at Guaymas, the Governor of Sonora, and many others."

"Did you not say the Governor of Sonora?"

"Yes."

"Ah, ah, ah!"

"Well?"

"Oh, nothing."

"Yes, you mean something; so speak."

"Indeed, why should I make a mystery of it? Do you know this governor?"

"No. I only know that he is colossally rich, that his name is Don Sebastian Guerrero, and he is a general."

"Is that all?"

"Yes."

"Well, you are mistaken in fancying you do not know him."

"Nonsense."

"Yes; and as it appears, you have even rendered him a great service."

"You are jesting; I never saw him."

"That is your mistake. Like the worthy knight errant, you are, you saved him from the hands of the miscreants."

"Come, speak seriously."

"I am doing so. In one word, you saved his life and his daughter's."

"I? You are mad."

"Not the least in the world. Indeed the father, and especially the young lady—who, between ourselves, is delightful—entertain the most affecting reminiscences of you."

"Who on earth told you that fine story?"

"Who? why the general himself."

"That is a little too strong."

"Come, think a little. About three or four years back, I do not know exactly which, did you not after leaving Guadalajara——?"

"Wait a minute," the count said hurriedly. "It would be strange if the person I saved were really the same——"

"Strange or no, it is."

"Well, then, that is famous for us."

"By Jove! We have a powerful friend, who will defend us tooth and nail against all comers. That is famous. I really believe Providence is declaring for us."

"I did not know that the Mexicans were gifted with so excellent a memory."

"I rather think it is the Mexican ladies in this case."

"No matter; the circumstance is of good augury."

"I hope you will profit by it."

"As much as I can."

"Bravo! And now that your affairs are settled, or nearly so, when do you intend to make a move?"

"I have certain arrangements still to make; so I cannot leave San Francisco before ten days."

"Can I be of any service to you?"

"None here; but over there, great."

"That is to say——"

"Are you fatigued?"

"Fatigued of what?"

"Why, of riding about in the fashion you have done, for some time past?"

"Once for all, and let that be carefully understood between us, remember that I am never tired."

"Good! Then you can render me a service?"

"What is it?"

"Though I cannot start for ten days, you can be in the saddle by daybreak, I suppose?"

"Of course."

"You must return by land to Sonora, to deliver three letters I will give you, one for Don Antonio Pavo, consular agent at Guaymas, the second for the Governor of Sonora, and the third for a certain Canadian hunter whom you will probably find at the Hacienda del Milagro, in the neighbourhood of Tepic."

"I will do it. Is that all?"

"Yes. You understand that I do not wish to arrive there, before preparations have been made for my reception."

"You are right: so I start——"

"Tomorrow."

"You mean today: it is now two o'clock."

"By Jove! That is true. How time slips away."

"Where shall I wait for you?"

"At Guaymas."

"That is understood. Write the letters while Curumilla and I saddle the three horses."

"Will you take your Spaniard with you?"

"Yes, he will be useful to me there."

"As you please."

Valentine and Curumilla went out, while Louis began his letters. Valentine, after saddling the horses, was conducted to the room where Don Cornelio was asleep. We must do the Spaniard the justice of saying that he offered the most obstinate resistance to the hunter, and it was not till he was compelled, that he left the bed in which he slept so comfortably. At length, when Valentine had succeeded, part by persuasion, part by carrying him, in placing him on his saddle and confiding him to Curumilla, he returned to the room where he had left his foster brother. The letters were ready; and Valentine took them.

"Now, brother, good-bye," he said, "and may you be fortunate."

The two men remained for a long time in an affectionate embrace. Louis knew the hunter too well, to try and induce him to take a few hours' rest; he, therefore, accompanied him to the gate, where the four men exchanged a parting greeting, and, at a sign from Valentine, the horses started at full speed. They soon disappeared in the darkness, but the sound of their horses' hoofs re-echoed for a long time on the hardened soil. Louis remained motionless in the gateway, so long as the slightest sound reached his ear, and then went in again, murmuring:—

"A man must be accursed who does not succeed, with such devoted friends."

The count worked through the whole night, not thinking of taking a moment's rest. The sun was already high on the horizon, and he still remained bent over the table, writing figures after figures. The door opened; and the person we saw talking confidentially with the count on the previous evening entered. Louis started at the noise, but on recognising his visitor a smile played over his stern countenance.

"You are welcome, consul," he said gaily, as he offered him his hand; "you could not have arrived at a better moment. Have you come to breakfast?"

"Yes, my dear count; for I wish to talk seriously with you."

"All the better, for I shall keep you the longer. Take a chair, and pardon my being surprised in this state, but I have spent the night in arranging these documents. Deuce take the man who invented writing and accounts."

The consul, for the gentleman was no other than the French representative in California, sat down, smiling; and, by the count's orders, an appetising breakfast was served almost immediately. The two gentlemen sat down opposite each other, and began a vigorous attack on the dishes.

"Well," Louis said presently, "any news?"

"Bad."

"Ah, ah! That worthy Jonathan is yelping, I suppose?"

"Louder than ever."

"Look at that! And why, may I ask?"

"You can guess it."

"Nearly so; but no matter, out with it."

"You are aware that you have made a number of enemies here?"

"Well, it was not my own fault."

"That is true! Well, these enemies are stirring, and making loud remarks."

"About what?"

"Why, you know people can always find something to turn into scandal. They say that the expedition will fail, that you are reduced to expedients, and that you do not know how to escape from your present position."

"Is that all?"

"No. They add, that you have contracted enormous debts, which you will never succeed in paying."

"Good again!"

"You understand that these calumnies produce a very bad effect."

"Naturally."

"I have therefore come to you, my dear count. I am not rich, unfortunately; still, I have at my disposal some 20,000 piastres. I am a shareholder in the company, and it is therefore my duty to come to its assistance; so I frankly offer you the money, which may be of some slight service to you."

The count cordially pressed his guest's hand.

"Thanks!" he said to him, with suppressed emotion, touched by the delicacy of this noble and generous procedure.

"Yes," the consul continued, ransacking his pockets, and producing a bundle of notes; "we must silence these scoundrels. Here is the amount."

And he offered the notes to the count, who declined them with a gentle smile.

"You are mistaken as to the meaning of the word I used," he remarked. "I thanked you, not because I accept your generous offer, but because it proves to me the esteem in which you hold me."

"Still——" the consul urged him.

"Again I thank you; but all my debts will be paid within an hour. I have at this moment nearly 200,000 piastres at my disposal."

The consul looked at him, open-eyed.

"But yesterday——?" he said.

"Yes!" the count interrupted him quietly, "yesterday I had nothing, today I am rich. I will explain to you this very simple miracle."

When the count ended his narrative, the consul pressed his hand joyfully.

"Good gracious!" he said, "you do not know, my dear count, what pleasure you cause me at this moment; you have staunch friends."

"Among whom I may reckon yourself."

"Oh! As for me," he said simply; "that is not astonishing; for am I not one of your shareholders?"

As soon as breakfast was over, the count set out to settle with his creditors, or rather those of the company, in order to destroy all excuse for malevolence, and close the mouth of the envious. After this, the count lost no time in making his final arrangements, and enlisting the few men he was still short of.

In a word, as he told Valentine when he left him, ten days had scarce elapsed since their nocturnal meeting, ere all the preparations were ended, and the company only awaited a favourable moment to embark and start.

The day on which the French company embarked for Sonora was a memorable one for San Francisco. The North American, beneath his cold and straight-laced appearance, conceals a warm and enthusiastic heart. When the Frenchmen entered the boats which were to bear them to the ship, for a moment and as if by enchantment, all enmities were silenced; and an enthusiastic mob, congregated on the pier, accompanied them with shouts and wishes for success, while waving their hats and handkerchiefs.

The count, as was his duty, was the last to embark. Several of his friends, among them being the consul, bore him company. As he leaped into the boat, the count turned, and pressed the consul's hand in parting.

"Good-bye," he said. "I will succeed, or Sonora shall be my tomb."

"Good-bye, till we meet again, my friend," the other answered. "I will not say farewell; I feel convinced that you will succeed."

"God grant it," Louis murmured, as he leaped into the boat and shook his head sadly.

A formidable shout burst from the crowd. The count bowed with a smile, and the boat started. An hour later, the white sails of the ship that bore the adventurers glistened, like a kingfisher's wing, on the horizon. The consul, who remained on the beach till the last moment, slowly walked homeward, saying to himself:—

"Whatever may happen, that man is not an adventurer, but a hero. He has more genius than Cortez. Will he be equally lucky?"

CHAPTER XVI
TWO MEN MADE TO UNDERSTAND
EACH OTHER

As several interesting events of our narrative will take place at Guaymas, we will describe that town in a few words.

Mexico possesses several roadsteads in the Pacific; but in reality has only two ports worthy that name, Guaymas and Acapulco. For the present, we will confine ourselves to the former.

Owing to a large quantity of islands which surround the port like a hill, and the lofty coasts, the roads are in all weathers as sure and calm as a lake. The sea breaks gently on shores adorned with mango trees, whose pale green forms a strange contrast to the earthy red of the beach, and gives the port a wild and desolate aspect, further increased by the continual silence of the roads, where a few ships seek shelter at rare intervals under the isle Del Venado, but, where usually only a few coasters are visible, or wretched canoes, hollowed out of trunks of trees, and belonging to the Hiaqui Indians.

The town stretches carelessly along the beach, with its white, low, and flat-roofed houses, defended by a fort built of red clay, armed with a few rusty and unserviceable guns. Guaymas, like all the pueblos of the republic, is dirty, ill built, and the streets are unpaved; in short, at each step you acquire proofs of that carelessness and egotistic incapacity which characterises the Mexicans. Behind the town, rise lofty and denuded mountains, which protect it from the cold winds of the Cordilleras.

Still, Guaymas, founded only a few years back, and whose population is but 6,000 at the utmost, is destined ere long, owing to the security of its port, and its magnificent position, to acquire a great commercial importance.

The day on which we resume our story, about an hour after the *oración*, or at seven in the evening, a man, wrapped in a thick cloak, and with the brim of his sombrero pulled down over his eyes, stopped at the door of a rather handsome house, and after casting a furtive glance around, to see that he was not watched, gave discreetly three separate knocks. This manner of rapping was evidently a signal; and the man we allude to must have been expected, for the door opened at once. The stranger entered, and the door was noiselessly closed after him.

The stranger then found himself in one of those inner patios found in all the houses of Guaymas; but he probably was perfectly acquainted with the place; for, without a second's hesitation, he turned to the left, mounted a few steps, and rapped at a second door, which was before him, in the same way as he had done at the first.

"Come in," a voice shouted from within.

The stranger pushed the door, which yielded to the pressure, and entered a large room, which might be considered to be furnished with a certain degree of luxury for Mexico, and especially for a province so remote as Sonora. But this luxury was in bad taste, and smelled of the *parvenu*. The furniture and pictures that decorated the room had been probably purchased or exchanged with the captain of the vessels that at times put into Guaymas, and presented the strangest possible discordance of style.

A man was seated in a butaca, almost in the centre of the room, and carelessly smoking a pajillo. When the stranger entered, he nodded to him, pointed to a chair, and said laconically,—

"Shut the door, and sit down."

The stranger took off his cloak and hat, which he threw on a sideboard; and, after closing the door as he had been recommended, he fell into a butaca with a sigh of satisfaction. We will describe these two new characters in a few words.

The first—that is to say, the master of the house—was a plump little fellow, as broad as he was long, with ordinary features, while his little sharp eyes gave his face an expression of soothing falseness and cowardly villainy. He was about fifty years of age, though he did not appear so, owing to the freshness of his apoplectic complexion, and long, flat, and greasy masses of black hair, which fell below his red and coarse ears. This worthy personage was dressed in the European fashion, with a profusion of jewellery, and rings on his fingers; and, through his costume and manners, which were made up of effrontery and timidity, he bore a considerable likeness to a butcher or a cattle dealer in his Sunday clothes.

His visitor, whom we have met before by the way, formed a perfect contrast with him. He was a half-breed, of Indian and Mexican descent, tall, dry, and thin as a lath; his face, like a knife blade, was adorned with an enormous beaked nose, which overshadowed a mouth stretching from ear to ear, and full of teeth white as almonds; round eyes with blood-shot eyelids, constantly agitated by a convulsive movement, completed the strangest and most sinister face that could be conceived. A cruel mocking smile continually moved his thin lips, and added to the feeling of discomfort his entire person inspired. In a word, his approach produced that clammy coldness felt in touching a viper or any other reptile. Beneath his cloak he wore the gold embroidered uniform of the higher Mexican officers. His name was Don Francisco Florés, and he wore the badge of a colonel in the Mexican service. We shall soon learn who was the hideous person, concealed under this borrowed name.

The colonel, after seating himself, took out some tobacco, made a cigarette, and began smoking with the most superb nonchalance. For some minutes the two men remained silent, examining each other with the corner of the eye. At last, the former, doubtlessly fatigued by this obstinate inquisition, which weighed upon him, and from which he could not escape, resolved to take the word.

"Caballero," he said, "you see that the instructions conveyed in the letter you did me the honour of writing to me, have been followed out point for point."

The colonel made a sign of assent, while emitting an enormous puff of smoke. The other continued,—

"Now I will take the liberty of observing that I do not at all understand your singular missive, and that I see no reason why you should surround yourself with so great a mystery."

"Ah!" the colonel said, with a laugh peculiar to himself, and which bore a strong likeness to a pile of plates breaking.

"Yes," the first speaker continued, annoyed by this irreverence; "and I should not be sorry, I confess, to have a clear and categorical explanation."

And, saying this, he drew himself up haughtily in his butaca; and regarded his visitor fixedly. The latter did not appear at all affected by this hostile manifestation; on the contrary, he stretched out his legs, and said, as he threw himself back in his chair,—

"Don Antonio, are you fond of money?"

"Eh?" the other remarked.

"I beg your pardon. I should have said gold: I will therefore modify my question. Are you fond of gold?"

"Really, sir——"

"Answer clearly, without any hesitation, as a caballero should do. I suppose that I am not talking Hebrew; so reply, yes or no."

"But——"

"*Capa de Dios!* if you go on in that way we shall never finish, master, *caray*. You are too sharp a greyhound, not to have recognised at the first glance with whom you have to deal. Answer clearly, then, without further tergiversation."

"Well, then, yes," Antonio answered, subjugated involuntarily by the man's accent.

"Very good. Do you love it much?"

"Well, tolerably."

"That is not enough."

"Very much, then, if you absolutely insist."

"I beg your pardon. It is a matter of indifference to me. It is not I who am in question, but only yourself."

"Well, well, I understand you."

"That is lucky; but you took your time to do so."

"Come, what is the business?"

"Ah, ah! You are coming to the point."

Don Antonio smiled.

"Well, I am only doing what you wish."

"That is true; so we shall not dispute about that."

"Go on; I am listening."

"You received my letter, as you allowed. Now, do you know why I arranged this meeting?"

"I am waiting to hear it from your lips."

"I will tell you at once. You are aware that a society has been formed at Mexico, called the Atravida?"

"I have heard it mentioned."

"Of course, as you are a partner in it."

"That is possible; but the question is not about that, I presume?"

"Perhaps it is. Well, this company, established under the auspices of the first Mexican capitalists, supported by the government, is intended to work the rich mines of the *Plancha de Plata*, situated in the heart of Apacheria."

"I am aware of it."

"Very good. You see we shall soon understand each other."

"I doubt it."

"I hope so. This company, composed of Frenchmen, all resolute men, organised as soldiers, and under the command of a skilful chief——"

"Count Don Louis de Prébois——"

"I know him. Spare your praise of him. This company, supported by high influences, must not, however, reach the mines."

"Ah, ah! And what will prevent it, if you please?"

"Yourself first of all."

"Oh, oh! I do not believe it."

"Nonsense! You shall see. Let me finish first."

"Go on."

"How much do you think this affair will bring you in?"

"I cannot tell you."

"What, not even approximatively?"

"It is very difficult to calculate, for the mines are rich."

"Yes, but they are remote. Come, mention a figure."

"It is impossible."

"Nonsense! Even supposing I were to help you——?"

"Ah! If you help me——"

"I thought so."

"But stay," Don Antonio remarked sharply. "What great interest have you, then, in spoiling this affair?"

"I, none; it is you."

"I!" Don Antonio exclaimed in amazement; "that is a little too much."

"You shall see."

"I am most eager to do so."

"So soon as the Atravida company was established, another, under the name of the *Conciliadora*, was at once set on foot, as always happens, and naturally for the same object."

"Come, the name is a capital one."

"It is. Now you know that competition is the backbone of trade."

Don Antonio bowed in assent; and the colonel continued, with his dry and harsh smile.

"The Conciliadora, although powerfully protected at Mexico, required an active, intelligent, and upright agent in Sonora; and it immediately turned its eyes on you. Indeed, Don Antonio Mendez Pavo, performing the duties of French consul at Guaymas, was the only man capable of serving it efficaciously. As the result of this reasoning, you were put down for 200 paid up shares of 500 piastres each; the coupons of which were intrusted to me to deliver to you. That makes, if I am not mistaken, a very nice little sum, which I shall have the honour of handing to you."

And he felt in the pocket of his uniform; but Don Antonio disdainfully checked him.

"You are strangely mistaken about me, caballero," he said; "when a man has the honour of representing France, he cannot be bribed in so miserable a way."

"Nonsense!" the colonel said, laughing.

"My duty orders me to protect the French company; and whatever may happen, I will do so."

"Magnificently spoken."

"So now," Don Antonio continued with fire, "return to the persons who sent you, and tell them that Don Antonio Pavo is not one of those men who can be induced to forget his duty so easily."

"That is charming, and you really spoke it with proper emphasis."

Don Antonio rose, and with a majestic smile shewed the colonel the door.

"Begone, sir," he said coldly; "or I shall not answer for the consequences of my anger."

The colonel did not stir; he made no change in the carelessly insolent position he had adopted from the outset. Still, when Don Antonio ceased, he threw away his cigarette, and giving the last speaker a glance of most peculiar significance, —

"Have you done?" he answered quietly.

"Caballero!" Don Antonio exclaimed, drawing himself up majestically.

"Permit me, Don Antonio, I have no wish to remain any longer here and waste your precious time. Still, you will allow with me, that every man intrusted with a mission must accomplish it in its entirety; and you are too conversant with business to deny this fact."

"I allow it, sir," Don Antonio answered, suddenly calmed by these words.

"Very good; then, be kind enough to sit down again and listen to me a few moments longer."

"Be brief, sir."

"I only ask for five minutes."

"I grant them."

"You are generous, sir; I will, therefore, profit by your permission. I go on, then. You are inscribed for 200 shares, representing, if I am not mistaken, 100,000 piastres, which I consider a very respectable sum."

"Not a word more on that subject, sir."

"I know," the colonel continued imperturbably, "what you would object; a bird in the hand is worth a vulture in the air."

Don Antonio, troubled by the meaning attached to his words, could find no reply. The colonel continued;

"The chiefs of the company employed the same line of reasoning as yourself, sir. They understood that they must act fairly and above board with a man holding so high as yourself, and so worthy in every respect of their confidence; consequently, they commissioned me to hand you, in addition to the shares — —"

"Sir," Señor Pavo essayed again.

"Fifty thousand piastres," the colonel said distinctly.

Don Antonio made a bound of surprise.

"What!" he exclaimed. "What did you say, señor?"

"I mentioned 50,000 piastres."

"Ah, ah!"

"In good bills, payable at sight."

"On what house?"

"Torribio de la Porta and Co."

"An excellent house, sir."

"Is it not?"

"Most assuredly."

"But," the colonel said as he rose, "since you refuse our offers, and my mission is now accomplished, I need only withdraw, after begging to pardon the loss of time I have occasioned you; for you *do* refuse, I think?"

Don Antonio had turned green; his small grey eyes, obstinately fixed on the papers the colonel toyed with, sparkled like live coals.

"Permit me," he said stammering.

"Eh? Can I be mistaken, señor?"

"I—I—I fancy you are."

"This time, bear in mind, we must understand each other thoroughly, in order to avoid any future misunderstanding, which might entail regret."

"Be at your ease. I believe there will no longer be any misapprehension between us. An affair, as you know, does not always strike a man at the first glance."

"That is true; but now you fully understand it?"

"Perfectly."

"All the better. Now we can have a frank explanation."

"Yes," Don Antonio said, with a mocking accent; "and, to begin, Señor Garrucholo, doff for a moment your borrowed character, for I like to know with whom I am dealing."

El Garrucholo, for the ex-bandit was really hidden under Colonel Francisco Florés, shuddered involuntarily at finding himself thus detected. He cast a viper's glance at the man who had unmasked him, and seized him fiercely by the arm.

"Take care, Don Antonio, there are secrets which kill those who hold them."

"That is possible, my master," the other answered, triumphing in his heart at the effect his revelation had produced. "But as, if I am not mistaken, we are about to complete together a very dirty transaction, I wished to prove to you that, if you held my secret, I had yours; and that it is to your interest to deal fairly by me."

"Threatened persons live a long time," the bandit said with a shrug of his shoulders.

"I do not threaten; I merely take my precautions—that is all. Now, let us converse."

The two men drew their chairs together and commenced a conversation, ear to ear, in so low a voice that no one could have overheard them.

CHAPTER XVII
GUAYMAS

The Mexicans are only children, though terrible children we allow, on whom it is impossible to calculate, no matter in what way. Their deplorable conduct, under all circumstances, since they succeeded in constituting themselves an independent nation, proves that, unless an entire change takes place in their character, no more is to be hoped from them in the future than they have effected in the past.

Curious, fickle, cowardly, rash, distrustful, cruel, and superstitious—such is the Mexican.

Let it not be supposed that we speak thus through a hatred of a people, among whom we lived so long; on the contrary, we love the Mexicans, we pity them, we should like to see them regard seriously their position, as a free nation, and behave as men; but we repeat it, they are terrible, stormy, and obstinate children, from whom no good can be derived, we are honestly afraid.

One of the manias of this people is to attract, by the most handsome promises, fallacious offers, and most friendly demonstrations, those strangers whom they fancy may prove useful in any way. They receive these foreigners with open arms, weep with joy while embracing them, offer them the most tenderly fraternal caresses, and give them more than they ever ventured to ask. Then one fine day, without any reason, motive, or slightest pretext, they change from white to black, begin hating with their whole soul the foreigners they have so greatly petted, insult and betray them, lay snares for them, and eventually ill treat or assassinate them, and that, too, while offering them a hand, and smiling on them.

If we wished to recriminate, how many names could we quote, how many shades would it be easy for us to evoke in support of our statements, without counting the noble and unfortunate De Raousset Boulbon, and the impetuous and generous Lapuillade, victims offered in a cowardly way to that hideous Mexican prejudice—a prejudice which is the basis of the policy of this unlucky people, and which will ruin it—not through a hatred of the foreigner, for that is a noble and national feeling, but through a hatred of

Europeans, whom they despair of ever equalling, and to whom, in their ignorance and carelessness, they feel a mortal jealousy and envy.

It is evident that during the ten years' struggle Mexico had to sustain against Spain, the former country produced grand and noble characters; but it seems that, exhausted by that gigantic effort, it was incapable of casting others like them into the crucible, for since the first hour of its liberty to the present day, it has not produced a single man worthy of walking, even at a distance, in the footsteps of the illustrious founders of its independence.

This is very sad to say; and yet, if we passed it over in silence, we might be reproached for not stating the truth, and for recoiling from the task we imposed on ourselves in writing this story, in which we have merely changed the names through a feeling that will be appreciated.

The arrival of the French company, however, was anxiously expected at Guaymas. The most absurd and contradictory reports were spread about it, its chief, and the object of the expedition; and as is generally the rule, the most absurd rumours obtained the greatest and firmest credence. Even before the arrival of the French, malevolence was watching in the shade, and seeking darkly to arouse the ill will of the population against the new arrivals.

What Colonel Florés stated in his conversation with Don Antonio Pavo was perfectly correct. Hardly had the organisation of the Atravida company been completed in San Francisco, ere two American houses, perfectly comprehending the advantages of this enterprise in which they were not allowed to join, for reasons we will be silent about for their credit, treacherously established a rival company, intended to impede the operations of the elder company by all means, even the most dishonest.

Hatred never slumbers. The affair went on rapidly, so rapidly that the second company had all its batteries prepared for effective action before the French had quitted San Francisco. This operation was managed with such Machiavellism, and the secret was so well kept, that the count, in spite of his extensive relations, suspected nothing, and embarked for Sonora with his heart full of hope and illusions.

Valentine was awaiting his friend with the most lively impatience. The hunter had conscientiously fulfilled the commissions the count gave him; and all had, apparently, succeeded famously. A comfortable barrack was prepared for the company: the French agent had been most honeyed, and placed himself at the hunter's disposal to do all he might desire with the most charming affability. Still the latter was not satisfied. With no plausible reason, with nothing arising to contradict these offers of friendship, Valentine, by one of those forebodings which Heaven sends to those it loves and wishes to protect, felt that all this amenity concealed a snare; the lips smiled, it is true, but the eyebrows frowned, and the brow was wrinkled.

General Guerrero, while testifying his delight at the arrival of the company, and placing himself at the orders of the hunter, had continued under various pretexts to reside at Hermosillo, instead of coming to Guaymas to welcome the company, as he should have done; in the first place as governor of the province, secondly, as member of the company; two reasons more than sufficient to suggest his change of abode.

Valentine, hence, was very restless; and the more so because, while feeling that a storm was collecting, he could not foresee whence it would come. Hence, he remained a greater part of the day by the seashore, watching anxiously every sail that appeared, hoping to see his friend arrive at any moment; for he supposed, with some show of reason, that the presence of the count and his brave comrades would suffice to silence those who sought to injure him: for the majority of the people was not only far from being hostile to the expedition, but seemed well disposed toward it.

Things were in this state one morning, when, according to his custom, Valentine was preparing to proceed to his observatory, as he called the rock on which he passed whole days. All at once, Don Antonio and Colonel Florés rushed into the cuarto where he resided, crying, gesticulating, and repeating, both at once:—

"Here they are, here they are! They are coming!"

"Who?" Valentine asked them, hardly able yet to put faith in such blessed news.

"El conde! El conde!"

"He will be here in an hour at the latest," said Don Antonio.

"Perhaps before," the colonel backed him up. "We are going to meet him."

"And I, too," Valentine exclaimed.

They went out. The news had spread with the rapidity of a powder train. Guaymas took a holiday. Immediately, before any orders were given by the authorities, the houses were hung with flags; for, as it happened, Corpus Christi would be celebrated a few days later, and the banners had been got in readiness.

The inhabitants, dressed in their best clothes, the Hiaqui Indians, of whom a great number let themselves out to private persons as workmen and servants—in a word, everybody, hurried and ran toward the beach, shouting, laughing, singing, and uttering interminable hurrahs. It was really a curious sight, —this crowd, hastening joyously to meet a few Frenchmen, whose good intentions toward them they instinctively guessed.

The authorities of the town followed the popular movement; but it was easy to read that they did not act from their own will, but were carried onward by the current of public opinion.

When Valentine and the two men who had constituted themselves his companions reached the beach, it was already invaded by the whole population. A few cable's lengths from shore the ship that brought the French might be distinctly seen. It advanced majestically, impelled by a strong breeze. It had its top-gallant sails set, and its lower sails clewed up, which allowed a large crowd to be seen on the poop. When the vessel had passed a little beyond Venado Island—the usual anchorage of large ships—it tacked, and sent down top-sails; then the anchor was let go, and the main jib lowered.

Valentine leaped hurriedly into a canoe, and, before Don Antonio and the colonel could follow him, pushed off. Not noticing the signs his companions made him, the hunter proceeded rapidly in the direction of the ship, vigorously aided by the man already in the canoe, and who was no other than Curumilla. In a few minutes they reached the vessel. Louis perceived them from a distance, so that when they came alongside he received them, and helped them aboard. Even before embracing his foster brother, or pressing his hand, Valentine turned and looked searchingly along the beach.

"Good!" he said, "they have not found a boat yet. Come, brother, let us go down into your cabin, I must speak with you without delay."

"Let me, at least, say 'how do you do' to you," Louis remarked, with a smile.

"Come: we have not a moment to lose."

The count looked at the hunter, and saw that his face was grave. He understood at once that he had important news to communicate. He no longer resisted. He gave his orders hurriedly to one of his officers, to prepare everything for the debarkation, and followed his foster brother who was anxiously awaiting him. Louis led him into the modest berth which he had engaged during the passage, and prepared to shut the door.

"No," Valentine said, preventing him, "leave it open, on the contrary; in that way we shall see the persons who come."

"As you please. Speak."

"I have only two words to say to you; but they are two I would advise you to profit by."

"You may be sure of that."

"You have powerful enemies here. Who they are I know not; but they detest you."

"What do you say?"

"A thing of which I am certain."

"But, my dear fellow, whoever those enemies may be, I have nothing to fear from them. My papers are all regular, my grant is clearly and carefully registered. I have not only the authorisation, but also the support of the government. I only act by formal orders, and, therefore, fear nothing."

"Brother," Valentine answered sententiously, "when you have to deal with Mexicans, you must always apprehend treachery. I have known them many a long year, and unfortunately know also what dependence is to be placed in them."

"You startle me."

"No, I warn you, that is all. It is your duty to be constantly on your guard."

"Do you know that, before Heaven, I am responsible for the lives of all these brave fellows intrusted to me?"

"That is why I advise you to be prudent, and not to trust in any one. There are two men above all whom I recommend you to distrust."

"Their names?"

"Don Antonio Pavo, and Colonel Don Francisco Florés."

Louis could hardly refrain from a start of surprise, as he looked his brother in the face.

"It is not possible," he exclaimed; "you must be mistaken."

"Why so?"

"Because these two men, one of whom is agent to the French government here, and the other the delegate of the Atravida, are both shareholders in the company. I am specially recommended to them, and have letters for both."

"As you please; but I assure you these men are betraying you."

"Have you any proof?"

"None."

"How do you know it, then?"

"I do not know it, and yet I am sure of it. Believe me, brother; for you are aware that I am rarely mistaken."

Louis shook his head sadly.

"All this is strange," he said.

At this moment a man leaned over the companion, and uttered the one word, "Spies!" in a low voice, yet sufficiently loud to be heard by the two men.

"Halloh!" Louis exclaimed with a start.

"It is nothing," Valentine observed; "only Curumilla warning us that our two men are coming. Let us return to the deck, for they must not fancy we have any doubts of them. Examine the two men carefully, when you find yourself in their presence; and I am certain you will come over to my opinion afterwards."

Louis made no reply. They went on deck, and Valentine left him.

"I am returning to land," he said; "you will see me again on the beach."

The hunter leaped into the canoe, which Curumilla had allowed to fall behind the vessel, so that it might not be noticed; and he pushed off for land at the very moment the colonel and Don Antonio set foot on deck.

No people is possessed, to so eminent a degree as the Mexican, of the most refined politeness and most graceful gallantry. By their feline and gentle manners they can seduce and charm persons they have an interest in cheating, whenever they please. Unfortunately, in spite of all the efforts they made, and the cajolery they employed to convince Don Louis of their sincerity and profound attachment to him, Don Antonio and the colonel had physiognomies which so clearly revealed the disgraceful passions that moved them, that all their labour was thrown away.

As Valentine had warned him, on the approach of these two men the count had involuntarily experienced a feeling of repulsion, so strong, that he was compelled to make an effort over himself, to prevent them seeing the effect they produced upon him. The count, however, thought it advisable to pretend to be their dupe, in order to profit by the faults their fancied security might induce them to commit, and derive from them all the information he might need at a future date.

He therefore responded to their advances and offers of service with such frankness and cordiality, that he succeeded in completely duping the crafty scoundrels who fancied him their dupe.

The count had scarce arrived in Sonora, he had not yet set foot on land, ere he had to commence his diplomatic apprenticeship, and contend in craft and falsehood with people, from whom he should have expected the frankest friendship and most absolute devotion—a rude task for a character so loyal and thoroughly honest as that of the count; but the success of the expedition depended on his finesse, and the skill with which he eluded the snares which would be incessantly spread beneath his feet. He understood this, and made up his mind to his course of action, though it was against the grain.

After conversing for some time with the two men, the count, seeing that all was in readiness for the landing, gave orders for it. Immediately the adventurers took their stations with admirable order in the boats brought from the port to receive them. The small flotilla advanced steadily toward the beach, amid the shouts of the crowd assembled on the shore, and the clangor of all the town bells, rung as a symbol of rejoicing.

CHAPTER XVIII
THE FIRST FORTNIGHT

A man must have been essentially a pessimist, or thoroughly acquainted with the Mexican character, to apprehend treachery on seeing the warm reception accorded to the Frenchmen by the inhabitants of Guaymas. It was a madness—a delirium impossible to describe. Leperos, rancheros, campesinos, rich hacenderos, all pressed round the French, vying with each other in offering them a hearty welcome. It seemed as if this little band of adventurers, who were only passing through the town, brought to Sonora peace, tranquillity, and liberty; in a word, all those things the Mexicans want, and for which they sigh in vain. The cries of, *Viva los Franceses! Viva el conde!* rose on all sides with a deafening sound.

So soon as the company landed, by Don Louis' orders, the ranks were speedily formed; and the count, having Colonel Florés on his right hand, Don Antonio on his left, led his men to the barrack prepared for them, clearing his way with difficulty through the dense masses of spectators. In front of the barrack the alcalde mayor, and the juez de letras—that is to say, the two principal authorities of the town—flanked by their ragged alguaciles, were awaiting the arrival of the company; and on perceiving them, Don Louis commanded a halt.

The two magistrates then walked a few paces toward the count, whom they saluted respectfully, and began a long address stuffed with all sorts of pompous Mexican hyperboles, from among which Don Louis managed to discover that the Sonorians rejoiced in the depths of their hearts at the arrival of the valiant French company; that they set on his courage all their hope of being protected against their ferocious neighbours, the Apaches; that the French had not landed on a foreign shore, but amid brethren and sincere friends, who would be delighted to have it in their power to prove their devotion; and a thousand other things too long to repeat here.

When the alcalde mayor had ended his discourse amid the warm applause of the crowd, the juez de letras began one in his turn, equally long, equally diffuse, and equally perfidious as the first, and which met with the same success.

We will remark here that the Mexicans adore long speeches.

At length, when the two magistrates had finished speaking, the count bowed gracefully, and replied to them with a few of those words which come straight from the heart. They produced a perfect frenzy. The crowd yelled with joy, waving their hats and handkerchiefs; while from every window a perfect shower of flowers escaped from the dainty hands of the señoritas, and literally inundated the adventurers, who cordially responded to this delicate attention.

The company then entered the barrack; it was a large house, with an enormous inner court, admirably adapted for the use to which it was put at this moment. Within an hour, the adventurers, with that eminent knack peculiar to Frenchmen, were comfortably installed, and appeared to have occupied their quarters for the last six months.

The count fancied he had got rid of the alcalde and juez de letras: but it was not so; they had still several requests to make of him before they left him at liberty, and would not neglect them.

As in all other centres of population in Mexico, at Guaymas everyone lives pretty much as he pleases, without troubling himself greatly about the authorities. This liberty, or rather license, may be advantageous to one portion of the population, but is evidently extremely prejudicial to the other; in this sense, that the rascals, having entire liberty to commit all the wicked actions Satan constantly breathes in their ear, the honest people are obliged to defend themselves, and not count in any way upon the protection of a problematical police, which, if it happen to exist, naturally makes common cause with the brigands.

The magistrates had judged in their wisdom to profit by the stay of the Frenchmen at Guaymas, in order to disperse the scoundrels of every description, with whom the city abounds, with a salutary terror. Consequently, they begged the count to guard the principal posts of the pueblo with men belonging to his company, and to organise patrols to traverse the streets by night, and watch over the tranquillity of the citizens and public security.

When, after much circumlocution, the magistrates at length ventilated their request, the count answered them with a smile, that he was entirely at the service of the Mexican government, and if they considered his assistance useful, they might dispose of him and his men as they thought proper. The magistrates thanked him heartily, and, incited by the facility with which the count granted their first request, they ventured to bring forward the second, which, in their idea being of much more delicate nature, they feared would be refused. It was as follows:—

Corpus Christi is the most important religious ceremony of Mexico. This festival, to augment the splendour of which the people undergo the heaviest sacrifices, fell this year just a few days after the arrival of the French in Sonora. They wished the count to promise to have his little mountain guns fired during the whole period the procession went about the streets.

Guaymas had many guns in the forts; but unfortunately they were dismounted, and completely honeycombed with rust.

It may be easily understood, that in the mind of the superstitious Sonorians, on so solemn a festival as this, the bells were not sufficient, and that the ceremony would entirely lose its solemn character, unless a few gunshots were fired.

The worthy magistrates little expected that they were causing the count a lively pleasure, by asking of him two things as a favour, which, had he dared, he would have claimed as a right, for the following reasons.

Since the discovery of gold, so many scamps of every description had sought refuge in San Francisco, that the Californian population justly enjoyed a frightful reputation for vice, crime, and debauchery, in all the adjacent countries, and especially in the Pacific ports, on which they sometimes pounced like swarms of predacious birds. The count ardently desired on behalf of his undertaking, to show the Sonorians among whom they were destined to live, that the French emigrants had nothing in common with these sinister bandits, and that the men he had the honour to command were brave men, resolved to behave themselves properly, wherever chance took them, and never to molest the Mexican population.

As for the second question, it was even more serious in the count's eyes. The Mexicans are not only ignorant and superstitious, but even more. Although they do not understand a syllable of the religion they profess, or perhaps on account of that, they are exaggerated fanatics, and sooner pardon a murder than an insult, however slight in its nature, not to the religion itself, but merely to its exaggerated ceremonial. This fanaticism, carefully maintained during the Spanish dominion, was intended to keep foreigners, that is to say the English, whom they feared greatly, from the shores of New Spain. At that time, indeed, the English were almost the only Europeans who ventured to visit the Spanish colonies.

The monks profited by the difference of our religion, to make the most exaggerated portraits of the English to their parishioners, investing them with horns and claws, as the children of Lucifer must necessarily have. The Indians, credulous as babes, accepted, with closed eyes, all the fables the monks thought proper to tell them; and, with them, every foreigner became an Englishman, that is to say a heretic, a gringo.

The declaration of independence, while enabling the Mexicans to see foreigners of all nations, made no change in their convictions; for it is not so easy to destroy a prejudice rooted for centuries. They continued, as in the past, to see in foreigners only Englishmen, and consequently gringos; hence, that smouldering hatred which breaks out every time that occasion offers, and that secret horror they experience at the sight of every European.

Being on the point of burying himself with his company in the heart of Mexico—of passing through fanatic, credulous, and ignorant tribes, with whom it was important to live in peace, and give them no pretext for quarrelling—it was of the highest interest to the count to show by an undeniable proof that the French were not gringos, but, on the contrary, as good catholics as the Sonorians.

Hence he favourably greeted the magistrates' request—a request which probably concealed a trap—and promised them not only that the guns should thunder during the whole period of the procession, but that the company would be happy to accompany the holy sacrament during its progress through the streets of the town. The more so, the count added, because the French were catholics, and would eagerly seize the opportunity to manifest their fervour for their revered religion.

The magistrates, having at length obtained all they desired, took leave of the count with great demonstrations of gratitude and respect. The count breathed again, for the *sederunt* had been long. Still, all was not over yet, as the count soon perceived.

Don Antonio, and his inseparable friend the colonel, would not so easily loose their hold, and only consented to withdraw when the count promised to be present that same evening with all his officers at a banquet Don Antonio had prepared, to *fête* the arrival of the French company. The count gave his word, and was at length left at liberty for a few hours.

Now that the company had arrived at Guaymas, that is to say, the first halt on the road to the mines, the expedition had really commenced, the first obstacles were cleared. According to the count's idea, all required now was to give his men a few days' rest, and then push resolutely onward.

Profiting by the first impression produced by the Frenchmen, the count, without loss of a moment, had his papers put in order, and easily obtained his passports for the interior. Several days passed thus, the French reigned as masters in Guaymas, petted and caressed by the inhabitants whom their gaiety and carelessness pleased above all, and who, having hitherto seen a few ragged outcast Mexican soldiers, could not leave off admiring the training, martial aspect, and the perfect dexterity with which the foreigners manoeuvred and managed their weapons.

The company performed the police duties of the town with the greatest care; thefts and assassinations ceased as if by enchantment; and the Sonorians slept tranquilly, on the faith of their new friends.

On Corpus Christi day, as had been arranged, the French cannon were fired during a portion of the day, and the adventurers accompanied the procession, bearing bouquets in their muzzles, and behaving with the greatest decency. Their presence at church produced all the effect the count anticipated from it; and the certainty acquired by the inhabitants that the strangers were good catholics, still further increased the friendship they entertained for them.

Matters went on thus for several days, and nothing occurred to trouble the azure of the count's projects. In fact, the most perfect harmony prevailed between him and the magistrates, at least apparently; hence, with the native frankness of his character, the count began to reproach himself secretly for the distrust he had at first felt, or rather Valentine inspired him with; and in his heart he accused his friend of having yielded to unjust prejudices against men who seemed to study not merely to satisfy him, but to anticipate the slightest desires of the members of the expedition.

Indeed, how could the count suspect treachery? He had only come on the entreaty of the Mexican government. It was that government which demanded that his company should be trained, numerous, and well armed. The chief authorities of the country had a greater interest in the success of the enterprise, because they were nearly all shareholders. To suppose that, under such circumstances, these persons intended to cheat him, the count must have at first admitted that they were insane; for no one ever carries on war at his own expense, and the Mexicans are generally known to have a clutching hand for money.

In the meanwhile, time passed rapidly; the count was afraid, lest the *morale* of his comrades might suffer by a longer stay in the heart of a Sonorian city. He was burning to set out; but, unfortunately, it was impossible for him to do so, until depôts of provisions had been made along the road, and the government of the state had arranged with him the definitive movements of the company on its march to the mines.

Don Louis complained bitterly both to the colonel and Don Antonio of the continual delays he was obliged to suffer, and the pretexts, more or less plausible, employed to keep him in disgraceful inaction. The governor, who declined to quit Pitic, only made evasive answers to his letters, or declared that he had received no instructions.

This state of things could not, and must not, last longer. As there was a risk of the company dissolving, and all the fruit of the preliminary labours being lost, before the enterprise had been seriously entered on, Don Louis resolved at all risks to emerge from this equivocal position. Consequently, after having formally stated his wishes to Colonel Florés and Don Antonio, he informed them that since General Guerrero did not appear to understand the tenour of his letters, he was resolved to proceed himself to Pitic, and have a categorical explanation with him.

The two men started with joy at this news; for they required the count's absence for the success of the plans they had formed. Instead, therefore, of turning him from his project, they urged him warmly to put it in execution without delay, and start as soon as possible. Don Louis had no need to be stimulated and urged on thus. So soon as he left the two men, he proceeded to the barrack, assembled the company, and told them of his speedy departure, which was joyfully heard by all these energetic and ardent men whom rest fatigued, and on whom idleness began to weigh heavily. The count intrusted the temporary command to one of the officers on whom he thought he could most count, giving him the order that, if he heard nothing from him within four days, the company would start at once to join him, and after again urging the men to keep up the strictest discipline, the count finally quitted the barrack.

At his house he found Valentine awaiting him. The latter approved his conduct, but refused to accompany him, giving as his reason, that he believed he should serve the good cause better by remaining at Guaymas. The truth was, that the hunter did not wish to leave out of sight the men he had undertaken to watch, until he had discovered their machinations.

Louis did not insist. He knew that with a man of Valentine's character there was no chance of discussing, when he had once formed a determination. Followed by Don Cornelio and an escort of ten well-mounted horsemen, the count set out, after once again pressing his friend's hand, and proceeded toward Pitic, where—at least he hoped so—he should at length find the word of the enigma.

"Hum!" Valentine muttered, following him with a thoughtful glance; "either I am greatly mistaken, or, now that he is no longer here, to thwart by his presence the gloomy machinations of the scoundrels who wish to make him their dupe, we shall soon have something new."

After this aside, the hunter walked with his usual measured step toward the barrack, where he arrived in a few moments, and found the adventurers in a state of great excitement, produced by the departure of their leader.

CHAPTER XIX
PITIC

The distance is not great from Guaymas to Pitic, and the count covered it in a few hours.

Pitic, or Hermosillo, is a delightful town, enclosed with walls, and surrounded by kitchen gardens, whose produce is rather important. Unfortunately, the night had completely set in when the count arrived there, and he could only take a vague glance at the scenery, which, seen through the obscurity, had entirely changed its character, and assumed a gloomy appearance, which painfully contracted the adventurer's heart. The count had considerably recovered from his first illusions; the paltry annoyances of which he was the object now made him see the future under a different light, and he already doubted the success of an enterprise against which, from the outset, so many underhand obstacles were raised.

At the moment of mounting his horse, he had received from the general commandant of the province a note giving him peremptory orders to remain at Guaymas, with his company, and not to march forward until more ample information, that is to say, until the general had received positive instructions on the subject, from the central government at Mexico. As may be easily supposed, this order, intimated in so brutal a manner after all that had passed, had obtained the sole result of pressing the count's departure; for he was outraged by this flagrant violation of all the conditions stipulated in his treaty.

The little band entered Pitic without exciting the slightest attention. At this hour the streets were nearly deserted; and the few travellers they met *en route*, deceived by their Mexican costume, did not even take the trouble to look at them. The count dismounted in the Calle San Agostino, before a house which he had got in readiness for the occasion, without saying a word to anyone. After a gentle rap at the door, it opened, and the party entered. The house belonged to a Frenchman, who had gone on a journey in the interior, for commercial reasons; but during his absence, the servants, in obedience to his instructions, received the count with the utmost attention. The latter, after whispering a few words to Don Cornelio, who went out at once, retired to the cuarto prepared for him.

Don Louis was a man of powerful and energetic temper, a man of action before all. He understood that, after the turn that matters had taken, he must act energetically and without losing a moment, unless he wished to receive an irreparable check. His plan was formed, and he prepared to carry it out without delay.

Don Cornelio returned at the moment when the count, who had changed his costume, was giving a final glance at his appearance.

"Already!" he said, on perceiving the Spaniard.

"I have found the house, it is only a few paces from here."

"All the better, we shall have less distance to go."

"Five minutes at the most."

"Is General Guerrero in Pitic?"

"He is. Still I fancy you would do better by delaying your visit till tomorrow."

"Why so?"

"Because there is a *tertulia* this evening at the palace."

The count turned.

"What difference does that make?" he asked.

"Oh, as you please, señor; but, perhaps, you do not know what a tertulia is."

"Not exactly; but you will explain it to me?"

"Nothing more easy. A tertulia is a party, a festival—a ball, in a word."

"I understand. And you are sure, Don Cornelio, that there is a tertulia this evening at the governor's palace?"

"Positively sure, your excellency."

"Bravo! That will do our business."

The Spaniard looked at him in amazement.

"Don Cornelio," the count continued, "change your travelling dress. I mean to take you with me."

"The fact is— —," he said hesitating.

"What then?"

"I must confess to you, señor conde, that I have no other clothes save those I wear."

"Ah, that is of no consequence," the count replied with a smile, pointing at the same time to a heap of clothes thrown pell-mell on the furniture. "I suppose that you are sufficiently my friend not to feel annoyed at the cool way in which I treat you."

"Oh, not at all," the Spaniard exclaimed, with a movement of joy.

"I must ask you to make haste, though; for I am waiting."

"I only ask for five minutes."

"I give you ten. You will find me in the patio; I am going to give my escort orders to mount."

The count went out, and Don Cornelio eagerly set to work obeying him. We must add, to the glory of the Spaniard, that Don Louis' treatment of him, so far from annoying him, had caused him to feel a deep gratitude.

The Spaniard was not mistaken; there was really a tertulia at the governor's palace. General Guerrero was extremely rich: hence, the ball he gave this evening was sumptuous, and in every way worthy of the exalted post he occupied in the province.

The crowd filled his rooms, which glistened with light and dazzled with gilding. All the higher society of Pitic was assembled at the palace; tables, covered with gold, were surrounded by players, who, with that proud carelessness characteristic of Mexicans, risked enormous sums on a card. In a vast hall, a band, perhaps rather wild to European ears, regulated the movements of the dancers; while a private room was reserved for the ladies. Doña Angela, ravishingly beautiful, was seated on her throne, in the midst of this bevy of pretty women.

But, despite all the general's efforts to please his guests, and excite them to amuse themselves, the festivities languished. The young ladies, generally so impassioned for dancing, refused all invitations; they preferred to remain talking together in the apartment reserved for them. The fact was, they were discussing at this moment a most interesting point, which had the privilege of arousing feminine curiosity to the highest pitch. The news of the French landing at Guaymas supplied the staple of the conversation.

"Good gracious!" a young woman said, with a charming smile, "will the English come here?"

"Doubtlessly," another observed; "but they are not English, *Querida*."

"Oh, you are mistaken, Carmencita. All foreigners are English, that is to say heretics; my confessor told me so."

"They must be hideous," a third asserted, advancing her head in curiosity.

"Indeed not, I assure you; they are men like others," the second speaker observed, a pretty brunette, with black eyes that sparkled with malice. "I spent Corpus Christi with my uncle at Guaymas, and saw them. Some of them, indeed, are very good-looking."

"That is impossible!" they exclaimed in chorus. "They are heretics!"

"They will massacre us."

"They are said to be very cruel."

"Their chief especially."

Till then Doña Angela had remained silent, absorbed in silent thought; but at this remark she suddenly raised her head.

"Their chief is a caballero," she said in a loud voice. "He is a conde in his own country; and if he has come to Sonora, it is probably only on our behalf."

All the young women were silent; for they were amazed at this strange outbreak on the part of Doña Angela; then they began chattering together. The young lady, vexed at having thrust herself forward so imprudently, bit her lips, blushed slightly, and fell back in her reverie. At this moment Don Sebastian entered the room.

"Ah, here is the general!" three or four young girls exclaimed gaily, as they rose and eagerly surrounded him.

"Yes, here I am, señoritas," he answered with a smile. "What do you want of me?"

"Merely some information."

"About what?"

"We wish to know," Doña Carmencita began; then she corrected herself. "It is not I, general, but these ladies."

"I am persuaded of that," Don Sebastian said, gallantly; "be good enough, then, to be their interpreter. What do they desire to know?"

"Who are the Ingleses?"

"What Ingleses?"

"Those who have landed at Guaymas."

"Ah! Very good."

"You will tell us, will you not, general?" they all exclaimed at once.

"If it is agreeable to you."

"Oh! Greatly so."

"In the first place, they are not English."

"They must be, as they are foreigners."

The general smiled at this simple observation; but mentally recognising the impossibility of destroying an opinion so deeply rooted, he turned the question.

"These men are two hundred and odd in number."

"So many as that?" two or three young ladies exclaimed, with a gesture of terror.

"Yes, indeed, so many as that, señoritas; but reassure yourselves—you have nothing to fear from them. They are kind and obliging, and their chief is a perfect caballero."

"But why do they come here?"

"They came for the purpose of working certain mines."

"I beg your pardon, papa," Doña Angela observed, who had been attentively listening to the conversation. "Did you not say they came?"

"Yes, my child, I said so."

"But they are still at the port, I think?"

"Yes, they are; but it is probable that they will soon depart."

"For the mines?"

"No. To return whence they came."

Doña Angela contracted her eyebrows, a movement in her which denoted grave annoyance and great mental preoccupation, and was silent again.

"All the better. Let them go, the heretics!" one of the ladies exclaimed. "These accursed English only come to our country to plunder us."

"That is true." The majority warmly supported her.

"Besides, I do not care what is said; I assert that they are frightfully ugly."

"Well!" a young lady said, with a delicious pout, "I should have liked to see one—only one—to know what to think about them."

"I am very much afraid, Doña Redempción," the general remarked with a smile, "that it will now be impossible to satisfy your curiosity."

"All the worse; for a heretic must be an extraordinary animal. Are they as ugly as the Indios Bravos?"

"That is a different matter."

"Ah! And are you certain, general, that I shall not be able to see one? That annoys me."

"I regret it, señorita."

"And I, too. But supposing one of them were to come to Hermosillo?"

"That is peremptorily forbidden them. They will be cautious not to disobey the order they have received."

"Ah!" she said with a pout.

At the same moment, a door was thrown open with a crash; and a servant announced in a loud and perfectly distinct voice, —

"His Excellency the Count Louis de Prébois. His Excellency Don Cornelio Mendoza."

If the count purposed to produce an effect, his object was completely attained. His sudden entrance was a regular tableau, and caused a general emotion, whose immense extent it was certainly impossible for him to calculate.

All the ladies had risen, and, grouped round the general, examined with a curious and timid eye the chief of the adventurers.

The count, whose splendid ranchero costume, which he wore with inimitable grace, added to the fascinating charm spread over his whole person, walked a few steps with a smile, bowed around with a gesture full of elegance, and waited. The general had suddenly turned of a livid pallor.

The news of the count's arrival, spreading through the other rooms with incomprehensible rapidity, suddenly stopped the dancing and gambling; all the guests quitted the other rooms, and proceeded toward the one in which the count was said to be.

Still, each second that elapsed added to the embarrassment of the position; the general felt it, and sought in vain a mode of escape. Don Louis understood, or rather guessed, the general's perplexity; hence, advancing two paces, he said with exquisite politeness, —

"I am confounded, general, by the trouble I have involuntarily caused among your guests. It seems that I was not expected at Pitic."

The general succeeded in regaining a little self-possession.

"I allow it, caballero," he replied. "Still the impromptu visit you have deigned to make me must be most agreeable to me, be assured."

"I hope so, general; and yet, to judge by the glances directed upon me from all sides, I may be permitted to doubt it."

"You are mistaken, señor conde," the general continued, attempting to smile. "For the last few days fame has been so occupied with you, that the eagerness of which you are now the object ought not at all to astonish you."

"I should wish, general," the count said, with a bow, "that this eagerness were more friendly. My conduct, since my arrival in Sonora, should have attracted greater sympathy toward me."

"What would you? We are savages, señor conde," the general said with a sarcastic smile; "we have the misfortune not to love what comes from foreign parts; so you must forgive us. But enough on that subject, for the present," he added, changing his tone. "As you have been kind enough to become my guest, allow me to present you officially to these ladies, who are burning to become better acquainted with you."

Don Louis yielded gracefully to the general's wishes. The latter then, affecting the most exquisite courtesy, presented his guest, as he called him, to the most influential persons at the ball. Then he led him to his daughter, who, since the count's entrance, had stood motionless, with her eyes obstinately fixed upon him.

"Señor conde," the general said, "my daughter, Doña Angela. Doña Angela, the Count Don Louis de Prébois Crancé."

Don Louis bowed respectfully before the young lady.

"I have had the honour of knowing the count for a long while," she said with a graceful smile.

"It is true," the general said, suddenly pretending to remember; "we have been acquainted for a long time, caballero."

"It was not my place to remind you under what circumstances we met."

"That is true, count, it was mine; believe me that I have not forgotten it."

"Nor I," the young lady murmured; "for I owe you my life, señor."

"Oh, señorita!"

"Permit me, permit me, señor conde," the general said, with an emphasis assuredly affected; "we Mexican caballeros have a long memory for good as for ill. You risked your life to defend mine, and that is one of the debts we like to pay. I am your debtor, señor Don Louis."

"Are you speaking seriously, general?" the count asked, looking at him fixedly.

"Certainly, caballero; the subject is too serious for me to treat it otherwise. I will even add that my most lively desire would be soon to find the occasion to acquit my debt."

"If that be so, general, I can offer you the occasion, if you will allow me?"

"How so?" the general asked, somewhat taken aback by finding himself taken at his word. "I am too happy to be agreeable to you. What do you want of me?"

"I want nothing, general; I only wish to make a request of you."

"A request! You, Don Louis? Oh, oh, what is it? Pray speak."

"I would beg you to grant me a few moments of private conversation."

"This night?"

"This very instant."

"Come," the general continued, "I hoped to be free from business for a few hours at least, but you order otherwise. Your request shall be satisfied, Don Louis; a caballero has but his word."

"Pray pardon me, general. I am really confounded by pressing you so greatly; but imperious reasons——"

"Not a word more, I implore you, Don Louis, or you will make me suppose that you attach to this interview an importance which it cannot possibly possess."

Don Louis contented himself with bowing in reply. The general then turned to his guests, the majority of whom, their first curiosity satisfied, had returned to the various amusements they had quitted for a moment.

"Señoras and caballeros," he said, "I must ask you to pardon me for leaving you for a few minutes; but as you see, Don Louis has my word, and I must free it."

The guests bowed courteously. Doña Angela had summoned Don Cornelio to her side, and, profiting by the liberty Mexican manners give young girls, she was conversing with him in a low voice.

"Go, papa," she said with a soft smile, intended for the count; "but do not keep Señor Don Louis too long. Now that the ladies know him, they would like some conversation with him."

"Do not be alarmed, ladies; in ten minutes we shall return. Any discussion between myself and the count cannot be long."

"Heaven grant that be true," Louis said in his heart; "but I believe the contrary."

The general passed his arm through the count's, led him through the saloons, and stopped at a door he opened.

"Go in, caballero," he said to him.

The count entered, and the general followed, carefully closing the door behind him.

CHAPTER XX
DIAMOND CUT DIAMOND

The room to which the general led the count was a study. Don Sebastian pointed to a chair, and took another himself. There was a moment's silence, during which the two men examined each other carefully. On passing the study threshold, both doffed that gaiety they had imprinted on their faces, to assume a severe and thoughtful look, harmonising better with the grave questions they were probably about to discuss.

"I am waiting, señor conde," the general at length said, "till it please you to explain yourself."

"I hesitate to do so, general," Don Louis answered.

"You hesitate, count!"

"Yes, because, in what I have to say to you, there are some matters so delicate that I almost fear to approach them."

The general was mistaken as to the meaning of the count's words. How could he understand the exquisite delicacy that dictated them?

"You can speak without fear," he said; "no one can hear you. Precautions have been taken, so that nothing said in this room can transpire outside. Banish then, I implore you, all reserve, and explain yourself frankly."

"I will do so, as you demand it; indeed, it is, perhaps, better that it should be so. In this way, I shall know at once what I have to hope or fear."

"You are bound to hope everything from me," the general said in an insinuating voice. "I wish you no harm; on the contrary, I desire to serve you; and to give you an example of frankness, I will begin by declaring to you, that your fate depends on yourself alone, and that the success or ruin of your enterprise is in your own hands."

"If it be really so, general, the discussion between us will not be long. But, allow me in the first place to set forth my grievances, in order to throw full light on the state of the case."

"Do so."

"In the first place, permit me one question. Do you know the conditions of my treaty with the Mexican government?"

"Of course I do, count, as I have in my possession a copy of it."

Don Louis made a sign of surprise.

"That must not astonish you," the general continued; "remember what occurred at Mexico. Do you not owe to an influential person, whose name you are ignorant of, the removal of those insurmountable obstacles which prevented the acceptance of your treaty by the President of the Republic?"

"I allow it."

"That person, I can now tell you, was myself."

"You, general?"

"Myself. Then, do you remember that when all was concluded, I became the first shareholder who gave his signature, and supplied funds?"

"That is perfectly correct; but this only renders more incomprehensible the strange position in which I have been placed."

"How so?"

"Pardon me, general, the frankness with which I express myself."

"Go on, count. We are here to tell each other the truth."

"In reality, since my arrival at Guaymas, your conduct toward me has been inexplicable."

"You are jesting. I consider it most natural."

"Still, it appears to me— —"

"Come, what do you find so extraordinary in my conduct?"

"Well, everything."

"Mention details."

"I will do so."

"Let us see."

"Shall I start from the commencement?"

"Certainly."

"Very good. You know, as you have a copy of my agreement, that it is stated in it that I shall only stay at Guaymas just the time necessary for the company to settle the halting places, and prepare provision and fodder."

"Perfectly correct."

"I have been kept at the port nearly a fortnight under excuses, each more frivolous than the other. Comprehending how injurious inaction may prove to my company, I made repeated applications to the captain-general and yourself. All my letters were answered by want of instructions."

"Go on."

"Wearied with this abnormal position, I at length succeed in obtaining my passports to start for the mine. At that moment I receive from you, general, a note giving me orders not to leave Guaymas."

"Very good. Proceed."

Don Louis, confounded by the impassiveness of the speaker, whose face remained calm and voice tranquil, began to feel himself growing angry.

"Now, general," he said, raising his voice, "I have a right to ask you clearly what game we are playing.

"A very simple one, my dear count, I repeat to you; and you can, if you really desire it, hold all the trumps in your hand."

"I confess that I do not at all understand you."

"That is impossible!"

"On my honour! I should feel most sincerely obliged by your explaining to me clearly what is happening; for I assure you that I am in a fog from which I despair ever to escape."

"That depends on yourself alone."

"By Heavens, general, you will allow that you are jesting with me?"

"Not the least in the world."

"What? At the request of your government, I come to Sonora with permission to work the mines. Owing to your influence, as you yourself allow, my treaty is signed. Confiding in Mexican honesty, I organise an expedition—I arrive; and my partners, yourself first of all, turn against me and treat me, not as their friend, their representative, not with even the respect due to a gentleman, but affect to consider me as almost a filibuster."

"O count! You are going too far."

"On my soul, general, such things can only be witnessed in Mexico."

"My dear count, you are mistaken. No one is seeking to injure you, on the contrary."

"Still, up to the present, you, one of the largest shareholders in the company, whose interests are at stake, you in a word, who, owing to the influence you possess, should have helped us in the most effective manner, have only employed that power to impede our movements and injure us in every way."

"O count! What terms you are employing."

"Good Heavens, general, excuse me! But it is time for all these absurd annoyances to cease, and for me to be allowed to proceed to the mines. All this has lasted too long."

The general appeared to reflect for a moment.

"Come, frankly," he said at last; "did you not understand why I acted toward you in that way?"

"I swear it."

"That is strange. Pardon me in your turn, count; but I had a very different opinion of you."

"What do you mean?"

"Then you did not guess why I, general, military governor of Sonora, supported so warmly your petition to the President?"

"But——"

"You did not guess," he went on sharply, "why I demanded that your companions should be well armed, and organised as soldiers?"

"It appears to me——"

"You did not understand why I had you invested with a military power as extensive as if you were chief of an army? Come, count, you are not speaking seriously at this moment; or else you wish to play a cunning game with me."

While pronouncing these words with a certain degree of vehemence, this time real, the general had left his chair, and was walking about the room in agitation. The count listened to him with the greatest attention, while watching him closely. When he was silent, he replied:—

"I will tell you, general, what I did understand."

"Speak."

"I understood, that the Mexican government, too weak to recover for itself the rich placers of the Plancha de la Plata, which by its carelessness, had fallen once more into the hands of the Indians, would gladly see strangers carry out an expedition from which it would reap the greatest profit. I understood, besides, that the government, unable effectively to protect the inhabitants of Sonora against the incursions of the Apaches and Comanches, would be delighted if the same strangers took on themselves at their risk and peril to restrain these ferocious plunderers within their frontiers. I understood lastly, that General Don Guerrero, (whose life and his daughter's I had been so fortunate as to save, and who felt such deep gratitude toward me), had gladly seized on the opportunity to do me a service in his turn, by placing at my disposal that great influence he possesses, to obtain for me that which I had so long solicited in vain. That is all I understood, general."

"Ah! That is all?"

"Yes; but am I mistaken?"

"Perhaps."

"Then, be kind enough to explain yourself categorically, general."

"What use would it be now? It is too late," the general answered, darting at him a glance of strange meaning.

"Why, then, too late?"

Don Sebastian walked quickly up to the count, and stopped in front of him.

"Because now," he said, "we can never understand each other."

"You believe so, general?"

"I am sure of it."

"But, for what reason?"

"You wish me to tell it you?"

"I beg you."

"Well, then, señor conde, the reason is this: you are a man of too much sense and vast intelligence—in a word, you are a man in a thousand——"

"General, I implore you——"

"I do not flatter you, count; I tell you the truth. Unfortunately, though you speak Spanish with rare perfection, you are not sufficiently acquainted with *Mexican* for us ever to understand each other."

"Ah!" the count said, without adding another word.

"I am right, I think; this time you caught the meaning of my words?"

"Perhaps, general, I will reply in the remark you employed an instant ago."

"Very good. Now, I think, we have nothing more to say to each other."

"Permit me a few words."

"Speak."

"Whatever may happen, general, on passing the door of the room, I shall not remember one word of our conversation."

"As you please, count; we have said nothing the whole town might not hear."

"That is true; but others might possibly put a different interpretation on them than mine. There are so many ways of understanding words."

"Oh! But ours were remarkably innocent."

"They were. I trust, general, we shall not part as foes."

"Why should we be so, my dear count? I desire, on the contrary, that the agreeable acquaintance we have renewed this evening may be changed ere long—on your side at least, for on mine it has long been so—into a durable friendship."

"You overwhelm me, general."

"Do I not owe you my life?"

"So I may always count on you?"

"As on yourself, my dear friend."

These words were uttered by the two speakers with such delicately sharpened irony, that no one could have guessed, beneath the charming smile that played on their lips, the rage and hatred which swelled their hearts.

"Now," the general continued, "I believe we can return to the ballroom?"

"I am at your orders, general."

Don Sebastian opened the door of the room, and stood against the wall. The count passed him.

"Do you play, Don Louis?" the general asked him.

"Rarely; still, if you wish it, I shall be happy to cover your stake."

"This way then."

They entered a room in which several monte tables were established. The gamblers were collected before a table, at which a man, who had an enormous pile of gold before him, was enjoying extraordinary good luck. The man was Don Cornelio. After conversing for some time with Doña Angela, the Spaniard, attracted by the irresistible charm of gold, approached the monte tables, and, fascinated in spite of himself, he had risked the few ounces he possessed.

Luck had been favourable to him; so constantly favourable, that in less than an hour he had gained nearly all the gold of all the players who had ventured to hold their ground against him; so that he eventually won an enormous sum. At the moment the count and the general arrived near him, Don Cornelio's last adversary retired, completely cleaned out, and the fight ceased for want of combatants; so that the Spaniard, after looking around him, and seeing that no one cared longer to contend with him, began with unchangeable coolness thrusting into the vast pockets of his *calzoneras* the ounces piled up before him.

"Oh, oh!" the general said, gaily, "it seems that the Atravida company is in luck to-night, Señor Don Louis; it gains on all sides at once."

The count smiled at this double-edged compliment.

"Let us see if I shall change the vein?" Don Sebastian continued, "Will you play against me, Don Louis?"

"On one condition."

"What? I accept it beforehand."

"This: I have a peculiar custom of never playing more than three stakes."

"Good."

"Wait a minute. I play them, doubling each time."

"The deuce! And if you lose one of the three?"

"That is of no consequence; still, I do not think I shall lose," he said with perfect calmness.

"What! You do not think you will lose?"

"No; I confess to you that I have great luck in play. The reason is, probably, because I care very little about winning."

"That is possible; still, what you tell me is so curious, that I should like to convince myself of the fact."

"It only depends on you."

By degrees, the guests had drawn nearer the two gentlemen, and formed a group around them. Doña Angela had also advanced, and was now close to Don Louis' side.

"Come," the general said, "let us play three stakes."

"At your orders."

"How much shall we set?"

"What you please."

"Suppose we say 2000 piastres?"

"Agreed."

The general took up a pack of new cards.

"If you have no objection," he remarked, "we will neither of us cut."

"As you please."

"But who shall be dealer?"

"I," Doña Angela suddenly exclaimed, as she seized the pack of cards.

"Oh, oh!" the general said with a smile, "take care, Don Louis; my daughter is enlisted against you."

"I cannot believe that the señorita is my enemy," the count replied, as he bowed to the young lady.

Doña Angela blushed, but said nothing; she unfastened the pack, and shuffled the cards.

"Two thousand piastres," the general said. "Deal, my child."

She began turning up the cards.

"Lost!" she said in a moment.

"That is true," said the general; "I have lost; now for the second. *Caramba!* Take care, niña, we are playing this time for 4000 piastres."

"Lost!" she cried.

"Again! That is singular. Come, Don Louis, the last one."

"Perhaps it would be better to stop here; neither you nor I, general, care for this money."

"That is the reason I wish for the third stake; besides, luck may have favoured you hitherto."

"Did I not warn you?"

"Come, come; I wish to be certain."

"Lost!" the young lady said for the third time, in her harmonious voice.

"*Caramba!* This is really singular. I owe you 14,000 piastres, Don Louis. I allow that you have really extraordinary fortune."

"I know it," the count answered, still perfectly cool; "and now permit me to leave you. Señorita, accept my grateful thanks for the kind assistance you granted me in this matter."

The young lady bowed, ashamed and blushing,

"Tomorrow, at daybreak, the 14,000 piastres will be at your house, Don Louis."

"Do not hurry yourself, general; I shall have the honour of seeing you again."

The count thereupon took leave, and withdrew with Don Cornelio, obsequiously accompanied to the door of the last room by the general.

"Double traitor!" the count muttered, as he mounted. "Take care of yourself, for now I see your game. In spite of your cunning, you have let me read your thoughts."

The count, followed by his escort, thoughtfully returned to the house he inhabited. He was reflecting on the means to be employed in foiling the machinations of his enemies, and carrying out his expedition successfully. As for Don Cornelio, he only thought of one thing—the luck he had had during the evening; and, while galloping by Don Louis' side, he mentally calculated the number of ounces he had gained, of which fact he had not yet been able to assure himself satisfactorily.

CHAPTER XXI
THE TAPADA

The American character is made up of contrasts; and one of the strangest of these is the honesty and punctuality with which play debts are liquidated. The man who would remorselessly assassinate another to rob him of two reals, would not fail to pay him, within twenty-four hours, any gambling debt, however large it might be.

The next morning, on waking, Don Louis found on the table of his room several canvas bags, filled with ounces. They contained the 14,000 piastres, lost on the previous evening by the general, and which the latter had sent at sunrise.

Louis was annoyed at this punctuality, which, in his ignorance of Mexican habits, he was far from expecting. It appeared to him of evil omen. He dressed; and, after breakfasting, left Don Cornelio engaged in counting his previous evening's gains, and wrapping himself in his cloak, went out with the intention of looking at the town.

As, during his walk, he passed before the palace, he took advantage of this circumstance to give his card to one of the general's criados, not wishing, after the conversation they had held, to force himself upon him, but intending to call in person the next day.

The count employed several hours in traversing the town, visiting the churches, of which two or three are rather fine, and smoking sundry cigarettes on the Alameda, a delightful promenade shaded by noble trees, where the fair sex of Pitic breathe the fresh air every evening. At length, he returned home, shut himself up in his room, and earned on his correspondence till a late hour.

The next day, as he had resolved, he proceeded to the palace: it was closed. The general, summoned by an important affair, had started at four o'clock the previous afternoon on horseback, only taking with him a small squadron of lancers. But, the man added who gave the count this information, his excellency the general would not be long absent; he would probably return within four days. The count, try all he knew, could obtain no more positive information. The Mexicans, ordinarily so gossiping, can become, when their interests demand it, as dumb as fish; and in that case it is impossible, either by money or promises, to get a single syllable from them.

Don Louis retired, excessively annoyed at this *contretemps*, which seemed expressly prepared for him; still, in order to clear up his doubts, and not wishing, under circumstances so grave, to act lightly, and commit any imprudence, although the general's behaviour seemed to him highly improper, he resolved to wait a few days, in order that he might have right on his side, by proving that Don Sebastian's departure had been premeditated for the purpose of avoiding any further explanation with him.

Daily, the count sent one of his men to the palace to inquire whether the general had returned. The answer was always the same. The general was absent, but it was certain he would soon return: he was indeed expected at any moment. Eight days passed thus. Another subject of restlessness then arose, to increase the count's annoyances and the impatient feeling that was beginning to conquer him.

On leaving Guaymas, he had given orders to the officer to whom he gave the temporary command of the company, to start to join him after four days. The men, then, must not only have started, but must be close to Pitic, as the two towns were only fifteen leagues apart, a distance which an armed body can easily cover between two suns; and yet, since his leaving the port, the count had received no news—no reply to his letters; and the company did not make its appearance.

What had happened since his leaving Guaymas? What new obstacles had been interposed to the movement of his company? Whence resulted this incomprehensible delay of four days? Why had not the officer left in charge informed him of what had occurred? Or had his couriers been interrupted on the road? Why had not Valentine or Curumilla, those two resolute and devoted men, for whom the greatest obstacles had no existence, come to warn him?

All these suppositions, and many others that offered themselves to the count's perplexed mind, threw him into a state of moral excitement impossible to describe. He knew not what to resolve, what means to employ, in order to acquire a certainty a hundred fold preferable to the doubt that gnawed him. At length, he decided on sending Don Cornelio, in whom he believed he could trust, at full gallop to Guaymas. That gentleman was out, however, and was sought for without being found.

This new obstacle culminated the count's feverish impatience. He mounted his horse, and started with the intention of exploring the environs of the town, in the secret hope of discovering some traces of his comrades, or at least learning some news about them. During the four hours he galloped in every direction, he saw nothing, and heard nothing. He turned back—a prey to a mighty sorrow, and heavy discouragement.

On approaching his house, the sound of a jarana reached his ears, and he hurried on his steed. Don Cornelio, carelessly seated on a stool in the porch of the house, was strumming his guitar, singing, as was his wont, his inevitable romance of King Rodrigo. On perceiving Don Louis, the Spaniard threw his instrument far from him, and rose with a cry of joy.

"At length!" he shouted.

"Why at length?" the count answered. "I consider the exclamation curious, since I have been searching after you, and could not lay my hand on you."

The Spaniard smiled mysteriously.

"I know it," he said; "but this place is not propitious for talking. Don Louis, will you permit me to accompany you to your cuarto?"

"With the greatest pleasure; the more so, as I also wish to speak with you."

"Come, that is a charming coincidence."

On reaching his room, Don Louis turned to his companion.

"Well," he said to him; "what have you to tell me?"

"Listen. This morning, according to my daily custom, I was walking about after breakfast, smoking a papelito, when, at the corner of the Calle de la Merced and the Calle San Francisco, I felt a slight touch on my arm. I turned sharply. A charming woman, or at least I suppose so, for it was impossible for me to distinguish her features, so carefully were they hidden in the folds of her rebozo, made me a sign to follow her. What would you have done in my place, Don Louis?"

"I do not know, my friend; but I entreat you, be brief, for I am in a hurry."

"Well, I followed her. You know that I have an idea about Mexican women, and am convinced that some day or other— —"

"In Heaven's name, my friend, come to the point," Don Louis interrupted him, stamping his foot impatiently.

"I am doing so. I followed her then. She entered the church of la Merced, I at her heels. The church was deserted at that moment, which caused me a lively pleasure; because in such a case a man can talk at his ease. Do not be impatient, I have come to it. When I reached a rather dark corner, the young and charming female, for I assert that she is both, turned so suddenly that I almost trod on her toes. 'Are you not Don Cornelio Mendoza?' she asked me. 'Yes,' I replied.

"'In that case,' she said, 'you are a friend of the count.' I guessed at once that the stranger alluded to you. 'I am his intimate friend,' I continued. 'That is well,' she added, drawing from her bosom a small note, which she placed in my hand; 'give him this as quickly as possible, it alludes to very grave matters.' I seized the paper, on which I mechanically fixed my eyes; when I raised them again, my incognita had disappeared, fled like a sylph, leaving no trace. It was impossible for me to catch her up, for the confounded place was so dark."

"Well, and where is the note?" Don Louis asked.

"Here it is. Oh, I did not lose it! It was too warmly recommended to me."

The count took it, and, without deigning a glance, threw it on the table. Since his arrival at Pitic he had received twenty a day, and had not answered one; he did not even read them now, as he felt convinced they all meant the same thing.

"And now," he added, "you have finished, I presume?"

"Yes."

"Then listen to me in your turn," he continued, handing him the letter he had prepared for the hunter during his absence. "You will mount this instant, start for Guaymas; give this letter to Don Valentine, and bring me back the answer. You understand?"

"Of course."

"I can rely on your diligence?"

"I start."

He went out. Ten minutes later, Don Louis heard the hurried footfalls of a horse re-echoing before the gateway.

"Tomorrow, at this hour, I shall know on what I have to depend," Don Louis muttered.

He threw himself on a butaca; and, resting his elbows on a table, he buried his head in his hands, and fell into deep thought. In this position, his eyes were involuntarily fixed on the note Don Cornelio had given him, and which was just in front of him. A sickly smile played on his lips.

"Poor fools!" he muttered, "who only dream of love and pleasure, to whom life is only one long festival. What need have I of your false protestations, to which I cannot respond? Love for me no longer exists. Like all the women who have preceded her, this one, doubtlessly, offers me an eternal love, which she will forget tomorrow. Why trouble myself about such absurdities? My heart is dead to joy—only too dead, alas!"

And he thrust the paper away.

The night was rapidly falling, and the count kindled a lucifer match to light a candle; but, as frequently happens to people deeply engaged, when he held the lucifer to the candle, he perceived that the former was nearly burnt out. Then, mechanically, he took up the note he had spurned, folded it up, and was going to twist it into a spill; but all at once he stopped, threw the match on the floor, lit another, and read this note, so despised a moment previously. The following were the contents:—

"A person interested in the Count Don Louis begs him, for his own sake, to go this evening to the Alameda at ten o'clock, under the first walk on the left. A person seated on the third bench will say to him 'Guaymas,' he will answer 'Atravida,' and follow her at a distance, without addressing other questions to her, to the spot where she is directed to lead him, and where the count will learn matters which, for his own safety and that of his comrades, it is important for him to know."

This strange note was not signed.

"What is the meaning of this?" the count said to himself. "Is it a mystification? For what object? Is it a snare offered me, in which they wish me to fall? By Heaven, I will know the truth! What hour is it—nine? I have still an hour before me. If my mysterious correspondent meditates an assassination, he will find with whom he has to deal. Who knows? Perhaps it is really a warning a good friend wishes to give me? I shall soon see."

While saying this, the count had changed his clothes for others of a dark hue. He put on his waist belt, through an iron ring of which, according to the Mexican fashion, he passed a sheathless machete; he placed two excellent revolvers in his girdle, wrapped himself carefully in the folds of a wide cloak, pulled his broad brimmed hat over his eyes, and prepared to go out.

"By Jove!" he said, as he crossed the threshold of the house, "armed as I am, the brigands who attempt to attack me will have their work cut out."

At the moment the count entered the street, it struck a quarter to ten by the clock of the Cabildo.

"I have just time," he said.

And he began walking quickly. The night was dark, the streets were deserted. As the count had expected, he reached the Alameda exactly as the clock struck ten.

"Let us see," he said.

He then walked with a firm step, though looking carefully around, and with his hand on his arms, in fear of a surprise. Conforming to the instructions of the note, he proceeded toward the walk indicated to him. He soon distinguished a dark form, which he recognised as that of a female seated on a bench. The count was then ashamed of his suspicions, left his hold of his arms, and, after reflection, was on the point of returning, supposing that this rendezvous was not so serious as he had at first supposed. Still, after a moment's reflection, he resolved on carrying out the affair to the end, and walked toward the stranger, who remained perfectly calm. At the moment he was passing her she coughed gently, and the count turned to her.

"*Guaymas*" she said in a low voice.

"*Atravida*" the count replied in the same tone.

"Come."

"Go on."

The strange woman rose, and not turning once, proceeded with a firm and hasty step along the Alameda, and turned into a narrow street inhabited by leperos, stopping before a house of rather wretched appearance. She then opened the door with a key she held in her hand, and went in, being careful to leave the door ajar. The count was close at her heels, and entered without any hesitation. He found himself in dense obscurity, and heard the door close behind him with a spasm at his heart.

"It is plain that I am in a wasp's nest," he said to himself.

"Fear nothing," a soft and melodious voice suddenly said, almost in his ear; "you have no occasion to alarm yourself, for these precautions are not taken against yourself."

The affectionate and almost mournful accent of this voice completely reassured the count.

"I fear nothing," he said. "Were I afraid of a snare, should I have come?"

"Listen, moments are precious. I have only a few seconds at my command."

"I am listening."

"You have powerful enemies; one especially has sworn your destruction. Take care! You would not serve his plans and become the agent of disorder, in order to help that man in gaining the object of his ambition; so that man has resolved your death."

"I despise the man's threats, for I know him."

"Perhaps so, I mention no names. Still, he is not alone against you. If you wish to foil your enemy's plans, act vigorously; above all be prudent. Treason is everywhere in Mexico, it is breathed in the air; so trust to none but well tried men. You have traitors even among those who come nearest to you."

"What do my enemies want?"

"To destroy you, I tell you, because you have refused to become their accomplice."

"Oh! I will avenge myself."

"Take care! Above all, do not remain long here. Your enemies can act the more surely in the dark, when, they know you are away from your company. Rejoin your comrades."

"I will do so this very night."

"Yes, start at once for the mines. If you can reach them before your enemies are in a position to raise the mask, you will be saved."

"Thanks for your advice, I will follow it."

"So now, good-by."

"Good-bye," the count said, with an accent of regret.

"We must not meet again."

"What! After the signal service you render me at this moment— —"

"It must be. Everything parts us."

"Tell me one thing, pray."

"What?"

"Whence comes the interest you deign to show me?"

"Is the motive for a woman's actions ever known?"

"Oh, you are jesting with me, señora; that is wrong."

The strange lady sighed.

"No, Don Louis," she continued, "I am not jesting with you. What need that you should know me? Sufficient for you that I watch over you. Seek not for the motive."

"On the contrary, I am anxious to know it."

"Were I to tell you that I loved you, would you believe it, Don Louis?" she said, sorrowfully.

"Oh!" he said, with emotion, "I would pity you, madam, if you attached yourself to a wretched being like myself, whose life has only been one long suffering."

"Do you not know, then, that we women love the unhappy before all? Our mission upon earth is to offer consolation."

"Madam, I implore you, do not let me leave you thus. I should carry away in my heart a grief which nothing could cure."

"I was wrong to come," she murmured, mournfully.

"Oh! Say not so, as you have perchance saved my life."

"Farewell, Don Louis," she replied, with an accent of ineffable gentleness; "we must part. Whatever may occur, remember that you have a devoted friend—a sister."

"A sister!" he remarked, bitterly, "be it so. If that is your wish; madam, I do not insist."

"Take this ring, as you wish absolutely to know who I am. My name is engraved upon it, but promise me not to read it for three days."

"I swear it," he replied, holding out his hand in the darkness.

A hand seized on his, pressed it gently, left a ring in it; and then he heard a slight rustling of silk, and a soft voice murmured farewell for the last time. The count heard a door close, and that was all. In a second, the door which had granted him admission to the house opened again. Don Louis wrapped himself in his cloak, and went out, a prey to considerable agitation. He reached his abode at full speed; from a distance he perceived a man standing before his gateway. The count, through a secret presentiment he could not explain, hurried onward.

"Valentine!" he suddenly exclaimed, with marks of amazement.

"Yes, brother," the other answered; "fortunately I met Don Cornelio. Your horse is ready; come, let us start."

"What is the matter, then?" he exclaimed, anxiously.

"Off, off! I will tell you all on the road."

Five minutes later, the adventurers started at full speed on the road from Pitic to Guaymas.

CHAPTER XXII
THE REVOLT

We will leave Don Louis and Valentine galloping on the road to Guaymas, and explain to the reader what had occurred in that town during the count's absence.

The French company formed at San Francisco was not completely made up, when the hunter brought his friend the money he required: about a dozen men were still deficient. Pressed by time and wishful to reach Sonora as soon as possible, Don Louis neglected to employ the same precautions in enrolling these men, as he had with the rest. He accepted almost anybody that presented himself. Unfortunately, among the new recruits were four or five scamps, to whom any restraint was unendurable, and who entered the company solely impelled by that instinct for evil which governs vicious natures; that is to say, with the secret intention of committing every crime that might prove profitable to them, so soon as they reached Mexico.

During the passage from San Francisco to Guaymas, and even so long as the count remained in the latter town, these persons carefully avoided showing themselves in their true colours, justly fearing punishment; but so soon as the count left Guaymas for Pitic, they threw off the mask, and in company with a few scamps of their own stamp, whom they picked up in the slums about the port, commenced a life of disorder and debauchery.

Colonel Florés and Don Antonio did not fail to profit by the irregular conduct of these men, and planted spies upon them, who excited them by all the means at their command to redouble their disorderly conduct. These emissaries cleverly spread the report that Don Louis had purposely deceived his comrades, that the mines of the Plancha de la Plata had no existence, that he had obtained no concession, and that his object was very different from what he had stated to his followers.

These calumnies, at first weak and as it were ashamed to expose themselves in broad daylight, in a short time obtained a degree of consistency; and a great fermentation was visible in the company. The officers, justly alarmed at what was passing, assembled in council, and resolved to warn the count of the alarming state of matters, and the dangers that menaced the expedition. Colonel Florés, as delegate of the government, was present at this council, and gave his opinion that a courier should be despatched to the count at once. The courier was really sent off, but almost immediately intercepted. This happened on the third day after the count's departure. The officer to whom he intrusted the command, reassured by the departure of the courier, and desirous to cover his responsibility by executing the orders he had received, ordered the assembly to be sounded at daybreak of the fourth day, and issued orders for immediate departure.

Murmurs broke out on all sides, cries and yells were heard, and for some time there was an inextricable confusion. Colonel Florés had hurried up, on hearing what was taking place. He insinuated that it would be probably imprudent to leave Guaymas, with the soldiers in their present state of excitement, and that it would be better to await the count's return, who, warned by the courier sent off the previous day, would doubtlessly arrive at once, and a hundred other more or less specious arguments.

But the temporary commandant was an old African soldier, trained in habits of discipline, and who only obeyed his orders. He replied sharply to the colonel that he begged him to attend to his own affairs, for what was occurring in no way concerned him. As for himself he had his orders, and would obey them, whatever the consequences might be.

Colonel Florés finding himself so sharply taken up, and perceiving that he was on the wrong road, immediately changed his batteries, and perfectly coincided with the officer, whom he urged to continue as he had begun, and not yield an inch to the insubordination of his soldiers. The commandant shrugged his shoulders contemptuously at these new suggestions from the worthy colonel, and walking into the middle of the yard, where the soldiers, forming scattered groups, were consulting together, he ordered the buglers to sound the assembly.

He was at once obeyed; but the adventurers yelled at the buglers, and redoubled their shouts and vociferations. The commandant remained motionless on the spot he had selected, with his arms folded on his chest; when the buglers had given the call, he pulled out his watch and coolly looked at the hour. The insurgents watched him closely, the other officers had come up, and ranged themselves round their chief.

"Return to your squads, gentlemen," he said to them in a clear voice, which, though not raised above the tone of an ordinary conversation, was distinctly heard by all. "Your men have five minutes to fall in; we shall start in a quarter of an hour."

A prolonged laugh greeted these words. The commandant returned his sabre to its scabbard, and walked with a measured step straight up to one of the scamps who had been the originator of the tumult, and who appeared to insult him most of all. The man started on seeing his chief walking toward him, and instinctively looked behind him. The shouts had ceased, and the adventurers, were waiting curiously the issue. When the commandant was only two paces from the man, he stopped, and looking him firmly in the face said,—-

"Were you laughing at me just now?"

The other hesitated to reply.

"It is not the chief who is speaking to you at this moment," the officer continued, "but the man you have insulted."

The adventurer felt that the eyes of all his comrades were fixed upon him; so he recalled all his effrontery.

"Well, supposing I was?" he said insolently.

"In that case," the officer continued quietly, "you are a scoundrel."

"A scoundrel?" the other retorted, in a passion. "You must be more careful in your language, I advise you."

"You are a scoundrel, I repeat; and I am going to punish you."

"Punish me?" he said, sneeringly; "come on then."

"Give the fellow a sabre," the officer said, turning to the spectators.

"A sabre? What for?"

"To give me satisfaction for your insult."

"I do not know how to use a sabre."

"Ah, that is the case, is it? You insult me because, you fancy yourself supported by your comrades, and that I am alone; but your comrades are brave men; they know me, and would not wish to insult me."

"No, no!" several voices exclaimed.

"While you are a miserable coward, unworthy longer to belong to the company. I dismiss you; you are no Frenchman; be off!"

Then, with a strength he little thought he possessed, the officer seized the man by the collar of his coat, and hurled him twenty paces. He jumped up, and ran off at full speed followed by a general yell.

The officer was not mistaken. The fellow was not a Frenchman. But why need we divulge his nationality? A whole nation must not be responsible for the villany of a single man.

When the officer turned round again after this summary execution, he saw that all the adventurers had fallen in, and were standing motionless and silent. The commandant reproached nobody, and did not appear to remember any longer the resistance offered to him. All men are alike. To subdue them, you must prove to them that you possess a decided superiority over them.

Colonel Florés was stupefied. He understood nothing of what was taking place.

"Hum!" he muttered to himself; "what energy! What courage! I fancy we shall not find it an easy matter to master men like these."

The commandant, after assuring himself by a glance that the company had really returned to its duty, gave the order for starting. This order, at once repeated by the subaltern officers, was obeyed without the slightest murmur; and the adventurers set out on their march, preceded by a long file of mules, carrying the baggage, and two or three carts, conveying invalids. The guns (for the count had judged it necessary to augment his artillery), were in the centre, dragged by mules. The march was closed by the cavalry, a detachment of ten men having been previously told off to form the vanguard.

The Frenchmen traversed Guaymas at a quick step, amid the shouts and wishes of success of the population collected on their road. Don Antonio accompanied the company to the Rancho de San José, which forms, as it were, a suburb of Guaymas. On arriving there, he took leave of the officers in the most friendly manner, repeating his offers of service; and after pressing the hand of Colonel Florés, who went on with the adventurers, and exchanging a glance with him, he returned to the port.

It was late when the Frenchmen started. The heat was stifling; consequently they could not cover much ground, retarded, as they were, by the mules and carts. At sunset, they encamped at the entrance of a village, about four leagues from the town.

The commandant imagined he had gained everything by inducing the company to leave Guaymas; but he was mistaken. The leaven of discord, artfully spread among the adventurers, was still at work, and was carefully kept up by the men to whom we have alluded. It was by no means the interest of these fellows to bury themselves in the interior of the country, where they would have no chance of finding what they had come to Mexico for, namely, opportunities for robbery and debauch. Thus, far from feeling discouraged by the check they had received that very morning, they intended to begin again, as soon as the occasion presented itself.

Valentine, who carefully watched all that went on around him, took the commandant on one side when the camp was formed, and warned him of the insubordination in the company. The latter, however, attached no great importance to the hunter's observations; for he was persuaded that, after the vigorous manner in which he had behaved, the adventurers would not dare to mutiny again.

Valentine's previsions were only too well founded, as the commandant had proof the next morning, when he wished to start again. The adventurers bluntly refused; threats or prayers were equally unavailing; they remained deaf to every observation. It was no longer mutiny, but a perfect revolt, followed only too soon by utter anarchy. The promoters of disorder triumphed; still they could not succeed in inducing their comrades to return to Guaymas.

Through a remnant of that feeling of duty which never deserts soldiers, the adventurers were unwilling to abandon the count; they returned merely to the old charges that had been suggested to them. They wanted a proof that the mines really existed, that their chief had a regular concession, and that they were not cheated. In addition to these demands they set up another, which would completely compromise the future of the company, were it granted. They demanded that all the officers chosen by Don Louis should be broken, and the company be permitted to choose others by vote.

Valentine remarked to them that they could do nothing during their chiefs absence. They must await his return, or commit a flagrant act of illegality; for Don Louis was at liberty to choose whom he pleased for officers, as he was the sole leader of the expedition, and alone responsible for its conduct.

The adventurers at length yielded to this reasoning, which appeared to them just; and, in order to stop as soon as possible these discussions which only delayed the affairs of the company, it was settled that Valentine should start the next morning for Pitic, and bring back the count with him. Valentine promised to do what they wanted, and tranquillity was gradually restored for the remainder of the day.

The next morning, at daybreak, therefore, Valentine mounted his horse, and started for Pitic. We have seen that he was fortunate enough to find Don Louis, and in what way he brought him off. On the road he told his friend all that had occurred, in the fullest details. Hence, the count was burning to arrive at the camp to check the disorder, and prevent the dissolution of the company, whose existence was seriously menaced, if such a state of things was allowed to continue only a few hours longer.

At daybreak, the horsemen reached the camp. All was topsy-turvy; confusion and disorder prevailed on all sides. The adventurers would listen to nothing. The officers, rendered powerless, knew not what to do, or how to turn away the storm that threatened them. But the sudden arrival of the count was a thunderbolt for the mutineers.

Don Louis leaped off his horse, and walked resolutely toward them. At the sight of him, the adventurers involuntarily felt the feeling of duty re-aroused in their hearts, which they had vainly striven to stifle.

"The assembly!" the count shouted in a thundering voice.

Yielding to this man's magical influence, which they had so long been accustomed to respect, they obeyed orders, and assembled around him.

"Not so," he continued; "fall in."

The first step was taken, they formed their ranks. The count surveyed them, looking closely along the ranks. The adventurers stood silent and gloomy; they felt themselves guilty. These hardened men trembled, not from fear but shame. The count addressed them.

"What have you to reproach me with, comrades?" he said to them, in his gentle and sympathising voice. "Since the moment I first collected you around me, have I not done all in my power to improve your position? Have I not constantly treated you as my children? Speak: if I have injured one of you, or committed a single act of injustice, tell it me? You have been led to believe that I am deceiving you, that I was not the owner of the Plancha de Plata, that this mine did not exist. Look here," he added, as he drew a document from his chest, "here are the papers; the agreement is regularly drawn up, the stations are prepared up to the mines. Now, have you faith in me? do you now suppose that I am deceiving you. Answer!"

He was silent for a moment; but not a voice was raised to answer him.

"Ah! That is the state of the case," he continued; "now listen to me. The mines to which I am leading you contain incalculable wealth. These riches will be yours. I shall only take what you give me. You shall settle my share. Will you now accuse me of wishing to cheat you for my own profit? You ask for fresh officers chosen by yourselves. I will never consent to such a condition. Your officers are men in whose capacity I have full and entire confidence: they well keep their positions. Among you there are cowards, who have become the tools of my enemies for the purpose of destroying us. These men all belong to the second squad. They had better spare me the trouble of discharging them with ignominy."

The adventurers, carried away by their chiefs frank and honourable language, rushed toward him, uttering shouts of joy. Peace was made: all was forgotten. The emissaries, so suddenly discharged, profited by the general enthusiasm to disappear without beat of drum.

"Here is a courier!" Valentine suddenly said.

The count turned sharply. A *lancero* was coming up at full gallop.

"*El señor conde?*" he asked.

"I am he," Don Louis answered.

The soldier held out to him a sealed despatch. The count took it with an indescribable flutter of the heart, and rapidly ran over the lines. Suddenly he uttered a shout of joy.

"Listen," he said; "here is the order I have so long been expecting. The President of the Republic authorizes us to set out immediately for the mines. Comrades, we will be off at once for the Plancha de Plata."

"To the mines!" the adventurers shouted.

On folding up the paper, Don Louis noticed a few words in French written at the foot of the envelope.

"What is this?" he muttered.

He then read:—

"Start at once. Perhaps counter orders have already been given. Your enemies are on the alert."

"Oh!" the count said, "what do I care now? I will manage to foil all their tricks."

The adventurers set to work gaily in preparing the carts for the long journey they would have to go. The two field pieces were carefully fastened on their carriages; in short, all preparations were taken to avoid the accidents inseparable from a journey across the desert.

The adventurers worked with such zeal to terminate their preparations, that within two hours the column was on their march for Apacheria. The joy was at its height, the enthusiasm general. One man alone doubted, and that man was Valentine.

The fact was, that the hunter was acquainted with the Mexican character, the groundwork of which is cunning, treachery, and roguery; and, in spite of himself, he trembled for his comrades.

[The further adventures of the gold-seekers will be found in the concluding volume of this series, which is called "The Indian Chief."]